YOU PROMISED ME FOREVER

YOU PROMISED ME FOREVER

MONICA MURPHY

Cover design: Hang Le
byhangle.com

PROLOGUE

Amanda

FOREVER AGO...

"Are you going to maul me on my front porch?" I ask Jordan.

The sexy look on his face tells me he's considering it. "Don't tempt me."

A shiver moves through me and he pulls me back into his arms. "Cold?" he asks.

"Yes." But happy. So happy. The porch is lit from the glow of the Christmas lights Dad puts up every year, and pretty much every house on our street is lit up as well. "Oh! I want to give you something."

He frowns. "What?"

I wiggle out of his hold and pull the small wrapped box out of the pocket of my cardigan. "This is for you."

His frown deepens as he stares at the box I'm holding before he lifts his gaze to mine. "I thought you were giving me my gift tomorrow."

"I have two presents for you. This is the special one. The other one can wait until Christmas." Tomorrow's gift is a bottle of cologne that will make me want to lick him every time I smell him. A real win-win gift, if you ask me.

He takes the present from me and slowly unwraps it to reveal a simple black box. He pulls off the lid and finds the men's silver link bracelet I bought for him. Lifting his head, he smiles at me. "I love it."

"Really?" I stressed over his gift so much. I took my friends to the jewelry store and had them help me pick it out. They assured me it was perfect, but I still worried he might not like it.

"Really," he says firmly, taking the bracelet out of the box. "Will you help me put it on?"

I take the bracelet from him and hook it around his wrist. It looks good on him and I smile, tracing my finger over the silver links. "You don't mind wearing a bracelet?"

"I will wear anything from you with no complaints." He drops a kiss on my cheek, then runs his finger over my new piece of jewelry. "Do you like your present?"

"I love it so much." I hold my hand out and spread my fingers, admiring my new ring. It's so tiny and dainty and perfect. A promise ring, he called it. "It's gorgeous."

"Not as gorgeous as you," he says, his voice low. I turn to meet his gaze and see the heat there. The hunger. Goose bumps sweep over me as he leans in and kisses me again, his tongue searching my mouth, his hand cradling my cheek.

The front door swings open, causing us to spring apart, and my brother Trent is standing there with a disgusted look on his little face. "Mom says you two need to come in before you freeze to death, but I'm telling on you. Mom, Amanda and Tuttle are making out on the front porch!"

The door slams before I can hear what anyone else said.

"Should we go inside?" Jordan asks, his eyes sparkling with amusement. That he can tolerate my pain-in-the-butt brother says a lot about his character.

"I guess so," I say with a little laugh.

"Hey," he says from behind me just before I open the door.

"What?" I turn to face him, startled by just how close he actually is.

He reaches out and tucks a wayward strand of hair behind my ear, his fingers lingering on my skin. "Did I tell you today that I love you?"

My cheeks go hot. Will I ever get used to Jordan so freely offering words of love to me? Probably not. "Yes, you did. But I'd like to hear it again."

Jordan tugs me into his arms and kisses me, his mouth warm despite the freezing cold air. "I love you, Amanda," he whispers against my lips.

"I love you too, Jordan Tuttle." I touch his neck, his hair. I can't get enough of him.

Ever.

"Forever?" he asks. It's our new favorite word and hearing it makes me smile.

"Forever."

ONE

AMANDA

Now

"So you're telling me that glorious hunk of man flesh..." My friend Lena points at the giant TV screen, where said glorious hunk of man flesh currently appears, his face on extreme close-up. "That guy right there. *He's* your ex-boyfriend?" Her voice turns into a squeak on the last word, like she can't believe it.

I nod. Take a sip of my drink. Heave an exaggerated sigh. "Yep."

Lena blinks, glancing over at the TV and tilts her head. We're at a bar on a Wednesday night, drowning our work exhaustion in cheap cocktails and salty appetizers. "You must be lying to me."

"I am so not lying." I almost wish I was lying sometimes.

It's really difficult to forget your ex when he's everywhere. Like right now. There he is on the seventy-five-inch TV screen, the camera zoomed in on his ridiculously handsome face that he can't hide even when he's wearing a stupid helmet.

The restaurant we're at replays the football games from the weekend. I know this, yet I still choose to come here. And that says a lot.

Like I'm a glutton for punishment.

"And you claim he was your first." Lena's eyebrows go way up—like disappear-in-her-hairline up.

"He was totally my first." Not my last, though. He promised me forever and that so didn't happen.

"I am having a really hard time wrapping my head around this." It's Lena's turn to take a drink, and she practically drains her glass before setting it on the round table between us with a loud thump. "You *really* went out with *the* Jordan Tuttle?"

"Oh yeah. For most of my senior year. And a little bit into college." That's where we fell apart. I was stuck at home, and he was gone, the new big man on campus at USC. Instantly famous, with adoring groupies and people wanting to be his friend and the media wanting to talk to him about his stats, his future, his charisma, his everything— and this all happened during his freshman year in college.

It only got worse as time went on. Not that I knew much about it, since I was a giant idiot and broke up with him.

Yes. You heard me right. *I* broke up with *him*.

What the hell was wrong with me?

When you're nineteen, broke and feeling alone with a brain full of insecurities and not much else, you make stupid, selfish choices. Now that I'm older and supposedly wiser, I can see there was a *lot* wrong with me.

And I have plenty of regret about it too.

"So what happened? Who broke up with who?" Lena asks.

When I admit my connection to Jordan, this is where it always gets sticky. "I, uh, broke up with him."

Her mouth drops open. She's quiet for a beat, two beats. Three. "Say what?"

"It's true." I take another sip of my drink, then shake the glass so the ice rattles. "It wasn't working between us."

Cheers erupt from the television and I glance up to see Tuttle throwing another touchdown pass to Niner wide receiver Tucker McCloud.

Of course he did. That's what Jordan does. He's one of the most accurate quarterbacks in the NFL.

Meaning he's very, very good at what he does. He's worth millions. Million dollar arm, million dollar smile, million dollar charm. He's got it all.

"Was he a complete dick?" Lena makes a sympathetic face. "Did he cheat on you?"

"No, he didn't cheat. And he wasn't a dick either. He just... didn't have a lot of time for me." Oh, that sounds pathetic, but it's true. He was so busy all the damn time. It's not like he meant to ignore me, but it felt that way. I was sad and all alone and massively insecure, which was a big problem throughout the entirety of our relationship. I never felt like I was enough in Tuttle's presence, even though he reassured me countless times that I was more than enough. That I was his entire world.

And I still ended things with him.

I felt stuck in my going-nowhere life, while his had taken off. It was like his life changed every single day, with opportunities being thrown at him from every direction. I couldn't compete. I hated being so far away from him, and I wasn't strong enough to deal.

So I broke it off. Via *text*.

Groaning, I prop my elbows on the table and rest my head in my hands. "I think I broke his heart."

"What? He doesn't look like he's missing you or anything." I look up to glare at my friend and coworker. "Come on! It's true! Look at him. He's wildly successful. He's *gorgeous*. And he always has a girl on his arm every time I see him in a magazine or on a gossip site. Wasn't he going out with that one famous model? The one who's always on the cover of *Vogue*?"

"Ugh, I don't even want to talk about him right now." I cover my face with my hands, tempted to scream. Tempted to straight up lose my crap and punch something.

But I don't. No matter what I say, people won't believe me. They take one look at gorgeous Jordan Tuttle and they're star struck. They have a hard time believing little ol' me could destroy him.

I did, though. I know I did. I broke my own heart and his too, and it sucks. Worse? I can't take back what I did. I have to live with my stupid decision for the rest of my life.

Instead of some stupid model who's always on the cover of *Vogue*, it could've been me on his arm. Me staring into his beautiful blue eyes. Me living with him, touching him, kissing him...

"Forget him." Lena waves a dismissive hand and smiles at me, leaning across the table like she's about to share a big secret. "At least you have Cade."

Hmm. Cade. Lena and I work for at a physical therapist office that specializes in sports medicine. I've always had a thing for football. My senior year I was a water girl for the football team, and that's how I got so close to Jordan. Well, that and the fact that we went to school together forever and supposedly he'd had a crush on me since middle school.

Oh, and then we messed around at that one party over the summer before our senior year, after I caught my then-boyfriend having sex with my supposed best friend and...

Yes. There's a lot of history between Jordan and me. History that I can look back on with a sort of nostalgic fondness.

Whoops. Wait a minute. I'm supposed to be focusing on Cade, not Jordan.

"Cade is sweet," I confirm. He's a new physical therapist who recently started working with us, and he's super cute. He asked me on a date today and I said yes. We're going to dinner and the movies on Saturday.

I think Lena is more excited about my date than I am.

"And he's extremely good looking," Lena adds, her eyes sparkling. "I think you two will make a great couple."

"Maybe." I shake my glass again, like that's going to make a fresh drink appear.

"Oh, stop—you always do this with guys. You're too cautious."

"More like safe," I correct. "And there's no such thing as being too cautious."

Another roar of the crowd sounds from the TV and I glance up to watch as they replay a terrific throw by my ex-boyfriend. I tell myself to look away. Look away now.

But I can't.

"I find it hard to believe you went out with that guy."

I turn to face Lena with a frown. "You think I'm lying?"

"No, not at all." Lena's eyes go wide. "But why didn't you ever tell me this before? We've known each other a long time. You'd think this type of information would've come up in conversation a while ago."

Lena and I have known each other for over a year, but it never feels easy to tell people about my connection to Jordan Tuttle. Her reaction is the reason why.

No one ever believes me when I admit Jordan and I were together. Oh, they *say* they believe me, but you know they probably tell their other friends, significant other, whoever, that I'm probably making this up. I mean, seriously.

Who in their right mind would ever turn away Jordan Tuttle?

"It just never came up in conversation." I shrug.

"Please. I'd shout it from the rooftops." Lena stares at the television. "He's sooooo hot. And look! Oh my God, they're going to have an interview with him Friday night!"

I check the TV to see Jordan sitting in a chair, his dark hair tame, his gaze intense, his smile restrained. That's his fake smile. I can spot it from a mile away.

"*Inside Football* premieres its new season this Friday night with an intimate look into the world of superstar quarterback Jordan Tuttle," the announcer's voice says.

Please. Jordan is a very private person. He wouldn't give anyone an intimate look into his world.

"We visit his home in the Sonoma wine country."

There's footage of him in jeans and a flannel shirt, walking through a vineyard while chatting with a beautiful female reporter, who stares up at him like a star struck fan.

I roll my eyes.

"And he offers *Inside Football* a rare glimpse into both his past—and his love life."

"Do you ever think about the one who got away?" the reporter asks, sounding so very, very serious.

He's sitting in a chair in a house. His house? Still wearing the dark blue and red flannel shirt, his hair a little wilder in this interview clip. There's scruff on his cheeks and he's... God. Extra sexy.

Looking directly at the camera, he says in that familiar low, melting voice, "I think about her all the time."

His words make me sit up straight, my entire body buzzing with electricity. Is he…

Could he?

Be talking about?

Me?

No. There's no way.

"Find out more on the season premiere of *Inside Football*," the announcer continues, just as Jordan fades to black.

"Holy shit, just listening to him speak turns me on." Lena shakes her head, her gaze meeting mine. "There's no way he's talking about you, right? Are you the one who got away?"

She sounds almost amused by the thought, while I say nothing. I'm trying to communicate everything with my eyes and one raised eyebrow.

Lena blinks once, twice, three times like rapid fire. "Wait a minute. You *do* think he's talking about you?"

"Maybe." I shrug, going for indifferent. I don't want to look like a total snob, like I believe the entire world revolves around me, but come the hell on.

The one who got away? He thinks about her all the time?

He *must* be talking about me.

I nibble on my lower lip, wishing like crazy I had another margarita to drown my sudden doubts in. *Maybe* he's talking about me.

But then again, maybe not.

TWO

AMANDA

IT'S Friday and I'm at work, and it's almost five. Appointments are light today, and I'm bored because no one is around, since most of the therapists who work here are already gone for the weekend. The only person left on shift is me and Cade, with Lena covering the front desk.

She's an assistant physical therapist like me, but we trade off every Friday afternoon to cover the appointment desk and phones, since our receptionist only works a half day. Her kid has some mommy and me gymnastics class, and considering we work at Atlas Wellness Center, which specializes in sports medicine, management goes bananas for that sort of thing and will automatically give employees time off when they ask.

Seeing Rhonda take off at noon every Friday with a giant smile on her face makes me wish I had a child I could put in mommy and me gymnastics class too.

But that feeling quickly fades, because kids? No. I'm too young, too non-committed, too selfish. I'm not ready for a wedding or a marriage or babies. I don't even have a boyfriend and I'm thinking I'd prefer to have one of those first to make it happen.

Though really, I guess you don't. I just prefer the more traditional route.

"Is it five o'clock yet?" I lean against the raised counter of the front desk, smiling down at Lena. She hates answering the phones. Customers make her angry even when they ask her innocent questions, and sometimes she has to watch her attitude.

"I wish." Lena glares at the elaborate phone system on the desk in front of her. "If I get one more call from a grouchy coach asking if he could get a release letter for his favorite *boy* playing tonight..."

"Yeah, I hate those calls." They make me uncomfortable. During football season, there's always a coach out there who wants to put his injured player back on the field too soon. It's only the end of August and we're already getting those calls. It's bound to get worse.

"Ladies." We both turn our heads to see Cade approaching the front desk, a smile on his handsome face. He just finished with a patient only a few minutes ago. "Are we the only three left?"

"Afraid so," Lena chirps, sending me a knowing look. I really hope Cade doesn't notice. I don't want to seem too overeager. "Though I'm perfectly willing to leave a little early if you'll let me."

"Since you've worked here longer than I have, don't you think you have authority over me?" he asks jokingly, sending me a quick wink.

Ugh. Winks. Are they cheesy or cute?

Hmm. I'll have to take it under consideration.

"Perfect. Then I'm out. Amanda, you can watch the phones." Lena throws open a drawer, yanks her purse from its depths and is gone in a matter of seconds.

I blink up at Cade as I settle myself in the chair Lena just vacated. "I didn't know she could move so fast."

"Me either." He smiles at me, our gazes lingering for a beat too long before I look away. Yes, yes, he's cute. He's really nice. Easy to talk to. Everyone seems to like him, and he's fit in here seamlessly since he started.

But do I feel a zing? A spark? Do we have actual chemistry? Not too sure yet.

Guess I'll find out for sure when we go on our first date tomorrow night.

"So tell me." He rests his forearms on the counter and I study them. His skin is golden, like he spends time outside but doesn't spray tan or anything gross like that. And they're corded with muscle, yet not too bulky. I have a thing for arms. And hands. Cade's are nice. "Do you have a restaurant preference for our date tomorrow?"

"Um." I press my lips together, my mind scrambling. Can't he just make the decision? "I'm pretty open."

"Not a picky eater?"

"No. Not at all." I shake my head.

"That's a relief." He smiles. "My ex-girlfriend was super picky."

Oh. Is he going to be one of those who talks about his ex all the time? I hope not. "That's...unfortunate."

His eyes widen, like he just realized what he said, and he holds his hands up in front of himself in an almost defensive matter. "Hey, don't get the wrong idea. I'm over her. We split up a long time ago."

How long ago? Days? Weeks? Months?

Preferably months. Maybe even years.

I can't ask, though. Not yet.

"No, that's fine." I try to sound easy breezy. Like nothing he says about his ex is going to bother me.

But if I'm being real? It sort of bothers me.

"She lives in a different state," he continues. "You don't have to worry about her."

"I wasn't worried." My smile feels brittle, so I let it fade. Thankfully, a call comes in and I answer it, sending it to the director's voicemail before placing the receiver back in its cradle. Cade is still standing there, though he's scrolling through his phone now, and I decide to put this all on him. "Listen, you're the one who asked me on a date, so why don't you pick the restaurant? And the movie?"

My voice is light and my smile is friendly. I want him to be the one to take command. I don't mind that sort of thing whatsoever.

He lifts his head, his lips curled upward. "You don't mind?"

"I definitely don't mind." Honestly, I'd rather not deal with it. I have too many other things occupying my brain space.

"Great." He glances at his phone's screen. "It's four-fifty-nine. I say we lock up."

So we do.

Is it wrong to admit I was dying to get away from Cade so I could head home? My commute averages about forty-five minutes, but on a Friday, it can take over an hour, which it totally did. Bay Area traffic at its finest, no?

But seriously, I was fine with it, because inching along the freeway makes the time pass, and that's what I wanted. Sitting on the bus, I pulled up an old playlist on my phone that I made during my senior year and I listened to it, letting all of those old memories wash over me. Memories of me and Jordan. All the fun we had together. The way my toes would curl every time he kissed me long and deep. How when I was with him, I felt like we were the only two people on this whole planet.

Basically, I tortured myself the entire ride.

I got off the bus at my favorite Chinese restaurant that's a couple of blocks from my apartment and ordered takeout, then sat around waiting the ten minutes it took them to prepare my half order of chicken wonton salad and sweet and sour pork with a side of fried rice. Tried to be healthy with the salad addition, but they smother it with this delicious sweet dressing that is probably about a million calories, so I guess healthy went right out the window.

It's definitely a wallow-in-my-misery Friday night.

By the time I got home, changed into an old pair of sweats and an oversized T-shirt that—yes, OMG, originally belonged to Jordan—pulled out that chilled bottle of rosé I'd been saving for a special occasion, poured myself a giant glass, and plated as much Chinese food as I could, it was nearing seven o'clock.

Almost time for *Inside Football* featuring Jordan mother trucking Tuttle.

The food smells delicious and I start shoveling it in, but when the TV goes black for the briefest moment and then a photo of Jordan on his NFL draft day magically appears, the announcer rattling off facts and stats, my stomach churns.

I'm instantly afraid all the food will go to waste. I set the plate on my coffee table, promising myself I'll eat more.

Later.

Curling up on the couch with the wineglass clutched in my hand, I watch with rapt attention. *This is ridiculous*, I tell myself as they show a few photos from his younger years. A class picture from fourth grade—yes, holy shit, I'm in it—a team photo from his youth league days, when they won the regional championships in the eighth grade.

The announcer gives the brief rundown on Jordan's life, talking about his parents, his successful father, his much older sister, how the family is extremely wealthy. They don't talk *to* any of his family, though, not even his pitiful mother or his wretched father.

Despite my feelings about them, this makes me sad. He never had solid parental support. My parents may drive me crazy, but at least I know they love me.

I'm not so sure Jordan knows his parents love him.

When the photo flashes on the TV of Jordan after our high school team won the championship game our senior year, I almost spill my wine. He's holding up his helmet in the air in victory, his other arm wrapped around...

My shoulders.

His gaze...

Staring adoringly in mine.

Me...

Smiling up at him like he's the love of my life.

The photo is there and gone in the blink of an eye. I rewind the DVR back a few seconds, then hit pause so I can study it. I own this photo. It's buried deep in a box somewhere, probably still at my parents' house. There's no reason to keep the photo with me.

God, we look so young and so in love with each other, it's downright heartbreaking.

"I'm seriously trying to drive myself crazy," I mutter before I hit the pause button and the show resumes.

The commercials go on forever and I eat some of my dinner, drink a lot more of the wine. When the show finally comes back on, I'm hypnotized as the stupid flirtatious female reporter—Liz Rockwell, at your service—is walking side by side with Jordan as he takes her on a tour of his freaking mansion.

He talks. I stare. She asks lame questions, he answers them, always with the faintest hint of irritation in his eyes, like he'd rather be anywhere else. I'd know that look anywhere. He hasn't changed much.

Well. I take that back. He's changed a LOT. He's filled out even more, and while he's not bulky, he has muscle. A broader chest. A more chiseled jaw. That same reluctant smile—he's never been a smiler, though he would just for me—and those beautiful blue eyes.

They're standing by his kitchen counter, Liz thumbing through a pile of photos, the ones they flashed on the screen earlier. She comes to a stop at the one of me and him, tapping her index finger on top of my face. "Who's that?"

The camera flashes to Jordan. His eyes are cold. "An old friend."

"Girlfriend?" Liz gives him a pointed look.

He shrugs like it's no big deal. The rat bastard. "I suppose."

Her smile is cunning. I bet she thinks she's going to get information out of him. "Bad breakup?"

He hesitates for a moment, like he has to think about it, and I realize I'm literally sitting on the edge of the couch, waiting breathlessly for his answer.

"Typical breakup," he finally says with a quick nod. "We were young."

Liz is staring at the photo once more, her expression thoughtful. "You two look very much in love."

Massive understatement.

"It was nothing," he says quickly.

"Nothing?" I leap to my feet, pointing my index finger at the screen. "Freaking liar!"

Liz sets the photos aside and focuses all of her attention on Jordan. "Is she the one who got away?"

"I guess."

Ugh. I fall back onto the couch. He's being his typical evasive self. I can tell you right now, I don't miss that shit for the world.

They talk about other stuff, but I can't hear anything. I'm too caught up on his *I guess* statement. I don't warrant much, do I? I shouldn't be surprised. I'm the one who walked away first. I deserve his indifferent treatment.

After the next commercial break, Jordan gives Liz a tour of his home, and it is beautiful. Gorgeous. Like out of a dream. They talk about his future, about football, and he chats easily. When she tries to talk to him about his past or his family, he hedges, changing the subject. It's all coming at me at a rapid-fire pace, throwing me off balance. Sending me into Tuttle overload.

I haven't experienced anything like this in years.

"So." Liz smiles. They're now sitting opposite of each other, the hot lights shining on them, Liz appearing as cool as a cucumber while I swear Jordan looks like he's sweating. "Do you ever think about the one who got away?"

My heart drops into my toes as I wait for it.

He stares straight at the camera, his expression sincere when he says, "I think about her all the time."

Oh my God. My heart just skipped like, five beats.

"You said it was nothing, though," she counters, looking pleased with herself, like she just caught Jordan in a lie. Which she totally did. "I'm guessing the relationship actually was serious."

"As serious as a relationship can be between two teenagers," he says. "We were young, sh—stuff happens. And then it was over."

"You have regrets?"

"I used to," he says.

Oh my God, what does he mean by that? His answers are so...unexpected. Confusing.

The tiniest bit annoying.

"What do you think she'd do if she saw you right now? During this episode?" Liz leans forward, her eyes gleaming. "Or what do you think she'd say if you two ran into each other in some random spot?"

"She'd probably tell me to grow the hell up and get over it." He chuckles. Liz actually giggles.

And then they break for another freaking commercial.

My head is spinning. He's making a mockery of our relationship, and I'm sorry, but that's not fair. I was young and stupid. He was too. How did we expect to make this work? Were we really that ignorant?

Apparently so.

I grab my phone and open up Instagram, then go to the search feature and type in his name. His profile pops up before I can type the u in his last name and I click on it, scrutinizing every photo he's shared.

Clearly this isn't a personal profile. He's catering to the fans, with photos of him poised and ready to launch a ball, or videos of some of his better plays over the last couple of seasons. Without hesitation, I hit the blue follow button, praying I won't regret this.

I stare at the newly appeared message bar, temptation making my fingers twitch. The commercials drone on in the background, but I'm not even paying attention anymore. I impulsively click it and send him a message before I can overthink anything.

I would never tell you to grow the hell up and get over it.

That's all I say.

Setting my phone down, I polish off my first giant glass of wine, wishing I'd brought the bottle into the living room with me. *Inside Football* starts back up with a quick interview with Jordan's current coach, talking about how great he is and his potential and how he's going to have an amazing career and a blah, blah, blah.

My phone buzzes and I check it.

Jordan_Tuttle8 has sent you a follow request.

What the hell? Talk about fast. I immediately go on Instagram and check my followers pending list.

Yep. There he is.

Glancing at the TV, I see he's back, still wearing the sexy flannel shirt and dark rinse jeans, looking like Hollywood's interpretation of a lumberjack. He's talking about wine and grapes and it's crazy to hear him ramble on about this stuff because he sounds so grown up and mature.

Not that he was immature when we were together, but this is a whole new side to Jordan that I don't know. That I will probably *never* know.

The realization makes me a little sad.

I accept his follow request, my heart hammering, my ears roaring. I'm staring at the phone, waiting for him to make another move, but after five minutes I give up and set the phone on the couch beside me.

Totally overreacting. Maybe it's some overzealous assistant who somehow remembers the name of her boss's old girl-friend so she sees it pop up and immediately decides to follow me back. That's logical, right?

Right?

My phone buzzes with another notification, and I check it.

Jordan_Tuttle8 has sent you a message

I almost drop the phone when I try to open up Insta, and when I finally do, I see his message.

Jordan: **Mandy.**

That's all it says.

The fucker.

THREE

AMANDA

I WAKE up to my iPhone vibrating next to my ear. I check the screen to see, first, it's 8:07 a.m.

And second, that it's my best friend from high school calling me. She lives in Texas so she's two hours ahead and completely thoughtless when it comes to time zones, I swear.

I greet her with, "Livvy, why are you calling me this early?"

Please. I know why she's calling me this early.

"Did you see Tuttle on *Inside Football* last night? He was totally talking about you. God, what a douche."

As all loyal high school best friends are wont to do, she can't forgive Jordan for our breakup, even though I was the one who broke up with him. In her eyes, he drove me to do it. You have to love a best friend like that.

We're not as close as we used to be, only because she lives in Austin now with her fiancé and true high school sweetheart Dustin, but we talk as much as we can.

"I think he made all of it up," I tell her.

Livvy pauses for a moment, like she has to consider what I just said. "Made it up? What are you talking about?"

"It makes for good TV." I lower my voice in a terrible imitation of Jordan. "'Oh yeah, that special girl from high school was my first real love, but we're not together anymore. So I'm broken hearted and all that crap.'" My voice goes back to normal. "He's so over me. You do realize this, right?"

"Maybe he's not."

"Please." I make a noise and sit up in bed. My head hurts. Too much wine. And my stomach hurts. Too much Chinese food, which I ended up devouring after I watched *Inside Football*. Twice. "He makes millions, he's world famous and he can have any woman he wants. He is not losing sleep over me."

"You never know," Livvy sing songs. "It would be what he deserves, wishing you two were still together."

"What do you mean by that?"

"He can want you, but he can never have you, because you are so done with that douchebag. He can go suck a bag of dicks."

Funny how when we end up talking about high school stuff, Livvy immediately starts sounding like her high school self. We're in our twenties now. We don't go around saying suck a bag of dicks anymore.

Well. I never really did. That's more Livvy's style.

"He doesn't want me," I reassure her. And myself. "He probably has a different woman in his bed every night. He's probably dated half the Kardashians." There was a rumor he had a minor tryst with Kendall Jenner about a year ago, but who knows if that's true? He takes one photo with her at a random event, and it's splashed all over social media claiming they're a couple.

"I wish he did. I wish he was begging for you to come back to him right now, just so you could have the satisfaction of telling him to kiss your ass," Livvy says.

I think about him following me on Instagram last night. How he sent me that one-word message and nothing else. The tease. The jerk.

Should I tell Livvy?

Nah.

"I'm not out for vengeance," I say. "I only wish him well."

"You have a bigger heart than me," Livvy mutters. "Dustin tells me my hate for Tuttle is ridiculous."

"It sort of is," I say gently. "Don't forget, I broke up with him."

"Because he practically made you!" she cries, forcing me to hold the phone away from my ear. She's loud when she wants to be. "He never called you, he always canceled on you when you had plans. I don't know how many times I had to comfort you while you cried over him bailing yet again."

Everything she says is true. I cried a lot over Jordan when he went away to college. I let the distance and his success and my insecurities destroy our relationship.

"He didn't make me end things. I didn't give him the choice," I tell her with a sigh.

"Well, whatever. I just hate seeing him on TV looking like such a smug bastard."

"I'm surprised you even watched it." Livvy's always busy working. She's a real estate agent in Austin and currently making a killing.

"Dustin told me we had to watch it," Livvy says with an irritated sigh. "He got excited when he saw himself in that one class picture."

"Ha, I was in that class too."

"I was in Haskell's class so no brief brush of fame for me. Dustin thinks he's some sort of celebrity now." She sounds amused. "He wishes he could go to one of Tuttle and Cannon's games."

Cannon Whittaker played football with Jordan in high school and was one of our friends. A big, sweet bear of a man now, he was traded onto Jordan's team last season, and the media went wild with stories about them being reunited.

"I could, not that I'm going to," I say. Their stadium isn't too far from where I work. It's almost like I went into sports medicine on purpose so maybe Jordan and I could cross paths someday.

Yeah. Right.

"Don't ever chase that man. He sucks," she says with total assuredness. "I have to go. I have an open house in forty minutes. I'll talk to you soon. Love you." Livvy ends the call before I can say anything else.

I check my phone, leaving Instagram for last. Snapchat—I'm not into it as much I used to be, though I do still like watching people's stories. Fast glimpse at Facebook to see my mother has posted a bunch of recipes that make me hungry. I click out when my stomach growls. Email inbox is full of nothing but junk sales stuff, so trepidation filling my veins, I open up Instagram to see...

I have a message.

And it's from Jordan.

Sorry got distracted. Glad you followed me. It's been a long time.

Oh my God, that's it? Though I don't know what I was expecting. A declaration of his undying love? That's never going to happen.

I start typing my response.

Me: **It has been a long time. I hope you're—**

What else do I say? I hope you're doing well? Doing shitty? Having the time of your life? Do you miss me? I miss him. I can admit that right now, early in the morning and all alone in my bed, I totally miss him.

Watching that show last night was absolute torture. I dreamed of Jordan, though it's fuzzy and I can't quite remember what happened. But he was there, like we belonged together, and it didn't feel weird.

It felt...

Right.

I erase what I typed and redo it.

I hope you're doing well.

Setting my phone on the table, I get out of my fold-out bed and go to the bathroom. Brush my teeth. Stare at my reflection, thankful my skin looks decent. I need to figure out what to wear on my date with Cade tonight. I want to look nice, but not like I'm trying too hard. There's a fine line and I don't want to cross it.

Sometimes I really hate this dating game bullshit.

I wander out into the kitchen and make myself a cup of coffee with the Keurig my parents bought me two Christmases ago. I toast an everything bagel and spread too much cream cheese on top. For some reason, I'm extra clumsy this morning, and my foot slips across the floor, causing me to almost drop the plate, and everything from my everything bagel scatters across the tile.

After I sweep it up, cursing under my breath the entire time, I sit at my extremely small kitchen counter, take a bite out of my bagel, sip from my cup of coffee, and realize I am totally stalling on checking my phone, which is still sitting on my nightstand.

I dash back to the end table to get it.

And holy shit, he answered me.

Jordan: **Are you doing well, Mandy?**

I wish he wouldn't call me that. And I wish he wouldn't ask loaded questions either, though I'm sure he doesn't see it that way. I'm the one who's being ridiculous. I'm the one who's reading too much into this.

I'm great, I tell him after I eat half my bagel. **Really busy with work.**

Jordan: **What do you do?**

Me: **I'm an assistant physical therapist at a place that specializes in sports medicine.**

Jordan: **You're here in the Bay Area, right? Where exactly do you work?**

I chew on my lower lip, wondering if I should answer him. Why does he care?

Screw it.

Me: **Atlas Wellness Center.**

He doesn't answer me right away, so I finish the rest of my bagel and down the coffee, though I need no caffeine. I feel jittery enough. When he finally responds I can't read it fast enough.

Jordan: **I know exactly where that's at.**

Of course he does.

We've had some professional athletes as patients, I tell him.

Jordan: **I hope you never see me in there.** He follows it with a winking face emoji.

He's making a joke, something Jordan Tuttle doesn't do very often. Yet I take it wrong. It feels like he's trying to tell me he hopes he never sees *me* again, which is totally ridiculous. I'm reading too much into his response, I'm overthinking this entire situation.

I need to chill.

We start talking about the *Inside Football* episode, and he's very modest, not making a big deal about it. I tell him Dustin feels famous because of the class photo they showed and he says Dustin should hit him up on IG. I say yeah, sure, but no way am I telling Livvy I had this conversation with Jordan. Not yet.

Not sure why, but I want to keep this secret all to myself.

It's weird, but we chat off and on all day. While I do laundry, he sends me a DM. I send him one back and a few minutes or even an hour later, I receive a response. We talk about everything else but the fact that we broke up. We play catch up about people and places, talking like old friends, which I suppose we are.

But it's finally near six and I still need to take a shower and curl my hair. Cade is picking me up at seven for our date and I haven't even really picked out an outfit yet. As fun as this stroll down memory lane is, I need to get on it. Focus on the guy who's interested in me now, not on the one from my past.

Me: **I'm afraid I have to go. It's been nice talking to you.**

I'm in the bathroom, shedding my clothes, the shower running when Jordan immediately replies.

Jordan: **Hot date on a Saturday night?**

Livvy would encourage me to say *hell yes, motherfucker* since that's her style. But is that rude? Is that me rubbing it in his face?

No. it's the truth.

Me: **Yeah.**

That's all I say. I jump in the shower before I say something I regret and hurriedly run through my usual ritual. I don't bother shaving my legs because hello, I'm not moving that fast with Cade. There will be no bare leg touching tonight. I don't wash my hair because it curls better when it's a little dirtier, and I've shut off the water and barely wrapped the towel around myself when I'm already checking my phone for a response.

Jordan: **Who's the lucky guy? Got someone steady in your life?**

My damp skin prickles at his words. For some reason, it feels like he spent a lot of time laboring over those two sentences. Should I be honest? Or make up some elaborate story about my hot sexy boyfriend who keeps me well satisfied in bed every night?

I'm not a liar, though. So I tell him the truth.

Me: **It's a first date with a guy I work with.**

He doesn't respond for so long, I'm dry, lotioned up, and halfway dressed with my makeup done and my hair partially curled by the time I receive a reply.

Jordan: **Have fun.**

My smile is smug at his words and my stomach bottoms out, but damn it, I *will* have fun.

Even if it kills me.

FOUR

JORDAN

DID I expect Amanda to reach out to me after the *Inside Football* interview?

If I'm being completely honest with myself, that's a yes.

What I didn't expect was the swarm of conflicting emotions that overwhelmed me while I chatted with her over social media throughout the day. In the beginning, I didn't know what to say. Should I be polite? Distant? Treat her like an old friend? An old lover?

She was all of those things to me. Friend. Lover. At one point, she was the most important person in my life—and then she ended it. When she reached out last night, my initial thought was to stick it to her. Remind her of what she could've had, but lost. When she broke up with me all those years ago, I'd been crushed.

Then I got pissed.

Fuck her, I thought more than once.

But as time went by, I realized what I did to her. What I did to every woman who tried to come into my life since her. I didn't have time for any of them. Worse, I didn't have time for Amanda—the supposed most important person in my life. College consumed me. Football consumed me. So many things were happening and I let them take me away from her.

So I felt like shit. After some time and distance, I realized I'm just as much to blame for the breakup as she is. She gave up on me.

I gave up on her too.

And that's hard to admit.

Yet now, at this very moment, here she is. Back in my life. Just like I knew she would be. Can we be friends again?

I'm not sure.

Knowing she's going on a date tonight with some undeserving jackass did something to me. Jealousy reared its ugly head, no matter how much I told myself that I'm over her.

Because I am. Over her.

We could never work. I'm still just as consumed by my too-busy life. I don't have time for anyone. I barely have time for myself.

And besides—I'm over her.

Over. Her.

Maybe if I keep repeating those same two words in my head, I'll start believing them.

FIVE

AMANDA

"I HOPE YOU LIKE CHINESE," Cade tells me as we walk toward the restaurant.

I smile as my answer, thinking of the crappy Chinese food I ate last night. Though this place looks way fancier than my neighborhood standby China Restaurant. When we enter the building, we're immediately enveloped in the cool, dark atmosphere. The interior is very chic, with dark walls and mirrors, golden lit sconces and sleek furniture everywhere. There's a gorgeous girl standing behind the black lacquered hostess stand, her blood red lips pouting as we approach.

"We have a reservation at seven-thirty for two," Cade tells the hostess in a hushed voice. It's quiet throughout the restaurant even though it's busy, and I can hear the tinkling music in the background.

The hostess shoots him a bored look before checking her reservation list. "Name?"

"Cade McDougal."

Any time I start dating a guy, I imagine his last name as mine. Amanda McDougal. Amanda Winters McDougal...

Has a decent ring to it.

Does this make me a psycho? Maybe.

Probably.

"Ah yes." The hostess taps her finger on the list, her black nail polish gleaming in the light. "McDougal. Two for seven-thirty." She lifts her head, sending us both a withering look. "You're late."

"By what? Two minutes?" Wow, look at me being so snappy. The hostess glares at me, quietly fuming.

Without a word, she grabs two heavy menus and heads deeper into the restaurant. Cade settles his hand against my lower back as we follow after her. I'm not surprised at all that she seats us at a tiny table close to the kitchen.

"What a bitch," I tell him after she's gone and we're seated at the table.

Cade winces. "I've heard this place has great food, but snotty service."

"She was definitely snotty," I agree, flipping open my menu. I try my best to contain my sticker shock, but dang, this place is expensive. And it's not just regular Chinese food either. It's fancy Asian fusion, which I love, don't get me wrong. I just have no idea what I'm supposed to order. Since Cade's never been here before either, we're clueless.

We're both going over our menus, comparing notes and trying to figure out what to eat when I hear my text notification ding from deep within my purse. I ignore it, fighting the impulse to check who it is.

When it dings again two minutes later, I must physically freeze up or give off a certain aura, because Cade says gently, "Go ahead and check it."

I offer him an apologetic smile as I reach down for my purse. "Sorry. It's just—no one ever texts me on a Saturday night."

Cade grins. "Not even for a hookup?"

My smile stays in place. I can't believe he just said that. "Not usually, no." I almost say, *I'm not that type of girl,* but I hold off. Sounds too over the top.

I pull my phone out of my purse to see I have a text from a number I don't recognize.

Unknown: **You still use this number?**

Frowning, I contemplate ignoring the text. But curiosity gets the best of me.

Me: **Who is this?**

The answer is immediate.

Unknown: **JT**

Who? Oh...

Jordan freaking Tuttle.

I shove my phone back in my purse and drop it to the ground, focusing all of my attention on Cade. This is about getting to know him tonight, not being hung up on the past. Good ol' JT is part of my past.

If I'm lucky, maybe Cade could be part of my future.

"Everything okay?" Cade asks.

"Definitely," I say with a smile, and I freaking mean it. I'm fine. Great, actually. I have a handsome guy sitting across from me at a nice restaurant and my hair looks fabulous. Life can't get much better than this.

We figure out what we want to eat, opting to sharing a few plates, and then we start asking each other questions. The usual first date thing.

"I'm from central Washington," he says when I ask where he grew up. "In a small town called Wenatchee."

Never heard of it. "Do you like it there?"

"It's okay. It snows in the winter and can get one hundred plus degrees in the summer, so that kind of sucks. But the Columbia River is right there, and I like the downtown area. There are cool restaurants and shops."

"That sounds nice."

The server appears, a friendly guy in all black, and he takes our drink orders. I can actually feel my purse buzzing against my shoe like it's an actual call, and I want to check my phone again, though I'm afraid it's stupid Jordan.

No way am I going to answer the phone and talk to him while out with Cade. That sucker *knew* I was going on a date tonight. It's like he's purposely trying to sabotage my evening.

"Have you ever been to Washington?" Cade asks after our server delivers our drinks and takes our dinner order.

"No." I shake my head, reaching for my glass of wine. "I've barely been out of the state."

"Really? Well, I guess I get why. Everything you need is here in California," Cade says. "I like to travel, though, so... I've been lots of places. Moved around some, too."

"How long have you lived here?" I ask.

"Almost a year. I was working at another physical therapists' office, but it wasn't what I really wanted. I was settling while waiting for a spot to open up at a place with a sports medicine focus, and luckily enough I found Atlas." He smiles.

I smile in return. "More like we were lucky to find you."

"How about you? Where did you grow up?"

"Oh, in central California. I moved here for college—went to San Jose State my junior and senior year."

"Went to community college first?"

I nod. Take another sip of my wine, which is crisp and delicious. Not too sure if I want to get overly liquored up tonight. I have to have some limits.

My phone starts incessantly buzzing again and I kick my purse, wishing I could send it flying. But I can't. And I swear Cade can hear/feel it too, because he sends me a concerned look, and I finally give in to see what's up.

It's not just a call from Jordan, he's trying to actually Face-Time me.

Un. Real.

Grabbing the phone, I clutch it in my hand with the screen against my palm as I rise to my feet, sending Cade another one of those apologetic smiles. I hope this isn't a habit I'm going to start. "I really need to take this. Give me a minute and I'll be right back?"

"Everything okay?" he calls after me as I start to leave.

"Everything is great. Don't worry," I tell him as I move through the restaurant. I hit the answer button just as I walk out the front door, and I glance at my phone, watching in disbelief as Jordan's handsome face fills the screen.

"Why are you FaceTiming me?" My greeting is rude, but I don't care. The past twenty-four hours has been filled with nonstop Tuttle and I'm kind of over it.

Well. I *should* be over it...

He raises his dark brows and I allow myself to really drink him in. His hair is cropped close on the sides but longish on top, and currently a bit of a mess. There's dark stubble on his face, giving him a bad-boy air, and his eyes are as blue as ever. He's wearing a plain black T-shirt that stretches across his broad chest and shoulders, and I'm instantly aroused—and annoyed.

It's so unfair that he's somehow gotten better looking over the years.

"Why so hostile?" he asks, sounding genuinely surprised.

I glance around, thankful no one is nearby. "I told you I was going on a date."

"Must not be going so well if you answered me."

Now he just sounds smug. And no way can I dignify what he said with a direct answer. "You need to stop."

"Come on. Aren't you curious?"

"What do you mean?"

"I wanted to see what you looked like. Your Instagram profile doesn't have enough photos of you on it," he says, being so blatantly honest it's downright disconcerting. He leans in close, like he's really checking me out, and I'm tempted to end the call.

But of course, we know I don't.

"You look good, Mandy," he says, his voice low. Sexy. "I like your hair."

I flip my long, wavy hair behind my shoulders so he can't see it anymore. "Thanks."

"Nice shirt." He sounds amused and I glance down at myself. I'm wearing a silky oversized shirt with a deep V-neck, and wouldn't you know it, there's a hint of cleavage going on. Not too much because I wasn't going for obvious, but just enough so that Cade would catch a glimpse and hopefully be...what? Intrigued?

Looks like I intrigued the wrong person.

"You're a perv," I mutter, bringing my hair back forward with my free hand so I can cover my chest.

He chuckles, and the sound ripples along my nerve endings, making me shiver. It's like he's actually with me, but he's not. It's weird. It feels...normal, talking to Jordan like this, even though it's been years.

"I have to go," I tell him when he still hasn't said anything.

"Where's your date?"

"Waiting for me."

"Where are you at?"

I almost swing around and show him the restaurant, but decide against it. "Wouldn't you like to know."

"I would." He's very serious. "Talking with you like this is... strange. But nice. I've missed you. Our friendship."

Ah. The two words that are like a splash of ice cold water in my face. Just the reality punch I need to get me out of this confusing conversation, so I can escape staring at his stupid gorgeous face. He just misses me as a *friend*. Nothing more. Gotta remember that.

"Right. I'll talk to you later, Jordan."

I end the FaceTime call before he can say anything else and hurry back into the restaurant, smiling at Cade when he spots me heading his way. I try my best to ignore the frustration building up inside of me. And the unease. Seeing Jordan like that unsettled me, and I don't like it.

Not one bit.

SIX

AMANDA

JORDAN TUTTLE DATING GIGI HADID!!

The headline on the gossip site is in all caps and uses two exclamation points, which I suppose makes it true?

As I read the short article that's filled with very few details, posted yesterday afternoon, it claims Jordan was spotted with Gigi on Saturday night at a very small, very exclusive restaurant in San Francisco.

Um, I FaceTimed Jordan Saturday night, and it looked like he was at home. Not that I've ever been there, but from the shadowy background I saw, I assumed he was in his living room. And seriously, I don't think he'd be talking to little ol' me if he had a chance to go out to dinner with a beautiful supermodel.

I'm also pretty sure Gigi is going out with someone even more famous than Jordan. Like one of those One Direction dudes, right? Maybe? I can't keep up.

None of that matters. I don't even know why I'm thinking about it. About her.

About *him*.

"You had fun with Cade Saturday night?" We're out to lunch, Lena and I, at a tiny hamburger joint not far from work. She's been dying to talk about my date since this morning, but we've been so busy with clients, we haven't had a chance. She made me promise that we'd chat during lunch so now here we are.

"We had a great time." After the unexpected call from Jordan, I went back into the restaurant and apologized profusely to Cade for temporarily abandoning him. We ate our dinner and it was delicious. We went to the movies and were entertained. He took my hand as he walked me to my front door and he gave me a sweet, simple goodnight kiss before I slipped inside my apartment.

Confession time: I thought of Jordan when Cade kissed me. I dreamed again of Jordan that night. I threw myself into cleaning my apartment all day yesterday and fell into bed a little after nine o'clock, totally exhausted. I purposely wore myself out so I wouldn't dream, but yeah. That didn't work.

Had yet another dream about Jordan last night. A rather vivid one involving naked body parts. I woke up in a sweat, irritably turned on.

No way am I telling Lena any of this.

"I bet you did. I think he's dreamy." For the quickest moment, I think Lena's talking about Jordan. But she's not. Of course she's not. "I like his hair."

"He has nice hair," I agree. There's no denying Cade is attractive.

"And eyes. Dark brown eyes get me every time," Lena continues with a sigh.

Wait a minute. "Are you crushing on Cade?"

"Me?" She rests a hand on her chest, her eyes wide. "No. Absolutely not." She takes a giant bite out of her hamburger...so maybe she doesn't have to say anything else?

Hmmm.

"Lena..." I draw out her name, sending her a look. I hope my suspicions aren't true, because if they are, this makes me feel like crap. Maybe she's been into Cade all along and she thinks I swiped him from her?

That makes me feel awful. So awful, I set my burger down, my appetite slowly disappearing.

If she does actually like him, I had no clue. Like none whatsoever.

"Oh my God." Lena buries her face in her hands, her voice muffled against her palms. "Please don't make me say this."

"I'm totally going to make you say it," I tell her firmly, curiosity getting the better of me. I have to know. The thing I like about Lena is she's always honest with me. We tell each other stuff straight up. "Come on."

"Fine." She drops her hands, her gaze meeting mine. "I've liked him from the very moment I saw him walk through the door, okay? He caught my eye, and I was totally interested. We started talking, I started flirting, he flirted a little bit back and then...he starts asking me about you." The disappointment on her face is painfully obvious.

"Oh, Lena." I feel terrible. Awful.

Especially since Cade isn't on my mind at all. Instead, I'm consumed with thoughts of Jordan.

"He's totally into you, and he just sees me as a friend." She shrugs. "Guess I missed my chance."

She's obviously miserable, and I'm miserable too, because honestly? I'm not that into Cade. He's kind. Funny. Good looking. Easy to talk to. I have nothing against him. He's a perfectly nice guy. We had a good time on the date, but there weren't really any sparks, at least for me.

Do I want to continue dating him? Can I imagine—having *sex* with him?

Um, that would be a no. Especially knowing that Lena likes him.

I'm about to tell her she can have Cade when my phone starts an incessant buzzing, rattling against the table where I left it. I glance at the screen to see it's the same number Jordan texted and FaceTimed me from on Saturday night.

For real?

I ignore it, flipping my phone over so it rests screen down on the table.

"You going to get that?" Lena asks. We're always worried we're going to get called back into work before our lunch hour is through.

"It's a spam caller. I've probably won another all-expenses paid vacation to Orlando." Perfect excuse. We gripe to each other about those calls from Elizabeth at Hilton Vacations all the time.

"Are you lying to save my feelings, Amanda?" I'm about to respond, but she keeps talking. "Was it Cade? Is he wanting to hook up for a quickie during lunch? I won't hold you back, you know. I'm all about the lunch break hookup."

"No. God, Lena, it wasn't Cade asking for a quickie. Just..." I lean across the table, peering at her. "Do you *really* have a thing for him?"

"Of course not." She sits up a little straighter. "Not anymore."

She's lying. I can tell by the tone of her voice, her body language. "I never knew—"

"I never told you, so don't feel guilty, okay? You have no reason to feel guilty," Lena says quickly.

"It's just that—"

She cuts me off again, rising to her feet as she keeps talking. "It's okay. Really. I need to use the restroom."

I watch her take off, my appetite leaving with her. This is a mess. If she really likes Cade, I don't want to ruin her chance with him. But does he like her? Or is he totally into me and won't even give Lena a chance? And then there's Jordan...

Grabbing my phone, I flip it over to find I have a voicemail. I immediately check it.

Hey Mandy. Checking to see if you and your boyfriend wanted to come to my game tonight. I left suite tickets at roll call so if you're interested, just give them your name at the window. Maybe we could catch up after the game? See ya.

I set my phone down on the table, my head spinning. Okay. I don't think I want to keep dating Cade, but I am so bringing him to this football game tonight. I'll just tell Lena I'm not into him later.

———

"You want to go to the game tonight?" Once we returned to work, I went in search of Cade and found him sitting in the break room, watching an old episode of *Jerry Springer* on TV and scrolling through his phone, an empty bag of snack-sized Doritos sitting in front of him.

He lifts his head, his gaze meeting mine. "You mean the football game?"

"Yeah." I nod enthusiastically, flashing him a smile. I am a bad person for using him like this, but come on. He'll want to go. What guy doesn't love football? And once we go to this game, I'll cut him loose. Maybe Lena and Cade can end up together and it'll be a beautiful, magical thing. "The Niners are playing."

"I know," he says carefully, studying me like I might have a mental problem. "This game has been sold out for months."

"Really?" I had no idea.

"Really. How did you get tickets?"

"I have a connection," I hedge.

"Who's your connection?"

Why is he asking so many questions? "Um, you'll never believe who it is."

"Try me." He crosses his arms, leaning back in his chair.

"Jordan Tuttle—we, uh, used to date."

Cade sits up straight, his mouth hanging open. "*You* dated Jordan Tuttle?"

I hate this. The notoriety that comes with dating a well-known athlete, even though it's been years and we were together before he became a big deal. I wonder how all of Tom Brady's exes feel. I find it a complete pain in the ass, if I'm being truthful. "It was a long time ago. High school stuff," I tell Cade.

"And he just so happened to give you tickets for tonight's game." The doubt in his voice is clear.

"We've, uh, recently reconnected." I'm not explaining it any further than that. I can't tell him Jordan FaceTimed me during our date. That'll sound crazy. "He offered me two tickets to tonight's game. In one of the suites. They're holding the tickets at will call. Would you like to go with me?"

His answer is immediate. "Sure. Definitely. Maybe I could meet Tuttle, or any other Niner who's around." He rises to his feet, smiling down at me. "You like football?"

"I love football." This is not an exaggeration. I've loved the game since I was little. I watched so many games with my father, even went to a few live ones, but those were rare since they're so expensive and we were a family on a budget. I swear I joined band just so I could go to all the games in middle school and high school.

"Great." Cade's smile grows. "We should leave from here then. We won't have much time to get over to the stadium."

Crap. Cade's right, I know he is, but I wanted to go back to my apartment and change first, reapply my makeup and maybe even take a quick shower. I want to look damn good for my first encounter with Jordan after all these years. Not see him wearing an Atlas Wellness Center red polo and a pair of black pants I bought on clearance from Athleta. My hair is in a high ponytail and I didn't wash it last night...

I am definitely not my best self right now.

"Yeah, okay." I don't have a car. Cade does, but do we want to deal with parking, or just take the BART?

"I'll drive," he offers like a mind reader, and I nod.

"Sounds good. Can't wait." I offer up a wan smile. I really should be more enthusiastic about this, but now I'm just a bundle of anxiety. "We'll leave around five then?"

"Yep. I'm really glad you asked me to go with you, Amanda." He leans in and drops a quick kiss on my cheek, smiling at me. "I've got to go. I have an appointment arriving in five minutes."

"See ya," I say softly just as I spot Lena standing in the distance, watching us with a hurt expression on her face.

She leaves before I can say anything.

SEVEN

AMANDA

I AM A NERVOUS WRECK.

No, seriously, I feel all hopped up on caffeine and I haven't drunk a drop since this morning's first and only cup of coffee. Cade has been a perfect gentleman during the entire sometimes-frustrating-because-of-awful-five-o'clock-traffic drive to the stadium, not asking me any questions about my past with Jordan, which I appreciate. He's accepting of the entire situation, though he did express worry as we approached the will call window.

"You sure those tickets are going to be there for us?"

"Yes," I say with as much positivity as I can muster. Deep down, I'm scared the lady at the window is going to laugh when I give her my name and tell me, "As if."

But she doesn't. I say my name, show her my ID and she hands over an envelope with my name handwritten on it in an unrecognized scrawl. "Go through that entrance," she tells me, and points toward a gate that has hardly anyone near it but two big burly security guards.

I show one of the burly dudes our tickets and he gives me a skeptical look, even though his eyes are covered by mirrored sunglasses. Cade doesn't say a thing, and I'm thankful he's not making a big deal out of this.

But oh my God, it feels like such a big deal. I haven't seen Jordan in the flesh since we were nineteen. We're twenty-five now. It's been six years. Six long years. And though I saw him for a few minutes on that FaceTime call and I see him pretty much every Sunday or when I'm watching ESPN, which is more often than you'd think, it's not the same as actually *being* with him.

Being in his presence. Seeing his beautiful face and smelling his delicious scent and waiting for him to flash one of those rare smiles at me...

"Tuttle's been the quarterback for only two seasons," Cade says as we make our way to the private suite where we're going to watch the game. The hallway is mostly empty, and I know we missed the start of the game, which bums me out.

"Yeah, I know." I wince the moment the words are out. I want to seem like a total Jordan Tuttle stalker.

"He's pretty damn good," Cade says excitedly and I nod my answer, not wanting to say anything else about Jordan.

Not right now, at least.

We keep walking, drinking in our surroundings. Our footsteps echo down the hall and I can hear the roar of the stadium crowd in the near distance, the announcer telling them something I can't quite make out.

"Do you come to the games often?" Cade asks, sending me a suspicious look.

I'm sure he's wondering if my ex leaves me tickets all the time. I suppose I can't blame him.

"No. My dad took us to a couple of the games when they were still at Candlestick Park, but that was forever ago." Back when he would get free season tickets from one of the guys he worked with who didn't want to go to the "boring" games. We made a day trip of it, Dad taking us kids while Mom stayed home since there were only four tickets. It was a lot of fun, but we were only able to do it twice.

"That's cool, that you were able to go to Candlestick," Cade says. The stadium was torn down years ago.

"It was a lot of fun," I agree, feeling nostalgic. Everything about the last few days has me feeling nostalgic, like I'm living in the past, which probably isn't the best thing. But I can't help it.

Thinking about Jordan—actually chatting with Jordan is making me feel young again. Like anything is possible.

"Oh look, here's the suite," I say, my voice coming out high pitched. I'm terrified, my hands shaking as Cade pushes the door open for me. I walk in first, gazing around the cavernous room filled with people. There's a table to the right covered with food, a bar set up to the left with two men serving drinks.

And ahead of us, a giant window that looks out onto the field, stadium seating directly in front of it.

"Wow," Cade says with a low whistle as we both stop and stare. The first quarter is almost over, and we can see the players out on the field. He's staring at them in wide-eyed wonder, looking like an excited little boy, and I can't help but feel the same way.

There's a chance I'm going to see Jordan tonight. Face to face. In the flesh. We'll be in the same room. Sharing the same air.

God, I feel a little faint.

"Hello, are you guests with us tonight?" A very tall, very pretty blonde woman stops in front of us, a friendly smile pasted on her face. "May I see your tickets, please?"

"Yes, we are." I hand the envelope over and the woman checks our tickets, then hands the envelope back over, which I stuff in my purse.

"Perfect. I'm your suite's 49er Ambassador for the evening, and I'm so happy to have you. As you can see, we have our buffet." She waves her hand like a game show hostess showing off the prizes. "And there's plenty to drink, including alcoholic beverages. All of it is complimentary."

"Thank you. It looks great," Cade says with an enthusiastic nod.

"Don't forget to check out the stadium seating so you can watch the game up close. We hope you have a great time," she says, her smile growing, showing off a straight row of perfect white teeth. "Enjoy your evening!"

The moment she walks away, Cade has his hand on my elbow, guiding me toward the buffet table. "Let's get some food," he suggests. "I'm starving."

I'm too nervous to eat, but I grab some crackers and cheese, a little dab of hummus and some carrots. We head over to the bar and the cute bartender hands me a glass of white wine with a wink and a smile. I go and stand with Cade in the corner of the room, watching as he downs chicken wings slathered in buffalo sauce and dipped in ranch.

"Are they any good?" I ask, wincing when he almost drops the half-eaten wing on his shirt.

"Delicious," he says, setting his beer on the table beside us so he can wipe his mouth with a napkin. At least he grabbed a napkin. The last guy I dated—and we went on exactly two dates—was anti-hygiene. As in, he didn't believe in deodorant because it was poison, he confessed to me he rarely bathed, and he basically lived in a dump with five other guys. He was a total dirt bag.

Lena has told me I make bad choices when it comes to men. I thought Cade would meet her approval and he did—to the point that she likes him more than I do. I still feel guilty about her lunchtime confession. And I hate that she saw Cade kiss me on the cheek after I asked him to go to the game. I don't know how long she was listening to our conversation, or if she actually heard me talk to him about tonight's game. I didn't get a chance to speak to her the rest of the afternoon since we were so busy with appointments.

I'll have to talk to her tomorrow and clear the air. Hopefully she's not mad at me...

"You're not eating," Cade says, knocking me from my thoughts.

I glance down at my still pitifully full plate "I'm not very hungry."

"Too bad, considering all the free food they're offering." He downs his beer, polishing it off. "Want another drink?"

"No thank you." I want to tell him to slow down on the drinking, that he's driving tonight, but I keep my mouth shut. The evening is young, and I don't want to be a nag. It's not like I'm his mama.

He tosses his plate in the trash and heads for the bar, and I watch him go before dropping my gaze to my plate filled with food I'm never going to eat. I toss it in the trash too.

The bar is crowded. I know Cade is going to be waiting a while, so I make my way to the stadium seating, smiling politely at everyone I pass. I don't know a single soul in this place. I have no idea who any of these people are, though some of them look important. Rich. Most of the men are wearing their Niner gear, though there are a couple of guys in full blown suits. Many of the women have massive diamonds in their ears and their giant boobs stretch their blinged-out Niner shirts tight across their chests. They examine me as I walk past, making me self-conscious.

I feel like the odd woman out in my Atlas Wellness Center polo and my faded black pants and my black Nikes. At least the polo is red, right? I'm sort of wearing Niner colors...

There's an empty seat at the far end of the first seat row and I settle into it, my eyes never leaving the field, searching out the number eight on a red-and-white jersey.

He got to keep his number. Eight is great, after all. I still have Tuttle's old high school jersey. I bet I could fetch a lot of money for it if I put it on eBay...

Like I would ever do that.

Ah. There he is. Out on the field, his butt looking extra fine in those gold uniform pants, not that I'm checking him out or anything. I watch him get in a huddle with his teammates and I wonder what they think of him. Do they respect him? Back in high school, he earned respect without hardly doing a thing. Like him or hate him, most everyone was at the very least drawn to him. He had a certain kind of magnetism that can't be described.

I bet he still has it. That gravitational pull that makes everyone want to be near him. The same pull that makes every woman he encounters want to be with him. I'm sure it's still there. That's not something that's just...snuffed out like a lit match. It burns forever within him.

And if I'm being completely honest with myself, I'm dying to see if there's still a spark between us.

Cade eventually joins me and our conversation is minimal as we watch the game. During the first half, neither team scores. I suppose you'd think the game is boring when there are no touchdowns, or even a field goal, but that makes the impending first touchdown count even more. So no, this game isn't boring. I'm praying Jordan throws a touchdown for the Niners as they start the second half, and I'm squirming in my seat once Jordan and the rest of the offensive team comes out onto the field.

"This game is insane," Cade says with wonder, his gaze glued to the field.

I say nothing, but he's right. It's so insane, I feel like I'm about to lose my mind.

Tuttle gets into position. Is it fair that all his muscles seem to flex and work as he pulls his arm back, looking for his receivers out on the field? A sigh escapes me before I can stop it and I clamp my lips shut. When is life ever fair?

Not when it comes to me and Jordan Tuttle.

Jordan throws the ball, and it spirals through the air until out of nowhere—intercepted! The commentators are yelling, the entire suite erupts in jeers and screams, and all I can do is sink lower in my seat.

My gaze flies to Jordan, and I can see the anger and frustration in his posture, blazing in his eyes, even from where I'm sitting.

"Man, is he nervous or what? He's not on his game tonight," Cade says.

Again, I don't answer. I'm too busy chewing my thumbnail.

This could end up being a long and terrible night.

"A FEW OF the players are going to join us after the game, so please do stick around."

I hear the 49er Ambassador say this to everyone as she moves about the suite with that giant smile pasted on her face. The game just finished, and oh my God, they won, but barely. It had been such a fight, especially during that tortuous second half. I could tell Jordan was so freaking pissed.

If he's anything like his high school self, he will *still* be pissed. And disappointed despite the win. He was always hard on himself.

He learned that from his asshole father.

"You'll want to stay, right?" Cade asks me. "To see your ex? Or is he even going to show up?"

"I want to stay," I tell him quietly, trying my best not to betray my nerves, because they're fluttering like a million and one butterflies in my stomach, dipping and swirling and reminding me that I drank two glasses of wine on an empty stomach and my head is a little spinny.

Jordan will show up. How I know this, I'm not exactly sure, but I have complete confidence that he will be here within thirty minutes, mark my words. There's a reason he gave me those tickets and wanted me to watch his game in the fancy suite. It wasn't out of the graciousness of his heart.

He brought me here on his turf because he knew I wouldn't be able to resist his request. Maybe he wants to show off and rub it in? Let me know what I've been missing all these years? Remind me of just how successful he is and how I'm a complete idiot for dumping him?

Or maybe those are my own petty thoughts, my own insecurities shining through.

The suite clears out pretty quickly. There are two guys in suits who are sticking around, clutching watered down drinks as they talk in low murmurs, their expressions intense. And there's an older couple still standing in front of the giant window who are practically vibrating with excitement, making me think they might be related to one of the players. There are a few women here too. Beautiful women of various shapes and sizes, all of them eyeing each other up like they're in some sort of competition.

And maybe they are. God, maybe they're all waiting to see... Jordan? No, they can't *all* be waiting for him.

Right?

"I hope they don't take too much longer." Cade stifles a yawn, his eyes droopy. "I'm exhausted, and I have to be at work at seven tomorrow. Have an early appointment."

Oh wow, I feel terrible for making him stick around. He does have a life, after all. But I kind of need him by my side too, for emotional support. I'm working hard at playing it cool, calm and collected on the outside, but inside? I'm a total wreck. I'm so nervous I feel like I could hyperventilate.

"Do you want to go ahead and leave?" I offer like an idiot, praying he says no.

He sends me a relieved smile instead. "Maybe? Yeah, we probably should. Sorry we can't meet your ex, but I'm tired. We still have a long drive home too."

Disappointment crashes within me as I let Cade take my hand and lead me out of the suite. My mind is racing, screaming at me to stay. Stay. STAY. But I don't protest, I don't tell Cade to stop, I just follow after him like a good little girl.

What the hell am I doing?

We're barely down the expansive hallway when I see them. Two giant men headed in our direction. I know without a doubt who one of them is.

Jordan.

And to his left, walking directly toward me? It's our old friend from high school, Cannon Whittaker.

"Amanda Winters, is that you?" Cannon holds his hand at eyebrow level and squints at me like I'm a shining sun too bright for him to stare at. Without thought, I let go of Cade's hand, making my way toward Cannon, keeping my eyes averted so I don't have to look at Tuttle.

I am a coward, but at least I'm aware of my faults.

Cannon's arms open and I throw myself at him, giving him a long hug. I haven't seen him in person since the summer after we graduated high school, and he looks great. Somehow, he's bigger and taller, though his dark blond hair is shorn close, like usual. He definitely looks more grown up now, and I squeeze him as close as I can, though really it's like hugging a stone wall.

"It's so good to see you." My voice is muffled against his hard-as-a-rock chest.

"It's great to see you too." He shifts away from me, his hands on my shoulders, his gaze taking me in. "You look amazing."

"You are too kind," I say with a laugh, suddenly feeling shy. And inadequate in my rumpled work clothes. I can feel Jordan watch me, his glowering presence making my legs wobble, the intensity of his gaze making me feel faint. Thank God Cannon still has a grip on me or I'd probably collapse to the floor.

"Mandy." Jordan's deep voice rumbles along my nerve endings, causing me to shiver, and Cannon turns me toward him just before he releases me, like they planned it beforehand. I'm face to face with Jordan Tuttle for the first time in six years—six freaking years!—and I do the dumbest thing ever.

I stick my hand out for him to shake it.

EIGHT
JORDAN

WHAT THE FUCK? Of course, I'm not going to shake Amanda's hand.

Instead I grab hold of it, that unmistakable jolt of electricity sparking when our skin connects, just like every other time we've touched. I pull her to me and wrap her up in my arms because I can. I'm the one who offered up the tickets so I could...what? Put on a show? Let her know exactly how great my life is?

I can't lie. My life is pretty damn great. I have everything I could ever want—except for one thing.

"Hi Jordan," she breathes against my neck, and I swear she melts into me a little. Like she can't help herself. Like we somehow still fit together even after all these years.

Either she got smaller or I grew bigger since the last time I touched her, and I'm guessing it's the latter. She smells familiar, yet different. Better. I recognize the scent of her shampoo, but nothing else. Her hair is longer. Thick. Dark and wavy, up in a ponytail and a little disheveled, like she's had a long day. Her body is curvier, something teenaged Amanda would've never believed could happen.

She still has those sexy long legs, though.

Finally, she pulls away from me, her lips curled, her eyes sparkling, nervousness written all over her face, and I watch her carefully in return, my expression as neutral as I can make it. Honestly, I'm still a little pissed over that garbage game we just played, and I'm tense like I usually am after a tough game. Her understanding gaze meets mine and I know she knows what I'm feeling.

We've always been in tune with each other...

She's my Mandy, all grown up. But not my Mandy anymore. In fact, there's a guy standing off to the side, silently watching us, and Cannon's watching us too. Like we're putting on some sort of performance and they're judging our interaction with each other.

With Cannon, I get it. He was there from the beginning. He knows me, he knows Amanda. But the guy with her? I don't know him.

And for some reason, I immediately don't like him.

"Cade." Her voice is light and high, and she steps toward the guy, grabbing his hand and pulling him closer to us. "These are my friends, Cannon Whittaker and—Jordan Tuttle."

She hesitates when she says my name, and I wonder at her choice of the word *friends*. Does this guy—*Cade*—not know we used to be together?

"Nice to meet you." I stick out my hand before Cannon gets a chance and squeeze Cade's hand extra hard, like an asshole.

"It is so great to meet you too," Cade says enthusiastically, wrenching his hand from mine. Then he's shaking Cannon's too, though Cannon is a lot kinder. He doesn't try and break the bones of Amanda's date. "Thanks for the tickets. You guys played a fantastic game tonight," Cade says to both of us.

Cannon nods enthusiastically. He did play great. I didn't.

It was a bullshit game. We barely won. But whatever.

"Thanks," I say easily. I can feel Amanda's gaze on me, but I refuse to look in her direction.

Once I start looking, I might not be able to stop.

"It's wild to see you here tonight," Cannon tells Amanda, staring at her like she's a ghost from his past.

More like she's my ghost, still haunting me.

"Jordan invited me," she says, her gaze cutting to mine, and this time I look back. She did not dress to impress. I'd guess she came to the game straight from work, and so did her date, considering their matching polo shirts.

It doesn't matter. She could be wearing a paper bag and I'd still think she was beautiful.

"Thank you for letting us watch you in the suite," she tells me, her voice soft, her brown eyes seemingly extra dark. Full of secrets.

I used to live for those brown eyes to look at me. And now, all those old feelings swamp me, taking me back in time.

Leaving me confused as hell.

"Yeah, thanks again. And what a view, watching the game from here," Cade adds way too enthusiastically. He reminds me of an exuberant puppy, wanting to please everyone.

"You're welcome." I glance over at Cannon. "Should we head to the suite?"

"Yeah." Cannon nods. "My aunt and uncle are waiting."

"I need to talk to the sponsors." I study Amanda once more. "Were you guys leaving?"

"Yeah. It is so awesome meeting you guys. Like seriously, lifetime memory-type stuff. But I hate to say it, I'm beat. It's been a long day," Cade says with a yawn he stifles behind a closed fist. "Have to get to work early tomorrow, too. You know how it goes."

Our lives couldn't be more different. I have no idea how it goes.

The disappointment on Amanda's face is clear at hearing Cade's words, and seeing her like this gives me a strange kind of satisfaction. As if I want her to miss me. "I guess we're leaving," she says softly.

"You need a ride home?"

She blinks up at me, clearly shocked by my question. As am I.

What the fuck am I doing?

"I can stay a little longer," Cade interjects, slipping his arm around Amanda's shoulders like he owns her, the prick. "I'll drive Amanda home."

"Cool," I say with a nod, but deep inside I'm seething. I don't like how he took control of the situation. I don't like how he's touching Amanda possessively.

More than anything, I don't like the way seeing her after all this time is making me feel.

This is, after all, the girl who held my nineteen-year-old heart in her hands.

And crushed it.

NINE
AMANDA

WINCING, I brace myself just before I splash cold water on my cheeks, then reach blindly for a paper towel. I pat my face dry, careful not to smudge mascara beneath my eyes, and blink once, twice, staring at my reflection in the mirror in the suite bathroom, where I made my escape a few minutes ago.

I look awful. There are no mascara smudges because it's all gone. There's not a lick of makeup left on my face. My skin is pale, though the icy water brought a little color to my cheeks. There are dark circles under my eyes and my hair is a total disaster. I drop the paper towel into the trash and then finger comb the messy strands, trying to calm them down, make them look better, but it's hopeless.

I am hopeless.

Knowing I can open the bathroom door and Jordan will be in the next room makes my heart want to gallop straight out of my chest. It was downright exhilarating to see him again after so long. Despite what happened to us in our past, despite my breaking up with him like the stupid teenaged girl I was, he's perfectly polite. Sweet, even.

Okay, fine, I can't exactly call our encounter *sweet*. Hugging him had been like that first snort of cocaine after being clean and sober for years. An addict finding her long-lost fix. I might've held him a little too long, though at least I was the one who shoved away first.

He had been a little growly, a little moody. I know it's because he didn't feel good about that game. Throwing that interception must've infuriated him.

And then there's the fact I tried to shake his hand like a dork.

I mean, seriously. I've had *sex* with him. Multiple times. He was my first. I was *his* first. I see him six years later and the first thing I want to do is shake his hand? What the hell was I thinking?

Dumb. He makes me dumb. Staring into his blue eyes and seeing him like that, all big and gorgeous and masculine and beautiful and handsome and oh my God, I sound like an idiot even in my thoughts.

With fumbling fingers, I find my favorite pinky-nude lipstick in my tiny purse and slick it on my lips, rubbing them together, pleased with the results. That's about as pulled together as I'm going to get, and yet again I hate that I'm wearing my work polo. I don't look half as beautiful as the women who are still hanging out in the suite. Their eyes lit up when Jordan and Cannon first entered the room. I just knew they all wanted a piece of them, and seeing the women's reactions filled me with an old, familiar and ugly emotion.

Jealousy.

Lame. I'm also super-duper lame.

Resting my hands on either side of the sink, I look myself in the eyes and tell my reflection, "Don't be stupid."

I drop the lipstick back in my purse and go to the door, throwing it open with firm determination.

Only to find Jordan standing there in the tiny hall, like he was—oh, I don't know—*waiting* for me?

No. Way. Just a coincidence. It has to be.

"Hi." I come to a stop, the bathroom door almost hitting me in the backside.

"Hey." He sounds grim. Looks uncomfortable. He hasn't smiled, not once since we locked eyes, and I remember how stingy he used to be with those smiles. How I felt like I unlocked a treasure chest of unlimited riches when he started smiling more. Only for me.

There were a lot of things he did only for me.

"Are you mad?" When he frowns, I further explain myself. "About the game. About the interception."

He nods, his perfect lips twisting to the side. "It wasn't a good game for me."

"I thought you looked great."

"I played like shit. Disappointed my team."

So typical for him to beat himself up over it. "You guys still won."

"By the skin of our teeth."

I tilt my head. "I've never understood that saying. Our teeth aren't made of skin. Like, where did that saying even come from? It doesn't make sense." *I'm* making no sense. Why am I talking about this when I really want to ask the important questions? Like:

How are you?

Are you happy?

Are you sad?

Is your life fulfilling?

Are you dating someone?

Do you miss me?

His lips curl the faintest bit. An almost smile. "Only you would overthink a cliché."

"What's that supposed to mean?" I'm vaguely offended.

"It's what you do, Mandy. You've always overthought a lot of things." The meaningful look he sends me is full of all sorts of unspoken messages.

Ones I don't necessarily want to confront right now.

"You've done it, though," I tell him, trying to change the subject. "You're a big deal, Jordan. You're one of the most respected quarterbacks in the NFL."

"I don't know about that." He shrugs. Always modest. Like everything he does is no big deal, when it's a *huge* deal.

"Please." I roll my eyes, but he doesn't laugh or smile.

"It's only the start of my third season," he points out. "We've had some good luck and a great team, including our coaches. They're all waiting for me to screw up."

"Who's waiting for you to screw up? Your *team?*" I don't believe it.

"No. Just—everyone. The media. The other teams. Their coaches. People who hate me." He rubs his hand against his jaw. "There are a lot of people who hate me."

"It comes with the territory." I wish I could tell him that I would never hate him. But maybe he wouldn't listen. Or worse?

Maybe he doesn't even care.

"You're right." He stands up straighter, glancing around. He appears pleased that no one is paying attention to us. "How are you, Amanda? How's work?"

His quick change of subject doesn't faze me. "It was busy today." I wave a hand at myself. "I had to come straight to the game. That's why I'm still in my Atlas polo."

"It looks good on you." His eyes drop and lock on my boobs, and I almost want to thrust my chest out.

I restrain myself. Barely.

In high school, I was flat chested. They grew a little bit over the years, but I can never say I have big breasts. Because I don't. I have nice little 34B-sized boobs that don't quite fill up the cup size; they look extra good in a padded, lifted bra, and that's about it. My legs are better. They're long and lean and I'm tall, which I used to hate, but I can now deal with it. Most guys I've gone out with have been the same height or a little taller. There had been that one blind date with the guy who was five-foot-four and wore lifts in his cowboy boots.

I'm not into cowboys. Or short men. This probably makes me prejudiced. Or sexist. I'm not sure which.

Jordan is taller than me. He's six-foot-three, I think.

Oh please, I *know* he's six-foot-three. I read his stats online. He weights 225 pounds. He could crush me.

I find that unnaturally arousing.

"Thanks," I finally say when I realize he's still staring at my chest. He lifts his head, our gazes clashing, and all we can do is look at each other, all those unspoken questions floating between us. My skin is tingling, my blood flowing hot through my veins, making me vitally aware of my existence. It feels like I stuck my finger into an electrical socket and shocked myself.

"You're welcome." His voice is a deep rumble, and he clears his throat, looks to the side, rubs his jaw again, suddenly appearing anxious. Twitchy. "I need to go. Talk to the sponsors."

No! Don't go! Not yet!

My brain is an overdramatic lover of exclamation points.

"Sponsors for what?" I ask casually, trying to stall him. Keep him with me, if only for a few more minutes.

"Oh, you know." He shrugs those broad shoulders of his. "Marketing reps from a huge sportswear chain. They like to stop by and schmooze us. Take us for drinks or dinner, when they should just email our agents and put something together for us to consider. They all say they can offer the personal touch." I can tell he wants to roll his eyes.

"They're talking to just you?"

"And Cannon. Marketing people love our high school connection." His smile is rueful.

All those old insecurities come rolling back, forcing me to remember how different we are. His world is nothing like mine. He's making million-dollar-plus endorsements and I'm working at Atlas Wellness Center. He's worth millions on his own and comes from a wealthy family, and I almost live paycheck to paycheck.

"It is pretty neat, how you two are playing together again." I want to punch myself in the face the moment the words leave my lips. *Neat?* How lame can I get?

"We don't even play together that much, at least not on the field. He's defense, I'm offense." His gaze lingers on mine. "But you already know that."

He's always respected my football knowledge. Sometimes I think I even impressed him. Taking a deep breath, I part my lips, ready to say something, but we're interrupted.

"Hey." We both turn to see Cannon headed toward us, his expression urgent.

"What's up?" Jordan asks coolly.

"We need to go. They want to take us to dinner." He jerks his thumb toward the two men in suits who stand nearby, covertly watching us.

"You get to see your aunt and uncle?" Jordan asks.

"Yeah." Cannon smiles. "They're so excited. Came all the way from Ohio to watch the game. I'm going to take them to Fisherman's Wharf tomorrow."

"Good idea." Jordan claps him on the shoulder, his expression grave, his voice going deliciously low. "Give us one more minute, okay?"

"Take your time." Cannon smiles in my direction. "Good to see you again, Amanda. Let's get together soon, okay? Go out to dinner or something?"

I would love, love, *love* to go out to dinner with Cannon. I've always had a soft spot for him. And maybe I could ask him questions about Jordan. Ones I would never actually say to Jordan's face, because I'm a complete chicken. "Sounds good."

He walks away and Jordan remains silent. As do I. I don't know what to say next. I feel like he's going to bust out something momentous on me, but what? A declaration of love? That he's never stopped caring about me, thinking about me, wanting me? Please.

That's wishful thinking on my part.

"I'm really glad you came to the game," Jordan finally says, his voice so low I have to step closer to hear him. "I wish I had played better."

"You did fantastic," I say softly, tempted to reach out and touch him, brush his hair away from his forehead, touch his arm, his chest. But I don't. I need to keep my impulses under control.

He's not mine anymore to touch.

"It's good to see you. In person." He offers up one of those barely there smiles again. Here and gone in a flash, no teeth revealed. "I'm glad we were able to reconnect."

Does he still want to stay connected? Yes?

Maybe?

"I'm glad we reconnected too." My cheeks are flushed. I can feel the heat in my face and I'm smiling so hard, it hurts. "I've—missed you."

The confession is out there. The truth, baldly stated and hanging between us like the crackling chemistry that's been on low boil since we first laid eyes on each other.

Yet his expression remains stoic. No flicker in his beautiful blue gaze, nothing. No *I miss you too*.

My smile falls and I know he sees it. He takes a few steps closer, definitely within touching distance, more like in *kissing* distance, and he reaches out. Settles one of those big, magical hands on my shoulder, gives it a light squeeze.

"Take care," he murmurs.

And then he's gone.

TEN

AMANDA

CADE KEEPS up the nonstop chatter the entire drive back to my place. He tried his best to play it cool when we were in the suite, but the moment we got in his car, he was practically bursting with the need to talk about his experience.

"I can't believe you know those guys," he says again and again with a shake of his head. "That you actually went to school with them."

I don't have the heart to tell him what dicks Cannon and Jordan used to be. Maybe they still are, I don't know. But during our senior year, both those boys treated me fairly, like we were actual friends. Cannon because he respected me, and Jordan because, well...

He was in love with me.

And I was deeply in love with him. Seeing Jordan tonight, talking to him, those fleeting moments when his gaze was on me, or when he actually touched me, all those feelings came rushing back, flooding me with emotion. To the point where all I can do is sit here and think about him and wonder...

Am I *still* in love with him?

It's not possible. I don't even know who he really is anymore. Too much time has passed, too many things have happened. We could never get back what we had. I destroyed that chance by breaking up with him.

At least he was civil toward me.

I'm so wrapped up in my own thoughts I don't realize we're back at my apartment complex until Cade pulls into the tiny parking lot. He cuts the engine and watches me, an expectant look on his face. Like he might want to kiss me or something.

That is the absolute last thing I want to do, with the way Jordan Tuttle is still lingering in my head.

"Thanks again for taking me tonight." Cade's smile is bright in the otherwise mostly dark interior of his car. "I had a lot of fun."

"Thanks for going with me."

"We should do it again sometime. Maybe go to another game."

"Um, sure." Here's where I feel like complete shit. I don't want to go on another date with Cade. He's a great guy, I just don't feel...anything for him beyond friendship.

I think of Lena and how she likes him. I feel bad enough, bringing Cade with me tonight. I can't do this anymore. It's not fair.

"Or dinner again. I found a great Thai place I think you might like." His smile grows, and dread fills me. I don't want to dump him tonight. I just made him go to that game with me so I could have someone to lean on. I used him for support, so that probably makes me an awful person.

At this moment, I definitely feel like an awful person.

"Okay," I tell him weakly, hoping I sound noncommittal. "Good night." I reach for the door handle, ready to bust out like I'm making a prison escape, but he stops me, his hand going to my shoulder, his grip firm. I turn to look at him, not saying a word, and he leans in. His eyes start to close...

I avert my head at the last minute, his lips grazing my cheek.

He pulls away, disappointment flashing in his gaze, and I refuse to feel bad, yet I do. I'd rather be friends with him.

I hate the flicker of hope that's lit deep within me. At the idea of being seeing Jordan again. Possibly being with Jordan again?

"See you tomorrow," I say, pushing the passenger side door open and making my escape. I bend down to wave at him through the window once I shut the door and he waves at me in return, starting the engine and backing out of the space so quick, he's gone in what feels like less than a minute.

I hustle back to my apartment, hating how late it is, and how quiet. I can hear the distant thundering of cars on the freeway, a dog barking at one of the houses across the street, and I let go a big sigh of relief when I'm actually in my tiny place with the door firmly locked. It's not that my neighborhood is unsafe, it's just...being alone late at night is a little scary.

My evening routine is starting later than usual, but I keep to it. I take a shower and wash my hair. Slip into an old T-shirt—from high school, what a surprise—and then blow-dry my hair. Climb into bed with my phone, shocked to see I have a text message from that number I haven't put a name to yet.

It's Jordan's number. And he's left me numerous messages.

It was good seeing you tonight.

Sorry we didn't talk much.

We should get together again sometime.

If your boyfriend doesn't mind.

His texts make me smile. He's ridiculous in the absolute best way.

I'm glad we got to see each other too.

We should definitely get together.

And he's not my boyfriend.

My phone starts ringing, and it's Jordan wanting to FaceTime. I answer without thinking, immediately regretting it because I'm wearing that old high school T-shirt which proves I'm thinking of him or whatever conclusion Jordan will draw. Plus, I don't have a lick of makeup on. Don't have a bra on either, meaning I'm not at my best.

At least my hair looks good.

"Why are you FaceTiming me?" I ask the screen, scowling at his handsome face, ignoring the way my heart hammers in my chest at seeing him. At how intimate this moment is, even though we're not in the same room together.

Doesn't matter. It's just me and Jordan, staring at each other through a phone screen. And for whatever reason, that feels like enough.

At least in this moment.

"Felt bad that we didn't get a chance to talk much." He hesitates. I can see doubt flicker in his gaze for the briefest moment. "Your boyfriend seems nice."

"I already told you he's not my boyfriend."

"He was very possessive of you, Mandy." Jordan's voice goes a little deeper and I swear I can feel it vibrating in the pit of my stomach.

I know exactly what moment Jordan's referring to. "That's because you offered to take me home and we went to the game together. I think you intimidated him."

"I was just trying to be nice."

Uh huh. That innocent look on his face doesn't fool me. "You're my ex-boyfriend. You intimidated him," I say again.

"Whatever. I think he was star struck. He probably wished *I* was taking him home." There's that ghost of a smile again. Seeing it makes me smile a little too.

"He probably did," I agree.

"So he's definitely not your boyfriend?" Jordan raises his brows.

I want to shout at him, *why do you care?* But I don't. I guess he's just curious. This is what happens when you reconnect with an ex, right? We're curious about each other's lives, including romantic entanglements we're not involved in...

"Cade isn't my boyfriend," I say firmly. "We went out on one date."

Well, two.

"Two if you count tonight," Jordan says like he's living in my head, which he sort of is.

"Right. Two," I say weakly, leaning back against my pillows. He has to know I'm in bed. Where's he at? He appears freshly showered, his dark hair damp, and he's wearing a gray T-shirt that stretches tight across his shoulders and chest.

Too bad he's not shirtless. I remember Jordan always had great abs. I bet they're even better now.

"You in bed?" he asks, again residing in my head.

How does he make those three words sound so freaking suggestive? "Um, yes."

He takes a deep breath. Runs a hand through his thick, dark hair, messing it up perfectly. Hardens his jaw so he now looks extra sexy. Stares off into the distance for a moment like some sort of model in a photoshoot. "I won't make the first move," he finally says.

I'm confused. "What are you talking about?"

"You. Me. I refuse to make the first move. I've done that time and again over the years, and you still ended up destroying me." He takes another deep breath, like that was a lot for him to say. I suppose it was.

But I want him to say more.

He doesn't. He just watches me in that infuriatingly Jordan Tuttle way of his. Where I'm supposed to be able to figure out his moods and what he wants from me. I thought I was the only one who really knew him, yet I've wondered over the years if I only knew the image he presented to me. Did I really understand him, ever?

I'm not sure.

"Do you—*want* me to make the first move?" I am an idiot for asking. What if this is his one shot to turn me down? Humiliate me on the spot? He could've been wanting revenge for years, and now he's finally going to get it.

My heart is whoosh-whooshing in my ears as I wait for him to say something. Anything. It's almost painful, how long he takes to speak. My breath keeps getting caught in my throat and I wonder if I'll pass out from lack of oxygen.

"What do you think?" He sounds stubborn as hell. Defiant, even.

"I think that technically you made the first move by inviting me to your game tonight," I say tentatively.

"And I think you technically made the *very* first move by following me on Instagram and sending me a message." He sounds pleased that I did that.

"You're the one who said on national television that you missed the one who got away," I point out.

"Are you assuming you're the one who got away?" He raises a brow.

My heart stops. I'm gaping at him, closing and opening my mouth like a dying fish.

He actually laughs for all of two seconds before he turns into serious mode once again. "Of course I was talking about you."

My heart resumes beating, only now it's doing double time. "You're mean."

"So are you."

"How am I mean?" I rest my hand on my chest, then drop it. I don't want him staring at my braless breasts.

"You're the one who broke up with me all those years ago."

I say nothing. I don't know how to argue that point.

"Did you actually want to break up with me?" He peers in close, his face completely filling my phone screen. "Or did someone make you?"

"Who would make me?" I ask incredulously. No one forced my hand. I made that stupid decision all on my own.

"I don't know. Your parents. A new boyfriend." He leans back and I see those broad shoulders shrug.

"I didn't have someone waiting in the wings when we broke up, Jordan," I say, slightly irritated. "There was no backup plan."

"Then why did you do it?"

"I thought it was the right thing to do!" I cannot believe we're having this discussion over FaceTime. It's embarrassing. "You were so busy, off living your life in college, and there were so many opportunities being thrown at you. I didn't want to hold you back."

He's looking at me like I'm crazy. Or like there are horns sprouting from my head. "Are you serious? Did you really believe you held me back?"

"I don't know! I was so confused and worried and sad all the time. I couldn't take it anymore." I throw my hands up in the air, feeling stupid. Hating that we're confronting each other with all this old bullshit. Can't we just pretend it never happened?

Not that forgetting our past is the right thing to do. I guess we need to confront our mistakes if we want to—oh my God —make another attempt?

Is that what we're doing?

No way do I want to get my hopes up. I'm not even sure if that's what I really want. Do I want another chance with Jordan? Sometimes, I think yes.

And other times, I think...

No. Absolutely not.

"Why were you sad?" he asks, his voice gentle.

"I missed you," I confess, heaving a big sigh. "I thought I was losing you. I thought you didn't want me anymore."

"You never lost me," he says firmly. "I lost you. You're the one who didn't want *me* anymore."

My gaze meets his as I stare at my phone screen. Everything comes back at me, all those horrible old feelings, the memories, the tears. So many tears. Having a new daily reminder of how much I epically fucked up my life really sucks.

Jordan talking to me is that new daily reminder.

And I don't know if I can take it.

"Don't you have anything to say?" he asks when I still haven't replied.

Fine. He wants to hear what I have to say? Here I go.

"That's the biggest problem you have with me, right? I'm the dumbass who broke up with you. I'm the idiot who cut you off, who hurt you before you could hurt me. It's all my fault."

"Amanda, no. That's not what I'm saying—"

I end the call before he can finish his sentence.

And pull the covers over my head, too many painful thoughts running through my brain.

It hurts too much. Talking to Jordan. Remembering what I gave up, how I believed that's what he wanted as well. It hurts too, thinking that he could want me back. Knowing that I broke his heart—that's all on me.

Can we really pick up where we left off? Can we—*he*—forget I broke up with him?

Or are there too many years and too much distance between us?

ELEVEN

AMANDA

I SHOW up at work the next morning dragging ass. I didn't get much sleep, tossing and turning the entire night, thinking about Jordan and our stupid argument. How he offered me the chance to make the next move and I...didn't do it.

Yet again, I've ruined everything. I'll probably never see him again.

I even teared up a little on the commute to work, enough to make my mascara run and ruin my entire look, but who's really paying attention? Cade is too busy with endless appointments, and Lena's assisting him today, which is pretty typical. We swap out, assisting the various therapists each week, though our schedule is fairly regular. I like the change, though. It keeps me from getting bored.

Today, I'm not bored—I'm sleepy. It's hard for me to focus and more than once, whoever I'm working with has to repeat him or herself. Lena avoids me, and doesn't even sit with me at lunch. She must've gone out instead, because

I'm left mostly alone in the lunchroom, eating a dry sandwich and watching Dr. Oz on TV while I skim my phone.

I hate that Lena is keeping her distance, but I respect her unspoken wishes and keep my distance too, though I desperately want to talk to her. Tell her my Tuttle troubles, and let her know she can have Cade.

Not like he's mine to give away...

Will she believe me when I say that? God, she'll probably hate me for having two men supposedly chasing after me. One of them the guy she has a just-admitted crush on.

Turning off my phone, I slump in the chair and stare up at the TV. Dr. Oz is talking about a new lifesaving procedure and I sort of don't care. All I can focus on is myself. I'm having a pity party and no one else is invited—how silly is that?

Since when did my life get so complicated anyway? I swear, things were downright boring before I watched that episode of *Inside Football*. I send Jordan one innocent message— that's what I'll keep telling myself—and now it's like I'm living in this surreal world where nothing makes sense.

The Dr. Oz episode concludes and dejected, I go back to work. I'm in the rehabilitation room, setting up for the next patient I'm assisting with, when my phone buzzes. It's from our receptionist Rhonda.

There's a delivery here for you! The text is accompanied by a bunch of blushie faced emojis.

Curious, I pocket my phone and head for the front desk, racking my brain. Did I order something from Amazon in the last few days and forget? That's about the only packages

I get here at work. Sometimes I order clothes too, but that's rare. I have to watch my budget, and really, I don't need a lot of clothes. Wearing the various Atlas polos I own five days a week takes care of that.

As I round the corner and start to enter the lobby's parameter, I spot what looks like a gigantic flower arrangement before I can even see the front desk. I slow my steps, savoring the moment as I come closer, knowing exactly who the flowers are from before I even read the accompanying card.

"Look at these flowers!" Rhonda says, bouncing in her chair when she spots me. She actually claps her hands. "Aren't they gorgeous?"

I stop in front of the counter and stare at the wild arrangement. There are pink and yellow and white flowers of all shapes and sizes, mixed in with bursts of greenery. The vase is huge—it looks heavy—and when I see the card clipped to the plastic insert sitting there, waiting for me to rip into it, I hold back, letting myself soak up the anticipation.

"Who are they from?" Rhonda asks when I still haven't said anything. She leaps to her feet, her hands on her hips as she glares at me, dying for me to speak.

Ignoring her, I touch a soft pink petal with my fingertip, then lean forward and breathe in the fresh, floral scent. It's a riot of color, a mountain of blooms contained in one arrangement, and I almost want to giggle with happiness.

But I don't. I'm not a little girl anymore. I'm a responsible adult who just got sent the biggest floral arrangement I've ever seen in my life.

"You're holding out on us," Rhonda says, her gaze meeting mine as she plops back into her chair. She scoots it closer to where I'm standing on the other side of the counter. "Is it from Cade?" she whisper-shouts.

How does she know about me and Cade? I was trying to be discreet. Work romances are usually frowned upon.

I glance around, thankful no one is nearby. "Nope."

Rhonda appears surprised but recovers quickly. "Ooh, a secret admirer then." She pushes away, wagging a finger at me. "Naughty girl, working two guys."

"Um, I'm not working two guys." I'm mildly offended by what she just said. Working two guys? She makes me sound like I'm doing the nasty with both of them.

"You know what I mean!" Another casual wave of her fingers. "I'm just being nosey."

She's being totally nosey. But I like Rhonda so I offer her a smile, grateful when the phone rings, saving me. While Rhonda answers and talks in her usual upbeat chirp, I pull the tiny, cream-colored envelope from its clip and open it, recognizing the slash of bold handwriting within.

He didn't just call in this flower order. He actually went there and paid for it. Plus, he handwrote the card himself.

Fuck the first move. Go to dinner with me tonight.

I bite my lip so I don't break out into a shit-eating grin, but there's no use. I'm smiling like my life depends on it. Maybe I should be offended by his boldness, but...I'm not.

I'm so not.

"Must've said something good," Rhonda says with a low whistle after she completes the call.

I say nothing. Just pick up the heavy vase and start carrying it to the little office area where the assistant physical therapists have a shared desk. I carefully set the arrangement in the center of the mostly clean desk, then take a step back, admiring my flowers.

They're absolutely gorgeous. No one has ever given me flowers before. Not like this at least. I received flowers from my parents when I graduated eighth grade and high school. Mom would bring me bouquets for our last band performance of the year. Jordan gave me a beautiful corsage on the night of our senior prom, but he never brought me flowers. Not that I can remember. Honestly, I didn't need the gesture. If I'm being honest with myself, I just wanted him.

But now, the gesture feels...awesome. Like Jordan Tuttle is making this grand statement that he wants me.

That's heady stuff.

My phone buzzes and I check it to see I have another text from him.

Jordan: **What do you think?**

Pressing my lips together, I contemplate what I'm going to say. I go for simple first.

Me: **They're beautiful. Thank you.**

He answers me quick.

Jordan: **I mean about dinner tonight.**

So impatient. I ignore his question.

Me: **I don't know how I'm getting these flowers home.**

Jordan: **What do you mean?**

Me: **I commute to work. I don't own a car.**

Jordan: **Seriously?**

I start to laugh.

Me: **Yes. Seriously.**

Jordan: **I'll come pick you up.**

Me: **You don't have to do that. I'd rather go home first and change. You don't want to see me in the Atlas polo again.**

Jordan: **I'll take you any way I can get you.**

My skin goes warm at his words. The promise in them.

He's typing again. I see the gray bubble, the little white dots.

Jordan: **What time do you get off work?**

Me: **Five.**

Jordan: **I'll be in the parking lot waiting for you.**

"Wow, did Cade get you those flowers?"

I glance up from my phone to see Lena standing there, gaping at the giant arrangement sitting on the desk. I shove my phone into my pocket and offer her a tentative smile. "No."

"Oh." She sends me a confused look. "They look expensive."

"I think they are," I agree.

"Who sent them?"

"You'll never believe me."

"Uh huh." She approaches the desk, bends her head to breathe in the flowers' scent. The smile on her face can't be contained, they smell that good. "So. Are you seeing someone else?"

Her voice sounds downright hopeful.

"I don't move that fast." Well, someone else is moving fast, I'll give him that. "It's...complicated."

The smile disappears. "What about Cade?"

"Listen. Cade and I—he's nice. I like him a lot." Lena's face falls a little. "But I don't like him like *that*. More as a friend."

She backs away from the flowers, the doubt on her face clear. "Are you saying that because of what I told you?"

"No, not at all." Well, sort of. Our timing is all wrong. He's a nice guy. Probably a good catch. But I don't think we'd work out. Not now. Maybe not ever. "He's not my type."

"Really?" Even more doubt colors her tone. Clearly she doesn't believe me. "Who's your type then?"

A hot professional football player with dark hair, ice blue eyes and a brooding stare.

"I'm not interested in Cade," I say firmly. "You should go for it."

Lena's mouth drops open. "Are you serious? You just went on a date with him last night."

"It wasn't a real date. I just—I had tickets to the Niners game and asked him to go with me," I say with a small shrug. "Two friends going to a football game. That's it."

"Well, you might not think it was a date, but Cade definitely does. He was telling everyone outside earlier about how you two went to the game, and how you introduced him to Whittaker and Tuttle."

Okay. This isn't good. "He was actually talking about us with coworkers? I'm sure he knows work relationships are frowned upon at Atlas Wellness Center."

I don't want other people gossiping about me—and Cade. I'm sure Rhonda is telling everyone he's the one who sent me the flowers.

Lena starts to laugh. "You sound like the company handbook."

"That's because I've actually read the company handbook, and it said exactly that." I sound like a complete priss when I don't mean to. I'm just looking for any excuse to not be dating Cade.

"But they're not completely forbidden, right? I've gone out with someone who worked here before," Lena says with a little shrug. "It's no big deal as long as you're discreet and don't let your relationship affect the work environment."

"If Cade is telling everyone what a great date we had last night, then he's not necessarily being discreet," I say wryly.

"Then maybe you should've said something to him last night so he didn't get the wrong idea," Lena retorts.

She starts to walk away, like our conversation is finished, and I follow after her. "Wait a minute, are you mad at me for something?"

Lena turns, her eyes blazing. "If you don't want him, you should let him know. Not lead him on."

I take a step back. "I'm not leading Cade on."

"You so are. You're being incredibly selfish right now, Amanda. Cade's already halfway in love with you, but some other guy is sending you expensive flowers. It's making you look..." She clamps her lips shut and shakes her head.

"It's making me look what?" Unease fills me as I wait for her response.

Lena's upper lip curls. "Trashy."

And with that nicely dropped bomb, she walks away.

TWELVE
JORDAN

AMANDA SAID I should arrive after five at her work, but fuck it. It's 4:48, I'm already here and I'm walking inside.

The moment I enter the lobby, the receptionist sitting at the front desk stares at me with wide eyes, and rises unsteadily to her feet. "Aren't you Jordan Tuttle?" She breathes my name like a prayer.

I nod as I approach her desk, then lean against it, wondering if I should smile. I decide against it. "That's my name."

Her hand goes over her heart, like she's ready to say the Pledge of Allegiance. "Please tell me you're not injured."

"I'm not."

She breathes a sigh of relief, shaking her head. "Oh, thank God. How can I help you?"

"I'm guessing you're a Niners fan?" I lift my brows, tilting my head in her direction.

She nods, her eyes still wide and a little wild, her lips clamped shut, like she can't even speak. I tend to do that to people, render them speechless, and I don't mean to. It's why I say so little.

No one can hold your words against you if you don't say much.

"I'm looking for Amanda Winters," I tell the receptionist.

Her eyes are somehow even wider. "You are?"

"Yes, I am," I say slowly. "She works here, right?"

"Amanda? Yes!" She blinks. "Of course she does! Let me see if I can find her."

The receptionist bustles away before I can say another word.

I wander around the lobby, looking at the photos on the wall. A group photo of what I assume are the Atlas Wellness Center employees, everyone posing in their red polos. I squint as I study the photo, searching for Amanda, and I finally find her. Second to the last row, on the far right. Her face is scrunched, like the sun is too bright and her eyes are narrow slits, her nose wrinkled, though there's a smile on her face. She looks cute.

When was the photo taken? During a time when I didn't really know her, didn't talk to her. It hurts to realize that, not that I'd ever tell her. But it's kind of mind blowing, how we've gone for years without talking to each other. She went from being the most important person in my life to never seeing her again, just like that.

It took me a while to recover. I swear I fell into a depression, and those who knew me blamed it on going away to college. The readjustment to my life, the constant pressure I was under. That all made sense, so I didn't protest. No one would have believed me if I told them I was heartsick.

It was easier to keep my opinions—and feelings—to myself.

The receptionist is back, Amanda trailing behind her. My ex-girlfriend stops in her tracks, blinking repeatedly as she studies me. "What are you doing here?"

"I told you I'd be here at five," I remind her. It's a shock to my system every time I see Amanda, each time I hear her voice. Having her in front of me makes me instantly crave more. More looking, more talking, more touching...

She turns me into a greedy dick.

The look on Amanda's face tells me she didn't think I'd really show up, and I'm blown away. Does she really lack that much faith in me? "But you're early."

"Only by a few minutes." I take a step toward her, my gaze roaming, taking her in. She looks...frazzled. Tired. Her hair is pulled into a low ponytail today, and hangs bone-straight down her back. She's got faint dark smudges under her eyes and her polo shirt is halfway untucked from her black pants. "Are you ready to go?"

"Um." She glances over at the receptionist, who is watching us like we're a live-action movie playing out right in front of her. "Give me a minute."

The moment she's gone, the receptionist is sighing loudly, her lips curled into a smug smile. "Are you the one who sent her the flowers?"

I ignore her question. "You saw the flowers?"

"I'm the one who signed for them." Another sigh, this one softer. "They were pretty hard to miss. *Such* a romantic gesture."

Impulsive gesture, I want to tell her, but I keep my mouth shut. I don't even know this woman. Why tell her something personal? She'd probably sell the story to TMZ or whatever the hell gossip site is hot at the moment. For all I know she's covertly taking photos of me with her phone. I wouldn't put it past her. Shit, I wouldn't half blame her either.

Being grateful for success is one thing, but it's hard to celebrate the good times when you don't have many people in your life you can trust. This is why I'm glad Cannon and I are on the same team. I *know* that guy. He's my friend. He knew me before everything blew up and I became an actual celebrity.

Life is strange sometimes, isn't it?

Maybe that's why I'm drawn to Amanda too. We have so much history together. After seeing her last night, I couldn't stop replaying everything we said to each other. What was I thinking, telling her she had to make the next move? No surprise that I caved like I always do when it comes to her.

If I'm being real with myself, I have no idea what I'm doing right now, or why exactly I'm doing it, but I'm trying to just go with my impulses and see where they take me.

Even if I might end up getting hurt in the end.

THIRTEEN

AMANDA

"WHAT THE SHIT, Amanda? *Jordan Tuttle* is out there waiting for you!" Lena is hopping up and down, all of her earlier anger with me gone.

Her reaction is surprising. She gave me grief only a couple hours ago and implied I'm a heartless bitch who toyed with Cade's emotions, and now she's freaking out because Mr. Superstar Tuttle is in the lobby waiting for me.

"I told you he was my ex." I grab the flowers and hold them close, surprised at how heavy they are. I look terrible after a long and emotionally exhausting day, but Jordan didn't seem to mind. His actions made me realize I miss the way he always looked at me.

Like I was his absolute favorite thing.

"He's the one who sent you the flowers, huh?" I nod and she exhales loudly. "Very sweet. Are you two getting back together?"

"Right." Okay, now I'm pissed. She's totally pretending she didn't say such cruel things to me earlier. "Only a few hours ago you told me I was awful for leading Cade on."

Her mouth pops open. "I—"

"And now that you know it was Jordan Tuttle who sent the flowers, you're fine with it." I shake my head and start to walk past her, disappointment taking over my anger. "That's not very cool, Lena."

Lena grabs my arm, stopping me. "You're right," she says softly, her hand dropping away from my elbow. "I'm sorry. I just—I didn't know what was going on, and it looked bad, you know? I thought you were totally playing Cade."

Now is not the right time to remember—or admit—that I used Cade by inviting him to take me to that game. I don't know if I can ever admit that to Lena, though I should. "He's just a friend," I remind her.

I need to tell Cade that, though, and right away. I need to be honest with him.

"And is Jordan Tuttle just a friend?" She raises a brow. "Because if he is, what a very hot and famous friend you have."

Just like that, we both start to laugh.

Here's the deal. I don't like being mad at people. My mother says I'm too forgiving. That I let people take advantage of me, that I let them walk all over me. As I've gotten older, I've become better at not allowing someone to take advantage of me, but in turn, that can cause people to keep their distance. And sometimes, that leaves a person lonely, you know? This is why I've always been so thankful for Lena. Our friendship has never been distant. She's warm and fun and open, and I try to be the same to her.

It was surprising, how mad she got at me over Cade, but now I get why. Because she has feelings for him, and in her eyes, it looks like I'm using him. I get it.

I do.

"I'm sorry too," I say once our laughter stops. I'd hug her, but I've got my arms wrapped around the giant vase. "I really had no idea you liked Cade."

"That's my own fault. I never told you." She smiles, her eyes twinkling, and I know we're good now, which is a total relief. "Are you going on a date with Jordan Tuttle tonight?"

I shrug, purposefully nonchalant. "Just dinner."

No need to get my hopes up.

"Dinner, huh?" Lena fans herself. "I don't know if I could eat, with that gorgeous man sitting across the table from me."

Valid point. My stomach feels like a roller coaster is running through it. Ups and downs and twists and turns, shrieking through the free fall. My appetite has totally left me, replaced with a hefty dose of rattled nerves. "He's an old friend. It's—nothing."

I need to keep repeating that word.

Nothing, nothing, nothing.

That's what Jordan and I are doing—a big fat nothing. Dinner is harmless. Catching up with an old friend. An old friend I happened to have sex with. No big deal. We're adults now. we can handle it.

"I'm walking you out," Lena says assuredly, turning on her heel and heading toward the front lobby. "I'm introducing myself to him too. Hope you don't mind."

I don't think I'd really have a choice, not that I mind. I want her to meet Jordan. In fact, I sort of want to show him off to her. Like, *do you see this very fine male specimen? Once upon a time, he was all mine. He loved me. And I loved him.*

Okay, wait. That's just a reminder of what I threw away...

"Let's go," Lena calls as she starts heading for the lobby.

I chase after her, the vase jiggling in my arms, the water sloshing within, flowers batting me in the face. I sort of wish he'd never come to pick me up. I'm desperate to take a shower, to wash my hair, to change into a beautiful outfit and just...make myself look better than this. What I'm working with at this very moment is too close to hopeless, let me tell you.

"Hey." I can tell by the polite yet vaguely flirtatious tone of Lena's voice that she's talking to Jordan. "You're Jordan Tuttle, right?"

I come to a stop, the flowers still in my face, my eyes scrunching closed when I hear her ask if he's really...himself.

Lord, kill me now.

"Right." I hear the amusement in his deep voice, even in that singular word spoken, and my eyes pop open as a smile teasing the corner of my lips.

"I'm Lena." She takes a couple of steps, and I'd bet money she's holding her hand out for him to shake. "I work with Amanda. We're good friends."

"Nice to meet you." They're shaking hands, and I'm sure he's sizing her up. I'm guessing she's sizing him up too, and I sort of want to die. Or maybe sneak out so I never have to face either of them again, but that would mean I couldn't have dinner with Jordan tonight and I do, after all, want to thank him for the flowers.

There's more I want to do for Jordan, *with* Jordan, but I can't face those dirty details just yet.

I'm hiding at the end of the hall, just behind the wall so they can't see me. My spying is making me feel totally awkward, especially if someone found me doing this, which could totally happen. I should just walk out there and talk to them, yet I can't help but linger for a few minutes more...

Lena gets right to the point. "You two used to date."

"Yeah."

"Can I ask you a question?"

"Um..." He sounds wary, and I can't blame him. "Sure?"

"Did she really break up with you?"

Okay. I want to die.

He's quiet for a moment, as if he's weighing his words and what he's about to say next, and I lean against the wall, clutching the vase to my chest and pray I don't sneeze because of the flowers.

"She did break up with me," he finally says, his voice grim. "And she broke my heart."

Oh.

God.

I swear Lena gasps. "Really?"

There's nothing said so I can only assume he nods or whatever, and I can envision her offering him comfort, which makes me feel like...

Shit.

Without thought I stride out into the lobby, feeling dumb as I clutch the giant arrangement of flowers in my arms. "Hey, Jordan. Thank you again for the flowers."

His eyes widen slightly when he spots me and Lena takes a step away from him, her bottom lip caught between her teeth, her gaze guilty. Like she got caught talking to him, when I don't mind. Not at all.

"You're welcome. They're—"

"Huge?" I smile, my gaze going from him to Lena. "Yes, they are."

"I hope you like them." His beautiful blue eyes are only for me.

"She *loves* them," Lena gushes for me, sending me a look, like she expects me to gush too.

"They're gorgeous!" Rhonda calls from her spot at the front desk.

I have a total audience here. We need to leave, stat.

"You ready?" he asks, like he knows how much I want to bail.

The smile I send him is full of relief. He's once again my knight in shining armor. "Yes, let's go."

We walk out of the building, Rhonda and Lena's loud good-byes still ringing in my ears. I know I'm going to hear from Lena later. She'll probably apologize for not believing me when I told her I was the one who broke up with him, and then she'll lay it on thick about how handsome and wounded he is. Because he is. Handsome.

And wounded.

Makes me a little crazy because *I'm* the one who wounded him.

"You want me to carry those?" Before I can even answer, Jordan is grabbing the vase from me, ridiculously sexy carrying a giant assortment of flowers while wearing a dark gray Henley shirt, dark rinse jeans and rugged boots. He's got that sexy city lumberjack thing down well. All he needs is a beard and the vibe is complete. "Your friend seems nice."

"She's very nice," I agree. "She didn't believe me when I told her I broke up with you."

"Why not?" He veers right and I follow after him.

"Most people don't believe me when I tell them." He appears surprised and I shrug. "They all think you're the one who dumped me."

"Yeah. Not the case though, right?" He actually chuckles.

"I heard you tell her I broke your heart." When he glances over at me, I try my best to look hurt. Because I am—he's not the only wounded one in this old relationship. He shouldn't admit those kinds of things out loud, to other people, even if it is the truth. "Why would you say that?"

He shrugs those impossibly broad shoulders of his. "It's the truth."

I sort of want to hit him. I also want to hug him. The conflicting emotions swirling within me battle it out, my brain fully engaged in the struggle.

What do I say to that, how does he expect me to respond? He's acting like it's no big deal now, so maybe I should do the same.

"There's my car," he says, and we both come to a stop, my mouth hanging open.

He's driving a Range Rover. Still. He had one in high school, and we had many moments in that car. Most of them awesome teenage experiences, if you know what I mean.

The new one is matte black, and it's gorgeous. I turn to look at him and find he's already watching me, the first real smile on his face since we've started talking again.

Seeing him look so happy steals my breath, and I just stare at him for a long moment, wallowing in the beauty that is Jordan Tuttle's face.

"A Range Rover, huh?" I finally ask, my voice teasing.

He shrugs again, hits the keyless remote, and the car lights flash, the doors unlocking. "Old habits die hard."

"Oh yeah?" What's he saying? Am I an old habit he can't kick?

Because I'm starting to feel the same way about him.

"Yeah." He makes his way to the passenger side and opens the door for me so I can slip inside. "Once I find something I like, I tend to stick with it. Not like some people I know."

My mouth falls open once again, my brain scrambling.

Really. *Really?* Did he just say that?

I wince.

Ouch.

Jordan shuts the door firmly before I can manage a reply.

FOURTEEN

JORDAN

AMANDA LIVES IN A SHIT HOLE.

It's a three-story apartment building with a parking garage on the bottom floor, and I'm guessing it was built in the 1960s. Don't think it's been remodeled since then either. The windows face the extremely busy street, and it doesn't look safe. Not by a long shot.

Yet she's babbling on like it's the best option ever. Almost feels like she's making excuses to me for living there.

"It's so close to everything, including the bus stop I take to work." She sends me a relieved smile. "So glad you picked me up, though. It would've sucked to ride the bus home with the flowers. Though I guess I could've left them at work."

I say nothing. My brain is too busy trying to comprehend the fact that she takes the bus every day to and from work. That she lives in this shitty apartment complex we're about to park in front of. That she seems perfectly happy with her life.

If she would've stuck with me, I could've given her so much more.

So much fucking more than she could've ever dreamed.

"Just pull in right there," she instructs, and I park on the street, putting the SUV in park and killing the engine. I glance around, my gaze going to the side mirror as I contemplate getting out of the car when the light finally turns red. There is too much traffic coming at me to make a safe exit.

"How long have you lived here?"

When I don't move to get out of the car, she drops her hand from the door handle. "About a year."

"You like it?" I don't see how she could.

"I like that I have my own place versus having a roommate, like I did at my other apartment." She shrugs. "It's kind of old, but it works."

It's awful, but I refrain from saying anything insulting. I don't want to make her mad. Feels like we're walking a fine line together already. Didn't help that I say stupid shit without thinking.

Amanda's right—I should've never told her friend that she broke my heart, but the words came out without thought. Just the automatic truth. Though maybe she needs to hear it...especially since we haven't really talked about it.

Yet.

Once the traffic lightens up, I get out of my car, and Amanda does the same. I grab the flower arrangement from the back seat and follow her to the building and then up the stairs, relieved that none of the apartments are on the ground floor. At least that's semi-safe—a creeper has to climb up to get through the window and hopefully that's a deterrent.

But I'm constantly looking around as we head to her apartment, noting the dark corners, the scummy guy who leaves his door open so I can see inside his trashed place. She walks faster when we pass by that open door, and I practically growl my disapproval.

I keep my mouth shut and my thoughts to myself.

For now.

She finally comes to a stop in front of apartment number forty-two and whips out a set of keys, unlocking two locks before the door swings open. I follow her inside, coming to a stop in the center of the room when I realize this is it. This is the entirety of her home.

"You live in a *studio?*" My tone is accusatory and I immediately regret saying it like that, but come the fuck on.

"Well, yeah." She shuts and locks the door, then throws her arms up in the air. "But it's all mine."

It's not much. There's a tiny kitchen and, from what I can tell, an even tinier bathroom. The couch is still folded out into a bed, and the sheets and blanket are a haphazard mess, one of the pillows on the floor. Amanda makes a dash for the makeshift bed—her *actual* bed—tossing the other pillow onto the floor and trying to fold the bed away.

"God, how embarrassing. I'm so messy," she says, completely bent over the couch and giving me a perfect view of her perfect ass.

"Leave it," I tell her, and she stands up straight, turning to face me. "Don't worry about it," I say, my voice gentler. "Just—go get ready."

"Can I take a shower?" she asks hopefully.

Her question sends an immediate image to my brain. One of Amanda in the shower completely naked.

And me joining her.

"Yeah," I say, my voice gruff. "Go for it."

"I'll be fast," she assures me, and then she's gone, the bathroom door shutting behind her.

There was a time long, long ago, in high school, when I asked her to come back to my place, and I took a shower while she wandered aimlessly around my room. I do the same now, prowling around, my gaze busy taking note of everything in her tiny apartment. There really isn't one personal thing on display. Not even a photograph of her family, of her friends, of a past boyfriend.

Nothing.

I fold up the couch for her, shove the cushions back into place and then settle in, checking my phone. I ignore the texts from my agent—she can wait—ignore the text from my father—he can *definitely* wait—and read the one text I received from Mia.

My ex-girlfriend.

Miss u! Get 2gether soon?

We broke up over a year ago, after my career got in the way of our relationship. As in, I was rarely home, or always busy, so I never spent enough time with her, and she always complained. Now I see her on occasion because we're...

Fuck buddies.

And that's it.

Her "get 2gether soon" is total code for "wanna fuck"? And most of the time, I meet up with her, we have dinner, we talk, we have a few drinks and then we get down to business.

No fuss. No strings. She's the perfect hookup because she's become just as busy as I am. She's an influencer whose fashion blog and Instagram took off right after we split up. Mia likes to say that thanks to my breaking up with her, her life has never been better.

The last six months, I started to wonder if Mia and I could make the perfect relationship work after all. She doesn't demand much of my time, which is a plus. She's so busy now, she's not sitting at home wondering when she can see me again. That would be ideal. I always felt guilty, having to cancel plans with her. With the women I've dated in the past, I canceled on them all the damn time.

Not that there's been a lot. After Amanda broke up with me, I steered clear from women in general for quite a while. They were too much trouble. Too demanding of my time, which I have so little of.

And now here I am, sitting on Amanda's couch, waiting for her to finish with her shower so I can take her to dinner. Once dinner is over, I want to take her back to my place, and show her my bedroom. Just like I did all those years ago, when I was trying my damnedest to convince her I wanted her.

No one else.

Just her.

My phone buzzes with a text notification and I check to see it's another one from Mia.

U busy tonite? Wld luv 2 c u

One thing I've always disliked about Mia was her adolescent texting style. It's like she can't spell out a word to save her life, yet she somehow can string together coherent sentences in her blog and Instagram posts. But I usually never let that bother me.

Not really.

Until now, at this very moment. Amanda is one of the smartest people I know. I've always respected that girl—that's what drew me to her. I'm just as attracted to her face and body as I am to her very attractive, very intelligent brain.

Can't get together tonight, I text Mia. *Have plans.*

Her response is immediate.

Maybe some other time?

This is where it gets tricky. Where I have to admit to myself that I don't want to see Mia anymore because I'm hoping this rekindling with Amanda could possibly work.

Could it, though? Could it, *really?*

I stare at my phone screen for way too long. Long after the shower shuts off and I can hear Amanda open and close drawers, catch the sound of a muttered curse from behind her bathroom door. I smile, wishing I could barge in there and rip her towel off. Plop her sexy butt onto the edge of the counter and kiss her until she melts into me, lets me touch her, lets me...

My fingers fly over the keyboard without thought.

I've met someone else, Mia. Take care.

FIFTEEN
AMANDA

I WAS TOO anxious about taking the shower. As in, I forgot to bring in clothes with me to change into. I'm just a girl standing in front of a mirror completely naked, a towel barely wrapped around me, my hair done, my makeup done, and no clean clothes to put on. Not even a pair of panties.

Talk about awkward.

One of the drawbacks of living in my studio apartment is I don't have any real closet space. Meaning I have to get creative. Like, my dresser/armoire is sitting out in the living area. Where Jordan is. How am I supposed to walk out there and tell him, *hey, don't mind me! I need to grab some undies and an outfit to change into!*

I want to wear a dress. I want to wear a sexy pair of panties and a lacy bralette—or maybe no bra at all—and I wanted to come out of the bathroom smelling good and looking good. Instead, I have to exit the bathroom wearing only a towel and burning with embarrassment while I grab my sexy undies and my dress and tell him to ignore me as I dash back into the bathroom.

This sucks.

So bad.

My phone is sitting on the counter, taunting me. I could just...send him a text. That's lame, though, right? How am I supposed to go about this?

Grabbing my phone, I open up our conversation and start typing.

Me: **I have a question to ask you.**

He answers in seconds.

Jordan: **What?**

Me: **I have no clothes to wear.**

This time he takes a little longer to respond.

Jordan: **You literally have nothing to wear tonight?**

I smile despite my embarrassment.

Me: **I have clothes to wear. But they're out in the living room. In the dresser sitting against the wall on the right.**

A photo is my reply, and it's of my armoire.

Jordan: **You mean this?**

Me: **Yes. So maybe you could go out onto the patio for a minute? Or five?**

He takes literally two minutes to respond, and his lack of a response is making me anxious. When he finally answers, I'm relieved.

Jordan: **How about I pick out your outfit?**

Um, nooooo. No way. I unlock the bathroom door and peek my head out, ready to yell a response when he magically appears, clutching a dress on a hanger—the very dress I wanted to wear—in his left hand and a delicate pair of lacy panties dangling from his right hand. He stops short when he sees me, and winces.

"You think this is creepy," he says with a faintly disgusted look on his face.

I burst out laughing, ducking my head as I lean against the bathroom door. Kind of creepy, kind of sweet. Really sweet, actually. "That's the dress I wanted to wear," I admit once I lift my head, our gazes meeting.

He takes a few steps until he's standing directly in front of me, his gaze dropping to my chest, probably wishing he could mentally undo my towel. It's slipping, I can feel it, and I tighten my arms, trying my best to keep the towel from falling. "I guess I still know what you like, huh?"

In more ways than one, I want to tell him. "You didn't get me a bra, though."

This conversation is sort of embarrassing, but I'm a grown ass woman, he's a grown ass man, and we were in a relationship for a little over a year. As in, we had lots of sex and adult discussions and he's seen me naked before. Plenty of times. He's helped me pick out an outfit before too.

"Don't wear one." He hands over the dress and I take it, the door swinging open, revealing me completely, standing there in just the towel. He has the panties clutched in his fingers, and he starts to hand them over, then hesitates, glancing down at the scrap of lace crumpled in his fingers.

"Maybe you shouldn't wear these either."

Oh God.

My knees wobble, and I'm thankful I'm still holding onto the doorknob. Otherwise, I'd melt to the floor. "Jordan..."

He quirks an eyebrow. "Too soon?"

I laugh again, and so does he. This is the most non-awkward awkward conversation I've ever had. "What are we doing?"

"I don't know," he answers truthfully. I can feel the honesty in his words, the way he looks at me. "Tell me to stop, and I'll stop."

"Don't stop," I immediately answer.

He smiles, and his face—*God*—he is the sexiest thing alive. "Tell me to go, and I'll go."

Our gazes lock. Hold. "Please don't go," I whisper.

Jordan takes the panties and holds them behind his back, that smile still on his face. "Put that dress on, Mandy, and then let's go to dinner."

"Okay." I nod frantically, excitement bubbling up inside of me like a shaken-up soda can, ready to explode and fizz everywhere. All we can do is stare at each other like two dopes with matching goofy smiles.

We are ridiculous.

"Shut the door and put on that dress," he commands me, his smile fading, his voice deathly serious, "before I tear that towel off you and we end up staying in tonight."

Oh. That sounds like a way better option...

I slam the door in his face instead.

I AM in Jordan's fancy Range Rover, sitting in the passenger seat with a black, floral-print dress on that I love, wearing no bra and no panties. Oh, and I have on my only pair of stiletto sandals, shoes I rarely wear because I always feel like a too-tall amazon in them.

But not with Jordan. Not when he's six-foot-three and those shoes increase my height to five-eleven. Standing next to Jordan in these heels makes me feel downright dainty.

God, I forgot how much I love a big, tall man.

The interior of his car is like a Jordan Tuttle trap. As in, it smells like him. As if he rolled all over the leather seats, the dash, the center console, and imprinted his scent permanently. I try my best to be discreet as I inhale his essence. The forest on a warm summer day. A sunny morning by the beach. That mysterious spicy drink my grandmother serves every Christmas. These are all the things I think of when I breathe in the fragrance of Jordan's car.

"Are you okay?" he asks, and the amusement in his voice makes me want to sink into my leather chair and pretend I don't exist.

I'm clearly losing my mind.

"I'm fine," I assure him with the most normal sounding voice I can muster, but inside, I am shaken and stirred. We are sitting dangerously close to one another. He just picked out my outfit for me to wear on this date. I threw a denim jacket over it so I wouldn't freeze to death, but otherwise I am only wearing the clothing Jordan chose for me.

Is that weird? Maybe it's a little weird, but deep down I like it. His behavior is so very...primal tonight.

Going on this date sans underwear is by far the most scandalous thing I've ever done, which proves I haven't done very many scandalous things. It's hard to be daring when you're going to school, working endless nowhere jobs just to get a paycheck so ultimately you can find that job you love one day. That's been me the last few years, before I graduated college and finally got my dream job. My mom told me I was lucky to find it, but my dad pulled me aside that Thanksgiving after I started working at Atlas and I went home for the holiday. He told me how proud he was, what a hard worker I've proven to be.

Just hearing those words made my eyes well up with tears. Mom has been a solid support, but Dad has always believed in me, even when I failed and made mistakes and seemed hopeless.

"You're awfully quiet," Jordan says, interrupting my nostalgic, vaguely melancholy thoughts.

No way am I telling him what's going on in my brain. I need to focus on the sexy times that might happen tonight.

If I can be so lucky.

"Where are you taking me?" I ask.

"Have you ever been to Santana Row?"

"Once. Went to dinner at one of the restaurants there." With a date. Not that I want to mention that particular part.

"I made a reservation at a steakhouse," he says, pausing for a moment before he adds, "I live there too."

"But I thought you had a house in the wine country." Oh God, I sound stupid. Like a fangirl whose information was wrong. Like a stalker who's been scoping him out on the Interwebz.

"I do, but I also have a townhouse close by. It's not far from the stadium, and it's pretty private. Lots of guys from the team live there," he explains.

"Oh, that's nice."

"Yeah." He pauses. "Maybe I'll take you there after dinner."

If I immediately say yes, does that make me look too eager?

Probably.

I don't say yes. I don't say no either. Instead, I totally change the subject. "Did you have practice today?"

"We did, though it wasn't as intense the day after a game. We fly out this weekend for an away game."

"Who are you playing?"

"Tampa Bay."

"Really?" I think of the joke my dad used to tell us when we were kids. He still tells it now, though we all groan and beg him to stop when he asks the question.

Where are your Buccaneers?

On your Buccan-head!

Totally cringe worthy. But when we were little, we'd laugh and laugh.

"Uh huh. We're going to Florida," Jordan comes to a stop at a red light and glances over at me. "Doing anything this weekend?"

"Laundry," I tell him jokingly. "Need to clean my apartment too."

He chuckles. "What does that take? Ten minutes?"

"Are you mocking my fun-sized apartment?"

"Definitely." He shakes his head. "It's so small, Mandy."

"It works for me." I don't like how defensive his words make me feel, or how what he said is almost like an accusation. I've never had the money or the privilege that comes with being Jordan Tuttle. I had a taste of it when I was his girlfriend, but I always felt like I didn't belong in his world. That I was just pretending.

He hated that. He hated it so much, he'd get mad at me when I said stuff like that. He knew it was a huge insecurity, my Achilles' heel, yet he never understood why I felt like that. He worried he was the one making me feel that way, but it was never him.

That was my personal complex.

I'm starting to feel it now, as we head toward the upscale Santana Row, with its expensive, trendy restaurants and the even more expensive, mostly designer stores. Growing up, we didn't have a lot of money. Our house was small—and my parents still live there. They will die there, I'm sure of it. We're a simple family. We didn't have a lot of extras or fancy vacations. We went to the beach. We went to the mountains. And only because we were so centrally located that the drive to the beach or the mountains didn't take long. I knew from a young age that I had to find a career that would make me actual money, because my parents weren't going to support me forever.

And I did find a career that I not only love, but I make good money doing it too. I'd live like a freaking queen if I lived anywhere else but the Bay Area. I'm proud of what I've accomplished these last few years. Yet I still have that tiny bit of uncertainty nestled deep within me. That insecurity rears its ugly head whenever I feel less than. When I think I don't measure up.

Being with Jordan in the past made that insecurity rise more often than I care to admit. I really don't want to deal with it again. I'm older now. More sure of myself—most of the time. More capable of dealing with negative feelings and turning them around.

At least, I hope I'm more capable.

"I wasn't making fun of your place," he tells me once the light turns green and he starts driving again. "It just shocked me, how small it was."

"No surprise. I'd bet your bedroom is bigger than my entire apartment." I'm joking, yet I'm also fairly certain that I speak the truth.

"Yeah. For sure," he says, hesitating for a moment. I realize we're both being cautious around each other, almost like we're...scared. "Don't you want something bigger?"

"I can afford where I'm living now without stretching my income too thin," I explain. "I don't want to live above my means. That's something my parents taught me from a young age, and it's always stuck with me."

"Smart move," Jordan says. "Debt sucks."

Like he knows anything about being in debt. He's been given everything he could ever want, though he did work hard at football. It helps that he's just naturally talented.

Funny, how all those old worries and insecurities pop up when you're with someone from your past. Maybe trying to resurrect an old relationship isn't a smart move.

But when I catch him smiling at me, his appreciative gaze dropping and lingering on my exposed thighs, and his knowing I'm not wearing any panties, I can't help but think going out with Jordan again is the most fantastic idea I've ever had.

SIXTEEN

JORDAN

I'M TRYING to impress Amanda by bringing her here, to the place where I live, and to one of my favorite restaurants. Santana Row has a small, hip downtown neighborhood vibe, with plenty of shops and restaurants and bars. I've hung out here plenty of times, mainly with my teammates, sometimes out for a drink or a quick dinner with Mia, though I honestly can't remember the last time I took her out. Most everyone leaves us athletes alone when we mingle here, because they know more than a few of us live here too.

I like my house in Sonoma better. It's huge and private, but I don't spend much time there during football season. So my townhouse in the city will have to do.

Amanda and I walk to the restaurant side by side, making idle chitchat. I'm tempted to grab hold of her hand, but I don't. Probably moving too soon. She looks adorable in that floral print dress with the denim jacket over it, and those stiletto sandals make her legs look impossibly long.

Impossibly sexy.

She oohs and aahs over the stores as we pass them by, slowing her pace when we walk by Sephora or one of the many clothing stores. She practically presses her face against the window of the bakery, her eyes wide as she takes in the colorful rows of cupcakes.

"I want one of those," she tells me after I drag her away from the window. "Maybe after dinner?"

"Sure," I say easily. She's the only woman I know who'll readily indulge her love of sweets—of food in general. Every other woman I've been with watched their weight, watched what they ate carefully. Almost like they didn't want to slip in front of me, or somehow make a mistake.

Amanda's always just been real. Something I've appreciated —and missed.

We arrive at the steakhouse and it's packed, even for a Tuesday night. I place my hand at the small of Amanda's back as we make our way to the hostess stand, my fingers tightening ever so slightly on the fabric of her dress. She glances over her shoulder and smiles at me, and seeing that smile is like getting a direct shock to my heart, making it pump wildly.

Not over her. That's the thought that keeps running through my head at having her so close, having her with me, going out with her like we do this sort of thing all the time together.

Like we're still an actual couple.

I'm not over her.

The woman working behind the hostess stand blinks up at me in recognition, but she plays it cool as she leads us to our table, seating us in the more private area of the restaurant. Amanda is practically bouncing in her seat as she flips the pages of the menu, and I finally have to ask her why she seems so excited.

"I haven't had steak in forever." She sends me an almost resigned look. "I go on dates, and they all want to feed me exotic food."

I hate hearing her talk about going on dates with other men, but I do my best to stuff my possessive feelings down deep. "What do you mean, exotic?"

"Himalayan, Vietnamese, Brazilian, Ethiopian. One guy took me to a place that specializes in Russian cuisine." She wrinkles her nose. "I think they're trying to impress me, when really I'd rather have a steak. Or even pizza."

"Pizza?" I fucking love pizza. Who doesn't?

"Yeah, but I get enough of that because it's cheap, you know? I don't indulge in steak dinners much." She scans the menu, her expression giving me hungry vibes. Not of the food kind either. "Oh my God, it all sounds amazing. Look at the sauce options. And oh, they have lobster too!"

Her excitement over the menu is cute. She's cute. So damn cute. "Get whatever you want."

"Anything I want?" She raises her delicate brows, her tone, her entire being, flirtatious. "You sure about that, Tuttle?"

She hasn't called me Tuttle to my face yet—or via text, Face-Time, whatever. It feels...weird. I used to tell her to call me Jordan since no one else did. Only Amanda. "What exactly do you want?" I ask her, my question like a dare.

"Whatever you're willing to give me," she answers, her voice soft.

Damn. She keeps this up and I'll give her the whole damn world. Anything she wants. Everything I have.

Will be hers.

SEVENTEEN

AMANDA

DINNER IS TORTURE. He orders a very expensive wine and I drink a lot of it, though he doesn't have a drop. I semi-sober up once my steak dinner finally arrives, and it is by far the most delicious meal I've had in what feels like forever.

Jordan watches me avidly as I eat, his hungry gaze skimming my face, lingering on my lips. Emboldened by the wine, I moan a little every time I take a bite, letting him know just how much I'm enjoying myself without saying a word, and it's turning him on. I can tell by how dark his eyes get as he continues to watch me, how tense his shoulders become.

It's a powerful feeling, knowing that I hold this man, this extremely gorgeous man who's a freaking celebrity all over the country, maybe even the world, in complete thrall while I eat my dinner.

Totally ridiculous, right? God, truly it's the best feeling *ever*.

I consume everything on my plate, leaning back in my chair once I'm finally finished, satisfaction running through my veins.

"Best steak ever," I declare.

"You enjoyed it, hmm?" He lifts a brow, and it's that same sexy move he used to pull on me when we were eighteen and I was captivated by every single thing he said or did.

Seeing him do it now just renders me stupid.

"Definitely." I nod toward his plate, which is also completely empty, save for a sprig of some unfamiliar herb lying discarded. "You liked yours too?"

"This place is my favorite."

I prop my elbow on the table, resting my chin on my curled hand. "Is that why you brought me here? To share your favorite restaurant with me?"

He stares at me from across the table, his jaw working, like he's trying to figure out what to say next. There's a candle flickering in the votive between us, casting his gorgeous face in shadowy planes and angles, and I realize he's so close I could reach out and touch him. Trail my fingers across his jawline, cup his cheek, trace his lower lip...

Oh God. I sit up straight, my head feeling a little too wobbly. I've had sooo much wine. That must be it. That's why I feel so much...

Yearning.

Longing.

For Jordan.

"There are lots of things I want to share with you," he finally says, his gaze never leaving mine. I could get lost in his beautiful blue eyes. Drown in them. Die in them.

Oh, I am feeling downright poetic right now. This is crazy.

"Like what?" I prop my chin on my fist again, sighing happily. I don't want this moment to end. I feel like I'm having a dream. The best dream ever.

"I want to take you back and show you my townhouse. And eventually, my house in Sonoma," he says in that velvety low voice of his. I swear, all he did was answer my question and his voice alone made my nipples hard.

"I would love to see your house in Sonoma," I say breathlessly. "I've never been to Sonoma before."

"It's beautiful." His mouth curves into this closed-lipped, lopsided smile. "*You're* beautiful."

My cheeks go hot and I blink away from his intense gaze, staring at the table. "Thank you."

"You still have a hard time taking a compliment, Mandy?"

I lift my head, my gaze meeting his once more, defiance filling me. "No. Not anymore."

"Really?" He sounds doubtful.

"Really," I say firmly.

"So you won't get embarrassed if I tell you that I can't stop thinking about the fact that you're completely naked beneath that dress?" Both his dark brows are up now, looking so ridiculously sexy I wish I could whip my phone out and capture a photo of him like this. So I can keep this moment tucked away forever in my camera roll.

"You like the fact that I'm completely naked beneath my dress, don't you?" Ah, listen to me, being all flirtatious and daring.

This is so unlike me.

"Truth?" I nod and he continues. "I fucking *love* the fact that you're completely naked under that dress."

I swallow hard at all the need I see lingering in his eyes.

"And I'm dying to get you alone so I can take that dress off of you," he continues, so very matter of fact. "But we have to wait."\

Wait.

What??

Whyyyyyy?

"Why do we have to wait?" I press my legs together, fighting to calm the tingles between my thighs.

He smiles, but it's tight, and his jaw is hard, like he's barely containing himself. "It's a secret."

"A secret?" I am so, so curious.

"More like a surprise."

"I love surprises." I clap my hands together like a little girl and he actually laughs.

"You'll definitely like this one." His laughter fades, but that faint smile is still locked in place. "In fact, I need to go check on—things. I'll be right back."

He leaves the table and I watch him go, my gaze glued to his backside as he walks away. Damn, he is one fine looking specimen. How did I get so lucky to have this man come back into my life? What did I do to deserve this second chance? I could lie to myself and say this isn't going to work, but I actually think it could.

Yes. I *really* think it could.

He's gone for a few minutes and I reach into my purse, pulling my phone out to check my notifications. A couple of Instagram likes, one memory from Facebook today, plus Lena's sent me three texts, all of them with plenty of exclamation points.

How's your date with Jordan Tuttle??!!!!

Tell me what's going on!!!!

OMG it must be good coz I haven't heard from you!!!!!

Smiling, I type her a quick reply.

Me: **So far it's the perfect date.**

I add a couple of heart eyed emojis to my text and hit send.

I'm about to slip my phone back into my purse when she responds.

Lena: **I'm so happy for you!!!!!!**

Her excessive exclamation points almost make me laugh.

Me: **Thank you. I'll fill you in tomorrow.**

I'm dropping my phone back into my purse when I spot Jordan striding through the restaurant, heading straight for me. Our waiter is following behind him, carrying a plate with a silver dome covering it. Jordan settles into his seat, his expression serious as the server pauses in front of our table.

"A special treat for the lady," the server says, and with a dramatic flourish, he lifts the silver lid to reveal a plate filled with one, two, three, four, five, six...

Cupcakes.

"Oh." I cover my mouth with a shaky hand, barely realizing our server has already walked away. I'm too enraptured by my surprise. They're all so pretty, each cupcake frosted in a different color, a pastel blue, pink, yellow, green, purple and white. My gaze flies to Jordan to find him watching me, amusement and—yes, plenty of affection too—in his gaze. "The cupcakes. From that bakery. How did you..."

"I have my ways." He points at the plate. "I hope you like them."

"I *love* them." This is literally so sweet. Jordan didn't just notice me ogling the cupcake display at a bakery, he actually sent someone to go buy me a half- dozen cupcakes and had them brought to me. He always used to indulge my sweet tooth. "Thank you."

"You going to eat one?"

"Yes! Oh my God, will you think I'm a pig? I just ate all that food." I rest my hand over my stomach, contemplating which one I should eat first. I like chocolate, but truly, I'm a boring old vanilla girl—literally.

"You're not a pig, Mandy," he says, slowly shaking his head. "Pick one."

"Will you split it with me?" I grab the one with blue frosting and hold it up, getting a little bit of frosting on my hand. I bring it to close to my face, licking the frosting off my finger quickly, and my body goes hot when I realize Jordan is watching my every move. "I...don't think I can eat it all by myself."

"Yeah. Here." He holds his hand out and I set the cupcake in his giant palm, my fingers somehow brushing against his as I pull my hand away, sparks flying like they do every time we touch. He sets the cupcake on his never-used bread plate and peels off the wrapper carefully, getting some frosting on his fingers too. He licks it off just as quick as I did, and I feel a stirring low in my belly when I see his tongue.

God, this is like foreplay. I'm going to be a mess by the time we leave the restaurant.

Jordan grabs the clean butter knife and cuts the cupcake in half, then offers me the plate. "Which half do you want?"

It's hard to tell which side is bigger, he's cut the cupcake so precisely. The thick frosting is just as tall as the actual cake, and I seriously can't wait to taste it. I point at the half closest to me and he grabs the other one. Before I can say or do anything, he plops the entire cupcake half into his mouth, leaving a dab of pale blue frosting in the corner of his lips.

"Jordan!" I start laughing as he chews and chews. "What a waste. You ate it all in one bite."

He chews a little more before he finally swallows. "And it was delicious." He points at the remaining cupcake waiting for me on the plate. "Try yours."

"I will, but first." I point at his mouth. "You have frosting on your face."

"I do?" He frowns. "Where?" He wipes at his cheek and I shake my head. He dabs at the wrong corner of his mouth and I shake my head again. "Tell me where."

Leaning over the table, I touch my thumb to the left corner of his plush mouth, wiping the frosting off his lips with one swipe. My thumb tingles from where I touched him, my entire body lit up from within. "Got it."

"Thanks." His voice falters when I stick my thumb in my mouth and suck the frosting clean off.

"You're welcome," I say with gleeful enthusiasm right before I take a big bite of my cupcake. No way could I eat that all in one bite and besides, I want to savor it.

And oh God, this cupcake is so freaking good. It's, like, the best vanilla I've ever tasted in my life—and I've tasted a lot of vanilla, so I should know—and the frosting is perfect. Buttercream, sweet but not enough to give me a cavity.

"This is so delicious, it's practically orgasmic," I tell him just as I take another bite.

"Jesus, Mandy," he mutters, pushing his hair away from his forehead. He looks pained. Like I'm making him miserable and I guess I probably am.

It's *so* great.

Once I'm finished—and I lick my thumb again just to drive him crazy—I smile and point at the remaining cupcakes. "What are we going to do with the rest of them?"

"Do you want another?" he asks.

I shake my head. "I'm stuffed." I mean, I could probably attempt one more cupcake, but I don't want to make myself sick.

"I'll get a box for them then." He flags down our server as he passes by and asks, "To-go box?"

"Right away, sir," the server answers before he takes off.

"I already paid the bill," Jordan tells me. "Are you ready to go?"

I almost want to tell him no. That I don't want to end the most perfect date I've ever been on in my life. There's no real awkwardness when I talk to Jordan. We have this shared history, an easy camaraderie from being friends first, and our friendship started long, long ago. We played catch up while waiting for our dinner to arrive earlier, mostly gossip about people we went to high school with, but we never took it too deep. Or too personal.

We're probably too scared to try that just yet.

This is a good start, though. This is what I want. Ease into it, find our footing, find our old selves, the ones who made up Tuttle and Amanda, the teen years.

Wait a minute. Maybe we shouldn't try to find our old selves. We should be focusing on our new and improved selves. I've grown up a lot, learned a few things about myself, and now about Jordan too.

I don't want to be the same ol' Amanda, the one filled with too much self-doubt. The one who sabotaged the only real relationship I've ever had and gave up on it way too soon. The one I thought was hopeless from the start, because high school relationships never last, right?

That's what I thought.

But maybe I thought wrong.

EIGHTEEN

JORDAN

IT WAS EASY, getting her to come back to my town-house. I asked, and she said yes, and we haven't talked much since then. Together we went in search of my car and I drove us to the Levare housing development, where my place is. I park the SUV in the garage and lead her into my home, stepping back as she comes to a stop in the living room and slowly turns in a circle with her head tilted back.

"How many levels are there?" she asks.

"Three, if you don't count the garage or the roof deck," I answer.

"Oh my God." She stares at me, her mouth hanging open. "Jordan, this is amazing."

Her words fill me with pride. I can't help but want to show off. Does that make me an asshole? Well, great. Then I guess I'm an asshole. "I'm glad you like it."

She walks farther into the living room, stopping at the floor-to-ceiling windows for a moment before she turns to look at me. "How many bedrooms?"

"Three."

"Bathrooms?"

"Three. Well, two and a half," I correct.

"Wow." She's now in the kitchen, running her fingers along the marble counters, lightly touching the stainless steel refrigerator. "I've always wanted a fridge with French doors," she murmurs almost to herself, opening the refrigerator to reveal...

Nothing much.

"Jordan, you barely have any food in here," she chastises as she takes in what little I do have. She grabs the milk carton and checks the date. "It's expired."

I shrug.

"You have ketchup, expired milk, Kraft American cheese slices and a six-pack of beer." She shuts the doors, her accusatory gaze meeting mine. "That's it."

"I'm not home much." If ever. And when I am home, I'm not cooking. What's the point of that when there's takeout readily available? Uber Eats is the greatest invention ever.

"I'll say."

She continues her inspection of my home, examining the giant closet across from the half bathroom, stepping out onto the balcony so she can admire the view. I let her do her thing, following her up the stairs to the second level so she can check out the two bedrooms that only have beds and nothing else, the bathroom, and the huge hall walk-in closet that is completely empty.

"This house has so much storage space." She shakes her head as she closes the closet door. "I would die for this."

If she would've stuck with me, this would be hers. She'd be the queen of my castle and I would've worshipped at her perfect feet every single day for the rest of our lives.

My entire body aches at the thought. Confirmation yet again that I'm not over her.

Is she over me? I thought so. I've clung to that truth for years, but maybe...

Maybe I have a chance again. With her.

With us.

Amanda hesitates at the foot of the stairs, her hand on the railing as she stares up at me with wide brown eyes. "Your bedroom is up here?"

I nod.

"Is it huge?"

"You know it," I boast. "I could fit your entire studio apartment up in there." Exactly what I told her earlier.

"Ha, don't remind me." She starts up the stairs and I follow after her, my gaze locked on her ass since it's pretty much in my face, and yet again I remember she has no panties on under that dress.

I know I shouldn't rush things. As in, I shouldn't rush her into my bed. But my body isn't listening to my logical head tonight. All it can think about is fucking.

Fucking Amanda on my bed.

Fucking Amanda against a wall.

Fucking Amanda up on the rooftop deck...

"Oh, your bedroom is gigantic!" she exclaims, pushing me out of my dirty thoughts. She points at my bed. "What the hell size is that?"

"Custom." I'm tall and I wanted a big ass bed. So I had it made for me.

"Holy crap." She walks all the way around it, her fingers trailing across my pale gray comforter. "I bet you could fit ten women into this bed." Her cheeks go red the moment she says it, and she sends me a horrified look. "Not that you've ever had ten women in this bed. Well, maybe you have, but not all at once. Or maybe not at all? God, please tell me to shut up before I make this worse."

I approach her hesitantly, like one might approach a scared animal, and once I'm standing in front of her, I grab both of her hands in mine. "You seem nervous."

"I am," she admits readily. "This is—weird, being in your house with you."

"Why?" I tilt my head, contemplating her. I'm nervous too, but for an entirely different reason. I love that she's here, but I want more. I want her naked.

In my bed.

Beneath me.

I'm nervous with *anticipation*. I've done this before, specifically with Amanda, plenty of times. But it all feels new and different.

Maybe because we're such different people than we were six years ago.

"You're such a grown up, Jordan." She smiles tremulously. "You have your own house—*two* houses—and another fancy Range Rover in your two-car garage. You're a responsible adult, and it's hard for me to wrap my head around that fact. Plus, you're famous. Everyone knows who you are and they probably all want a piece of you too. It's...it's so mind blowing that you've come this far, that you've done so much."

"Is that why you're here with me tonight?" I ask, the doubt sweeping through me slowly, like the thick gray fog that rolls into the San Francisco Bay. "Because of what I do and the fame that comes with it?"

"Of course not," she says without hesitation. "I knew you before you were *the* Jordan Tuttle, you know. Back when you were short and a little chubby, with zits all over your face. Remember that?"

I wince. Yeah, I remember when I was shorter than her and hadn't quite shed the baby fat yet. My mom wanted to send me to a weight loss camp the summer after seventh grade, but thank Christ I grew like six inches in a matter of a few months. The diet lectures and camp mentions completely disappeared. "Why you gotta bring up the bad times?"

She laughs and squeezes my hands. "I'm just saying I've known you for a *long* time. And while we haven't been in each other's lives for over six years, I don't think that matters. I still know who you are, Jordan. And I don't care about the money or the fame."

I want to believe her. I also want to trust her. I do.

I take her in, staring blatantly at her and she smiles in return, her eyes shining with unrestrained happiness. I find myself drowning in them. Forgetting all my troubles and my earlier doubt.

Can't forget that she broke up with me though. She gave up on me first. I can't forget that. No matter how hard I try, the doubt is still there, reminding me I shouldn't trust her. Not completely.

Not yet.

NINETEEN

AMANDA

HE TAKES me up to the rooftop deck, where a breath-taking view of the city lights greets me. We're so high up, there's a strong breeze, causing me to wrap my arms around myself to ward off the chill.

"This view is great," I tell him as I lean against the railing, tipping my head down so I can see the traffic below. Not that there are many cars out at this time of night, but there are just enough to keep my interest.

Well, that and I'm avoiding looking at him. I'm on edge, unsure. What's going to happen next? He hasn't even tried to kiss me, or touch me beyond holding my hands. My body is demanding more, more, more, but it's almost like he's—withholding his affection on purpose, maybe?

I sincerely hope not.

"I never come up here," he says as he stops to stand right beside me, resting his arms on the railing.

I turn to look at him, surprised by his admission. "Really?"

"Yeah. Don't have time."

"Sounds like you don't have much time for anything." This worries me. This is what we ran into before, and after a while, it sent me packing.

Some might say I gave up on him, and I was stupid. Most of the time, I agree with that assessment. But then I remember sad, lonely me six years ago. Still living at home and going to community college while my hot and popular boyfriend was at USC and living the dream—without me.

"I'm busy, yeah. Like, all the time." He nudges his elbow against mine. "You know this, though. You remember."

"I do. Yes, I get it," I say, my voice cool, my thoughts haywire. Crap, I don't really get it, no matter how much I want to.

Brutal truth time: I want to be with a man who's able to give all of himself to me, no matter what. Not like I want to be attached at the hip and he has no outside interests or whatever—I want us to share in everything we do, and right now, with the way Jordan's life is going, I'm not sure if he can be that man.

No matter how badly I want him to be.

Only an hour ago at the restaurant I was telling myself this could totally work, and now I'm thinking it's near impossible.

Why is the truth so hard to face?

"Hey." He touches me, his fingers slipping beneath my chin to tilt my face up so our gazes connect. "I can practically see the cogs turning in your brain."

My smile is sad, I can feel it. "Reality sucks."

He understands what I'm really saying, and I appreciate that about him. Reality does suck. We're having a great time tonight. Being together feels familiar, yet different. Fresh and new, with that comforting, *hey we've done this before,* vibe too.

But tomorrow I'll go back to work and so will he. He's so busy who knows when I'll see him again.

For all I know, this might be my one last chance.

"Fuck reality," he murmurs as he lowers his head until we're so close, I can feel his breath waft across my cheek. "Don't worry about all the bullshit, Mandy."

"But I can't help—"

He cuts my words off with a kiss.

My stomach drops, tumbling over itself at that first touch of his glorious mouth on mine. Again, it's familiar yet new. Thrilling. Exciting. He's kissing me. *Jordan Tuttle* is kissing *me.*

His lips are soft. Not hungry, not demanding. More like a test, a question.

Are we really doing this?

Are you going to let me keep kissing you?

Do you want this?

Do you want me?

Yes.

Yes, yes, yes.

Our mouths meet again and again. Sweet, chaste kisses that make my entire body grow warm. He slips his arms around my waist and pulls me in closer, his lips parting mine, his tongue darting. Retreating. A tease.

A promise.

Feeling bold, I slip my tongue inside his mouth, circling it around his. He growls low in his throat, his arms tightening around my waist, the fabric of my dress lifting the slightest bit, reminding me that yep, I'm still naked beneath the thin fabric.

It feels so good just kissing him. Imagine what might happen once he puts those skilled hands on my bare skin?

We kiss and kiss, our tongues tangling, our hands wandering, until he finally breaks away first, his mouth on my neck, licking and nibbling. I keep my eyes closed, my hands coming up to wrap around his neck, my fingers sliding into his thick, soft hair. He pushes aside my denim jacket so it falls off my shoulder, his mouth on my collarbone, his hands sliding up, causing the dress fabric to draw up even more.

"Are you trying to expose me?" I ask breathlessly, a shiver moving through me when the cool breeze hits.

"Maybe," he murmurs against my throat, one hand dropping to flirt with the hem of my dress. His fingers brush against my thigh and I whimper.

Is it bad that I want to yell at him to just go ahead and do me? That sounds stupid, even in my thoughts, but it's so true. I want Jordan naked. I want to touch him, kiss him, feel him slip deep inside me.

I want it all.

"We're not going to do—this outside, are we?" I open my eyes and glance around, noting the outdoor table and chairs. The chairs look comfortable, but not for both of us. And there are no lounge chairs, which is a bummer because one of those would've worked just fine...

"Absolutely fucking not." He pulls away from me, grabs my hand, and we walk back into the house, both of us practically running down the stairs, our matching harsh breaths echoing. He stops at the doorway that leads into what looks like an office, pressing me against the wall, his hands cupping my cheeks just before he steals another kiss.

Oh, and it's a good one. Lots of tongue, his hands cradling my face, his thumbs skimming my skin, making me feel...cherished.

Loved.

Ugh, I shouldn't even think of that word when it comes to me and Jordan. That's the past. I need to focus on the here and now.

I tilt my head back and he takes the kiss deeper. His hands fall to my hips and then he's grabbing hold of me, his hands slipping low to cup my bare ass, and the moment he touches me there, a jolt of electricity pulses through my body, making me shudder.

"Fuck," he groans against my lips, his hands pulling me into position so my legs are wrapped around his waist, my feet digging into his rock-hard backside. I'm snug against his front, bare and rubbing the seam of his jeans. I can feel him.

He's hard beneath the denim and I press closer, a whimper escaping me at the delicious friction.

I could probably come like this. It's been a while since I've had sex. It's been even longer since I've had *really* good sex.

And it's been over six years since I've had the best sex of my life.

Ridiculous, right? That the best sex ever was with Jordan. But I think it's because we were so much in love, sex-obsessed teenagers driven by our hormones. We learned together. We experimented. We were comfortable with each other, but not in a boring way. More in the *ooh, let's try that* way.

Those times were some of the best I ever had. The memories have faded, but being with him like this, my body reacts instinctively, knowing exactly what to do and how to move in order to arouse him.

Muscle memory is an interesting thing.

Jordan pins me to the wall with his hips, his erection pressing against me, his hands gripping my bare butt. His mouth is on mine, his breath hot, his teeth tugging on my lower lip, his big body caging me in. "You're trying to get off, aren't you?" he asks in that growly, sexy voice of his after he ends our kiss.

"What do you mean?" I play stupid on purpose. I want to hear what he has to say. Right before I broke up with him, he started to get into dirty talk. Not too raunchy, but just raunchy enough to get my blood pumping.

"You keep rubbing against my dick." Oh God, his voice is so rough. I lift my hips and grind on him a little as an example, and he groans. "Yeah, just like that."

"You feel good," I admit as I rock against him, sinking my teeth into my lower lip to keep from moaning too loud.

"So do you," he murmurs, his fingers slipping lower, so tantalizingly close to where I want him the most. "You're getting my jeans wet."

Okay, that was the hottest thing ever. Clearly I have no shame, because I grind against him again, harder this time, and I can feel my orgasm hovering close. He knows it too. Probably can tell by the way I went still for that millisecond moment, can hear it in the way I sucked in a harsh breath and held it.

This man knows my tells like no other.

I both want to prolong this moment and get it over with right away, because my body is tightly strung, my blood running hot, my skin buzzing. It's urgent, my need to find release because holy crap, I *must* have it.

Now.

He kisses me again, his soft, hot lips melting into mine, our tongues dancing, his fingers teasing me from behind while I grind on his denim-covered erection, finding my rhythm, the rhythm I know that's going to take me straight to O-Town. My brain helps along with matters—reminding me what he looks like naked—to die for—and that gleam he'd get in his eyes just before he went down on me—seductive yet mischievous. Going down on me was something Jordan liked to do often.

Something I'd like him to do ASAP, if you get what I mean.

He slips his finger inside me and that's all it takes. Destination O-Town has arrived and it turns me into a gasping, whimpering, shuddery mess as I basically hump Jordan like a greedy, inexperienced teenager experiencing her first orgasm from someone else. My face is pressed against his throat and my fingers are curled tight in the hair at his nape as I cling to him, probably stabbing his butt with my stiletto heels. He holds me tight, one large hand smoothing up and down my back as my shivers slowly subside, yet I don't want to shift away from him. Not yet.

I like how he's holding me. Soothing me. Oh, and there's also the fact that I'm a little embarrassed that I just came so hard, so quickly.

"Mandy." His voice rumbles and I can feel the vibrations. "You all right?"

I nod, but still don't move.

"I'm going to set you down now, okay?" When I nod again, his arms loosen around me, and I slip my legs from his hips. My feet land on the floor and my knees are still weak so I wobble, but he catches me.

This tiny moment reeks of symbolism. No matter what happens, if we're together, Jordan is always there to catch me before I fall.

Or maybe I'm just totally reaching.

TWENTY
JORDAN

AMANDA IS GIVING me a serious case of blue balls.

I made her come and now she's freaking out. Once I set her on her unsteady feet, she tugged her skirt down, smoothed a hand over her hair and then mumbled, "I have to use the bathroom." She dashed into my master bathroom and has secluded herself in there for the last five minutes.

I'm sitting on the foot of my bed, running my hands continuously through my hair, tugging on it extra tight until it hurts. Maybe if I focus on the pain, my insistent dick will settle down.

Yeah. Not happening.

She's the sexiest thing alive. Seriously, no woman has ever done it for me like Amanda. Having her in my arms only a few minutes ago, our mouths fused as she rubbed her wet pussy all over the front of my jeans, *Jesus.*

Need to stop thinking like that. Remembering the moment is doing me no favors. As in, my dick is still painfully hard.

The bathroom door slowly swings open and she walks out, looking uneasy. The shoes are off. They're dangling from her fingers and she drops them on the floor with a plop, her teeth sinking into her lower lip as she contemplates me.

I say nothing. Just lean back with my hands braced on the mattress behind me, kicking my legs out. She's still studying me, her gaze doing a leisurely stroll from my head to my feet until she finally says,

"I think maybe we're—moving too fast."

Well, shit. So that's what it takes to deflate my dick.

"Man—" I start to say, but she cuts me off.

"No, let me finish." She takes a deep breath and exhales loudly, waving her hands in front of her face like she's trying to cool down. Or stop the tears from coming, I'm not quite sure. "Being with you tonight has been amazing, but I'm scared."

She's quiet for a moment, so I go ahead and ask the question. "Scared of what?"

"Of you. Of this not working," she admits quietly. She takes a step forward, the scent of her perfume wafting toward me, and all I can think is *so close*.

I was so damn close to having her naked and my cock buried deep inside her. Yet somehow, I messed it all up.

"Do you want this to work?" I ask. My chest goes tight. This is one of those hard truth moments, and I'm worried she'll say something I don't want to hear.

Amanda ducks her head, her long dark hair spilling over her shoulder, and gives a little shrug. "Do you?"

"I asked you first."

She bursts out laughing, shaking her head. "We sound like little kids."

"Right now, we're acting like little kids." I stand and go to her, close enough to touch her, but I don't. Not yet. "What do you want, Mandy?"

"I don't know." She keeps her head bent and I give in, slipping my fingers beneath her chin, tilting her face up so her gaze meets mine. Her eyes are shining with unshed tears and seeing them cracks my steel-plated heart. Damn, this girl wrecks me. She always has. "I want to, but..."

"But what." I touch her cheek. Trace her jaw. Her skin is still flushed from her earlier orgasm and she's so warm.

So beautiful.

Still mine.

"I don't want to get hurt," she whispers, closing her eyes and leaning into my palm. "And if we do this, I'm afraid you'll hurt me again, Jordan. I can't help it."

It's my turn to take a deep breath. I'm stalling, trying to figure out exactly what I want to say. How much I want to reassure her that if she just gave us a chance, we'd probably work. I'm not over her. Clearly, she's not over me. So why not give it another try?

"I can guarantee you'll hurt me again too," I admit. "If you put a stop to this right now, you'll hurt me. But if you don't take a chance, then you'll never know."

Her eyes pop open and she's frowning at me. "Never know what?"

"Just how great we could be." I skim my thumb across her lush mouth, tempted to kiss her again. "Once upon a time, we were pretty damn great, you know."

Until she dumped my ass with no real explanation. Didn't offer me a chance to correct my wrongs or whatever. It was just a simple *it's over*. And I wasn't allowed to try and change her mind.

So why am I willing to put my heart on the line once again? She'll destroy it. She's good at that—she has lots of experience.

Yet seeing her like this, touches something deep within me. Her expression is...raw. Vulnerable. Her lips tremble and the tears start to spill, one sliding down her cheek. Then another.

"We totally were," she says, her voice faint.

I say nothing. It's so much easier to clamp up. Shut down. I lean in and kiss her gently, communicating with my lips what I can't say with words.

Take a chance on me.

Take a chance on us.

Hopefully she'll listen to what I'm trying to say.

TWENTY-ONE

AMANDA

COME **to the game with me this weekend.**

The text from Jordan is a simple request, but the deeper message behind his words is one that scatters my thoughts into immediate chaos.

He wants me to go to Tampa Bay this weekend. To watch him while he plays. To possibly sleep with him in his hotel room at night, but let's be real—sleep is code for having sex. Which in turn, means we're going to *actually have sex.*

We've done it before. It should be no big deal. But he's gone on to have sex with supermodels and I've gone on to have sex with...regular guys. Not even enough to count on one hand. Will I measure up?

Does he think we're moving too fast? Do I seem too easy? I did, after all, grind on his dick until I came on his jeans. Talk about immature.

My cheeks are hot just thinking about last night. Worse, I never, uh, serviced him in return. I'm the most selfish, orgasm-seeking monster on this planet.

"What are you reading that's got you looking like that?"

The familiar voice startles me and I drop my phone onto the table with a clatter, glancing up to find Cade watching me with an amused look on his face.

He is the last person I want to see right now. Lena already gave me a lecture this morning about how I need to let Cade know that I'm not interested in him beyond being his friend, and I know she's right, but I don't want to hurt his feelings.

I also know I can't string him along. That's not right. Not at all.

"Nothing really," I say, keeping my voice purposely casual. I turn my phone over so neither of us can see if Jordan texts me again. I took a late lunch since it's been so busy today, and I'm in the lunchroom eating a sandwich I packed that isn't very good. It sits forgotten on the table beside my phone, and I grab it, rewrapping the sandwich in aluminum foil and then balling it up. I'll toss it in the trash when I leave the breakroom.

"How've you been?" Cade doesn't bother asking if he can sit with me. Instead he pulls a chair out and plops his butt in it, smiling at me. "Crazy morning, huh?"

"Very," I agree, flinching when my phone buzzes again. My fingers crawl toward the phone like I have no control of them, but I don't pick it up.

I refuse to look at it in Cade's presence.

"Can't believe it's already Thursday," he says.

"Same," I say weakly. More like it's *only* Thursday and my life has completely and totally changed in a matter of a few days.

"So." His hesitation is like a warning, and I know without a doubt he's going to ask me out. "What are you up to this weekend?"

What is up with the men in my life trying to be a part of my weekend plans? What's even crazier is that I go from having zero attention from any guy to two of them trying to get all up in my business in a matter of minutes.

Plenty of women would tell me I'm lucky. But all I feel is...

Conflicted.

"I'm not sure yet," I say haltingly, which is the absolute truth.

"Want to get together? Check out a movie, maybe?" He's smiling. His eyes are sparkling. Cade is a very attractive man.

But after everything that's happened with Jordan, and realizing my feelings for him never really died, I know Cade is not the man for me.

"Cade..." My voice drifts and I sit up straighter. His smile fades, and I know he knows I'm about to turn him down. "I'd like to go to the movies with you, but I'm actually— seeing someone else."

Making that declaration causes my heart to start racing. The words are out there. I've just turned Cade down because I am involved with Jordan. Again. I'm trying my best to fight against it, yet the doubt is there. Taking residence in my brain.

You've gone down this road before and failed—sure you want to do it again?

I ignore the negative voice inside my head and focus on Cade. His eyebrows are so far up they're practically in his hairline. "Well. You definitely move fast."

I'm slightly offended by his comment—and the tone of his voice. "It happened fast," I snap defensively.

"Let me guess." He rises to his feet and snaps his fingers like he just had a revelation. "You're getting back together with your ex. Tuttle."

My mouth drops open but then I clamp it shut. Guess he's more perceptive than I realized. "We're, um, kind of seeing each other again. Yeah."

"Right." He nods, his expression totally shut off. No more friendly Cade for me. "I should've known. You two were acting weird around each other Monday night."

"It was...awkward. I hadn't seen him in years." Were we that obvious?

Probably.

"And it's only Thursday," Cade points out. "Obviously he knows how to get to you. Sent you the flowers on Tuesday, took you out, and must've convinced you that you two belong together. Again. All in approximately...forty-eight hours. Am I right?"

I blink up at him, shocked by the venomous edge to in his voice. Why is he so angry?

Rising to my feet, I cross my arms almost defensively. "We have—history between us. And it's something we still want to explore."

Cade rolls his eyes. "Sure. Whatever you say. You brought me along to that game and play me like a fool."

I try to withhold my wince. He's sort of right. And I feel terrible about it. "We didn't mean for it to happen."

"I find that hard to believe."

Dropping my arms, I rest my hands on my hips. "Listen, you don't need to take your aggression out on me."

A huff of surprise escapes him. "What are you talking about?"

"I turn you down as nicely as I can, and you're downright—hostile." My blood is boiling. Like seriously, who does he think he is? "What gives you the right to start yelling at me?"

"I wasn't yell—"

I cut him off. "You raised your voice at me and you know it. You're not my boyfriend, Cade, not that the title gives you any right to talk to me like that. We've gone on two dates. That's it."

"You led me on," he accuses, and for the tiniest moment, I feel guilty.

Cade's not too far off the mark. I might've used him on Monday so I didn't have to go to that game and face Tuttle alone. That was wrong of me.

"Two dates aren't leading someone on." I lift my chin, trying to ignore how my body is starting to shake. "I apologize if I made you feel that way, though."

I am the bigger person for apologizing. That's what I'm telling myself. He really doesn't deserve my apology. *He* should say sorry to *me*.

Cade doesn't bother acknowledging my saying sorry either. The jerk.

"Jordan Tuttle is rich. And famous. I can't compete with that, when he's showering you with attention and money and gifts. But just know this. I'm a regular guy." He points his thumb at his chest. "I'll always be here when Tuttle won't be. Remember that."

And with those last words, Cade exits the lunchroom without a backward glance.

Shock courses through me as I pick up my phone with shaky fingers. I see that Jordan has sent me two more texts.

It'll be fun, I promise.

I want you there with me.

Cade's words ring through my mind as I try to come up with a response for Jordan. I hate how easily it is for me to doubt him after what Cade said. That's stupid. I barely know Cade.

And I've known Jordan forever.

Me: **I can't afford the plane ticket, is my response.**

He texts back immediately.

Jordan: **Give me a break, Mandy. I got you.**

I smile when the next text appears on my screen.

Jordan: **I got you in more ways than you'll ever know.**

Me: **Flirt.**

He sends me a bunch of kissy faced emojis, which is surprising. He was never one to express himself with emojis.

I send him blushy faced ones in return.

"Whoa, what happened between you and Cade?" Lena asks as she rushes into the lunchroom, heading straight for my table.

"What do you mean?" Apprehension ripples through me. I really hope Cade didn't complain to her about me. He only just walked out of here, so he couldn't have griped for too long.

"I passed him in the hall and he practically snarled at me when I said hi," Lena explains, her eyes wide. "He's always so nice. I didn't know what his problem could be until I saw you sitting in here."

"Gee, thanks a lot," I say sarcastically as I set my phone down with a sigh. I don't like how shaky that conversation with Cade made me feel, and I'm thankful it was Lena who walked in and not someone else. I need a friend now more than ever. "I was honest with him like you told me to be."

"Oh." Lena sits across from me at the table. "I guess he didn't like to hear what you had to say."

"Not at all," I agree.

"What did you tell him?"

"Well, first he tried to ask me out on another date." I see the flicker of disappointment in Lena's eyes, but I push past it. "When I turned him down and said I was seeing someone else, he figured out quick who that someone else was."

"Was he sad?" Lena asks.

"More like angry. He accused me of leading him on."

"Well, I guess most guys don't like to be turned down, and when you're turned down because the woman you're interested in is seeing a famous football player? That's gotta hurt a little." Lena winces.

"Yeah, I guess you're right, but that still doesn't give Cade the right to be mean to me."

"I totally agree," Lena says.

I hate how the doubt starts creeping up on me again. "I'm not even sure if this is the right thing to do."

Lena frowns. "What do you mean?"

"I don't know." I shrug. "Should I keep seeing Jordan?"

"Do you want to keep seeing Jordan?" I can see the surprise etched all over my friend's face. She probably thinks I'm insane.

I nod, startled by the sudden lump of emotion clogging my throat making me unable to speak.

"Then you should go for it." She makes it sound so simple.

"He invited me to go watch his game this Sunday," I tell her.

Lena's eyes light up. "Oh, that'll be fun. In the suite again?"

"No, in Florida." I suck in a breath. "He wants me to go to his away game."

"Oh. Wow." Lena blinks rapidly, her brows shooting up. "That feels serious."

It's almost reassuring to hear her say exactly what I was thinking. "I know, and it scares me. Getting back together with Jordan...scares me a lot."

As soon as I confess this, the relief that hits me is almost staggering. It feels so good, admitting my secret emotions to my friend.

Lena sits up straighter, her expression determined. "So. Is it a good fear or a bad fear?"

She's totally confusing me. "What do you mean?"

"I mean, does the thought of getting back together with Jordan make you feel...afraid? Like in a dark and foreboding way? Or is it more the fear of the unknown."

Jordan has never scared me in a dark or foreboding way. I always felt safe with Jordan. Now, not so much, only because of the uncertainty of everything that's happening between us.

I know him, but I don't. I understand him, yet I don't.

Confusing, right? I make no sense. My emotions are a mixed-up jumble of insecure teenage Amanda and confident, grown-up Amanda.

"It's the unknown," I admit. "It could be great, but what if I mess it up again?" Or he could mess it up this time around.

"The only way you'll know is if you try." Lena reaches out and grabs my hand, giving it a little squeeze. "Would you rather try one more time? Or have a lifetime of regret?"

"Well, when you put it like that..." My voice drifts and I start to laugh, squeezing her hand in return. "I don't like regret."

"Then I guess we know your answer then." She smiles.

I swallow hard, ignoring the way my stomach flutters with nerves.

I guess we do know my answer.

TWENTY-TWO

AMANDA

MY PHONE RINGS at exactly seven o'clock, which is when Jordan said he'd call—though he didn't tell me it would be a FaceTime call. Thank goodness I still look decent and I already changed out of the work polo.

I hit answer and wait eagerly for his face to fill my screen.

My breath catches when he's finally there, a little smile curling his lips when we make eye contact. "Hey," he says in that easygoing way of his. Like it's no big deal that we're talking like this. That the last time I saw him, we made out and I ended up coming all over his jeans.

Seriously, I need to get over my embarrassment. We're trying to make this work. I have every right to basically hump Jordan and have an orgasm.

"Hi," I say, trying to keep it together. "How are you?"

"I'm good," he says, leaning back against a headboard. Guess he's sprawled out on the bed in his hotel room. I wish I was with him. "Tired."

"Time change messing you up?"

"Kind of." He hides a yawn, and it hits me how much I miss him. Silly, considering how long we haven't been in each other's lives. I spend a few days with him, and now it doesn't feel like enough. "How are you?"

"Good. It was a crazy day." I already decided I won't tell him about my earlier argument with Cade. No need to fire Jordan up over nothing.

"Listen, I'm going to cut right to the chase." His expression is grim and worry makes my heart start pounding. "I don't think you should come to Florida."

"Oh." My voice is small. My heart is sinking. "Okay."

"Don't get all butt hurt." His voice is teasing, that smile coming back. "I have a better idea."

Curiosity fills me. "What's your better idea?"

"Do you have a passport?"

"Um, yeah. Got one two years ago when I went with friends to Mexico for a few days."

"Perfect. That should work then." He's got this far away look on his face. Almost like he's talking to himself.

"What should work?" I ask.

"I want you to come with me." He pauses. "To England."

"What? Are you serious?"

"Dead serious," he says with a nod.

England? Really? "When?"

"We're playing an exhibition game in London at Wembley Stadium a week from this Sunday. What do you think?" He lifts his brows.

My mind is racing with the possibilities—and the obstacles. I wish I could just pick up on a whim and go wherever I want, whenever I want to, but I don't have that luxury. "I-I don't know if I could get the time off."

"Don't you get vacation time?"

"Well, yeah. I get one week a year." As in, I have five paid days off. "But usually, we have to request the time off at least a month in advance."

"Think they could make an exception?"

"I don't know," I answer, chewing on my lower lip.

I go quiet for a moment, thinking of all the things I'd need to do before I leave—if I even *can* leave, when Jordan finally asks, "Do you *want* to go to London with me?"

He sounds so unsure, and that's unusual for Jordan Tuttle. He was—and still is—the most confident person I've ever known. He just always makes everything he does look so damn easy.

Throw a touchdown and win the game? He can do that.

Pass that test with an A yet never bothered to study? He can do that too.

Pursue his dream career with pure determination and end up playing for the NFL like it's no big deal? Yep, he sure did that.

He can do anything he sets his mind to.

"Yes," I tell him with a faint smile. "Yes, I definitely want to go to London with you. I've always wanted to go there."

His smile is one of pure relief. "We can make this work."

"Easy for you to say." I'm teasing, but then again, I'm not. It *is* easy for him to say. It's not so easy when I'm living a normal life and can't take off whenever I want.

If you would've stayed with Jordan through it all, maybe you'd be his wife. Maybe you'd be traveling everywhere with him right now.

I push that nagging voice to the darkest corner of my brain.

"Just put in for some vacation time or whatever," he says.

"It's hard to do it so last minute, though. They'll need to find someone to cover for me," I explain.

"And that might be difficult?"

"Sometimes." Truthfully? I don't know. But I've seen management scramble when someone calls in sick before, especially when it's for an unexpected and extended period of time.

"I really want you to go," he says in that determined voice I instantly recognize. "We could stay for a few extra days. Explore the city."

Hope fills me, along with a healthy dose of excitement. "That sounds amazing," I say softly.

He brings his phone closer to his face, and it's like a shock to my system. Will I ever get over how handsome he is? "I've never been to London before."

"Me either." I've never really traveled out of the U.S., minus my extended weekend trip to Mexico with some of my girl-friends. It was for a friend's bachelorette trip. We all saved up, shared one hotel room at a resort, and had the time of our lives. I got a little wild and crazy and hooked up with an extremely drunk, extremely cute guy from South Carolina. I liked his drawl. He liked my ass. I've never had a one-night stand before until then. Once I returned home, I never spoke to him again. It was a match made in wild-weekend-in-Mexico heaven.

"We could stay in a swank hotel," Jordan says, knocking me from my thoughts.

I almost laugh, keeping my gaze fixed on him. Why am I dwelling on some drunk guy from my past when I can focus on this very gorgeous, sweet man talking to me at this very moment? "Swank, huh?"

"We're provided rooms during the trip, but I could find another hotel. Somewhere nicer." His voice goes deeper. "More private."

The look in his eyes says it all. He's envisioning many hours in that hotel bed. With me.

So am I.

With him.

"I want to sightsee, not just spend the entire time in bed," I tease, going for bold. It feels almost...weird to talk to Jordan this way, since that sort of thing used to embarrass me when I was a shy teen.

But now, screw it. I'm a grown woman. I'm not going to play coy.

He smirks. "We can sightsee *and* spend plenty of time in bed," he reassures. "Trust me."

His words take hold of my heart, squeezing it tight. I'm desperate to trust him. To trust *in* him.

To trust in us.

TWENTY-THREE
JORDAN

THE WEEKEND WENT by so fast I barely had time to think, let alone sleep. We flew into Florida, practiced our asses off *and* sweated our asses off since it was so damn humid, and then proceeded to destroy the opposing team. We went out and celebrated at a brand new nightclub that wanted us there—specifically me—but I bailed after an hour. I had no interest in drinking, and I definitely had no interest in meeting any women.

Overall, the weekend was good. The only thing missing was Amanda.

It's Monday and I'm home now. Arrived only an hour ago and I'm already itching to see her. It's barely four in the afternoon, so she's still working.

As proud as I am of her career success, I can admit to myself I resent the hell out of her job. When I want to do something with her, treat her by taking her somewhere special with me, her job is the roadblock that reminds me of what we could've had if she'd just stuck by my side.

I know without a doubt we'd still be together if she hadn't broken up with me. We'd probably even be married by now.

But would I have been a total jerk and not let her pursue a career? I can provide her with anything she wants, but would I have convinced her not to work, just so I could have her all to myself?

That's kind of an asshole move. And though I used to be a complete and total asshole when I was younger, I like to think I'm not that same guy anymore.

Unable to stand it any longer, I finally hop in my SUV and head for her workplace. The drive should've only taken me twenty minutes but ended up being almost an hour. Lots of stop and go traffic on the freeway that tested my patience.

I have none right now. None whatsoever.

I'm dying to see her.

Finally, I pull into the parking lot right at five o'clock, and I spot her immediately. She's waving at her friend as they part ways, her steps determined as she starts heading for the bus stop that's located right in front of the wellness center. She's got on the red polo and black pants outfit again, and her hair is pulled back into a simple braid, little wisps of dark hair catching the breeze as she walks. When she draws closer, I roll down my window and call out her name.

She comes to a sudden stop, her eyes widening when she spots me. Without hesitation, she jogs toward the car, her eyes sparkling, her smile huge.

"Hi." She sounds breathless, and unable to help myself, I lean my head out the window, brushing her mouth with mine. "What are you doing here?"

"Get in," I tell her, ignoring her question. She can't figure out why I'm here? I want to see her.

I want her.

"Where are you taking me?"

"Get in and I'll show you," I practically growl. Having her so close is making me impatient. We're wasting time with idle chitchat when we could already be in my car and halfway pulled out of the parking lot by now.

"So bossy," she murmurs just before she rounds the car and slips into the passenger side of my Range Rover. The door slams and her scent fills the confines of my car, making me feel a little drunk.

Without thought I reach for her just as she leans in my direction, like she's expecting me. I curl my hand around her nape and pull her mouth to mine. Her soft lips part easily and I delve my tongue inside, my dick instantly hard. It doesn't take much for Amanda to arouse me.

It never really has.

She breaks the kiss first, even more breathless now. "We're making out in the parking lot of my work."

"Is that a bad thing?" I touch her cheek, stroke her jaw. Her skin is soft. Silky. Her lips are plump, a little red from our kiss.

So I kiss her again.

"A very bad thing," she says after she pulls away from me. "I already feel like I'm on their shit list for asking about taking vacation time at such short notice."

"Don't worry about it." She worries about a lot of things, and I wish she didn't. I'm probably overstepping my boundaries, but I want her to know that since she's with me, she has nothing to worry about. I'll take care of her every need.

If she'll let me.

"I'm just glad they approved my vacation request," she says with a tentative smile.

Pleasure rushes through me, heady and sweet. I'm so fucking glad she's able to come with me.

"Me too." I relinquish my hold on her and she settles in her seat, smiling over at me as she puts on her seat belt. "Ready to go?" I ask her.

"Yes, please. Get me out of here before you start kissing me again." She's teasing. I can tell by the smile on her face. How her dark eyes are sparkling.

Smiling in return, I put the car in reverse and back out of the space, then make my way toward the exit. "If you're lucky, I'll be doing a lot more than kissing you later."

She goes quiet for a moment, finally speaking up when I pull onto the freeway. "I...I thought we were going to take this slow."

I can't believe she wants to. Seriously, what's the point? We were together before, and it was good. Great, actually. Until she gave up, and I let her.

Well, I'm not going to let her any longer. What we had before was worth fighting for. What we potentially have now—I can't give up. I can't let it go.

And I definitely don't want to move slow.

"We've been together before," I start, and she's already talking.

"Exactly, so we should learn from our mistakes," she points out.

"We were young," I counter, shooting her a quick look. She's watching me, an incredulous expression on her face. Like she can't believe we're having this conversation right now. Guess that makes two of us, because I can't believe it either. "We didn't know what we had until we didn't have it any longer."

"Do you really believe that?" Her voice is quiet, and I swear she sounds surprised.

"I do." I want to punch the steering wheel in frustration. This is the last place I want to talk about this. We should be having this conversation at my house. Or hers. Alone, face to face, sharing our secret feelings.

Instead, I'm driving in rush hour traffic, barely able to look at her.

"Are you trying to say that ours was the most meaningful relationship you've ever had?" Her voice squeaks on the last word.

I decide not to hold back. What's the point? If I can't be truthful with her, then what the hell are we doing?

"Yes. It was. I've always had a thing for you, Mandy. You know this," I stress.

"A thing? Like what? A crush when you were twelve? Thirteen? That's different than an adult relationship, you know.

I had a crush on you too. A meaningless one at first, because I truly believed there was no way you'd be interested in me. In fact, I *knew* you wouldn't be interested in me, because you were you and I was...me." She ends her ramble with a sigh.

I fucking hate when she talks like that.

"Yet I was interested. I was *always* interested." From the moment I started to notice girls, I noticed Amanda first. Seventh grade is where my crush turned into full-fledged yearning.

There's no other word for it. I yearned for this girl like some sort of sap in those awful romantic comedy movies chicks dig. When you're thirteen, that shit is embarrassing. When you're eighteen, that kind of shit drives you to make the girl of your dreams the girl of your reality.

I had my moments. I wasn't perfect. I did some stupid stuff that I regret. But once Amanda and I were committed, I was all in. I firmly believed we were it for each other. I didn't want anyone else.

Just Amanda.

I may have had other women since we broke up, but she's always haunted my thoughts, and I didn't trust any of them. Not like I trusted Mandy.. I've only had one other serious relationship besides Amanda, and that one went nowhere. I cared about Mia, but I realized after we split that I wasn't in love with her.

I wasn't obsessed with her, like I am with Amanda.

"And you're still interested," Amanda says, pulling me from my thoughts.

"More like obsessed," I mutter, immediately wishing I could take the words back.

But fuck it. If I can't be my authentic self with this girl, then I have no chance of being authentic ever.

TWENTY-FOUR

AMANDA

OBSESSED.

The word has a bad reputation, am I right?

Stalkers are obsessed with the object of their so-called affection.

Psycho ex-girlfriends are obsessed with the one who wronged them.

Teenagers infatuated with the latest boy band are obsessed.

That amazing new book you just read with the swoony couple who should be together but aren't? Yep, readers are definitely obsessed.

Being so completely focused on something until you can't think of anything else is considered a bad thing. Unhealthy.

Wrong.

Yet I don't think there's anything wrong with the way Jordan just said he's obsessed with me.

In fact, I *like* that he just used that word. I like it a lot. Because guess what?

I'm freaking obsessed with him too.

"You think I'm insane," he says about a minute after he dropped my new favorite word.

"What? No. I definitely don't think you're insane." I wrinkle my nose, confused. "Why would you say that?"

"Obsessed—maybe that wasn't the right word choice for how I feel about you." He's staring straight ahead, which is a good thing since he's driving. But I can see the tension in his jaw. The firm line of his lips. He's stressed out because he just admitted he's *obsessed* with me.

It's taking everything I have not to start bouncing in my seat.

"Are you saying you're not obsessed with me?" I ask innocently.

"I don't want to scare you off." The tension eases from his face a little, though his jaw is still tight.

"You can't scare me off," I tell him, sounding way more confident than I feel.

He snorts.

Literally snorts.

"Yeah, right," he mumbles.

"What do you mean by that?" I'm vaguely offended.

"Trust me." He flicks his gaze toward me for a too-brief moment. "I can definitely scare you off."

Why do we always have these sorts of conversations? It's like we talk in circles. It's also like we're kids again, trying to outdo each other. We're sort of ridiculous.

Yet I fall right into his trap anyway.

"Just try me," I dare him, the smugness in my voice so very obvious.

Again, he glances in my direction, and I hold my breath, steeling my spine just at the look I see on his beautiful face. Oh lordy, maybe he *can* scare me off—just by looking at me. "Want to hear about my plan?"

"What plan?"

"I call it my *get Amanda back to my house and naked in my bed* plan." He says it casually, like it's no big deal, that he wants to get me naked in his bed. "As in, I'll take you back to my place, we'll chat. Maybe we'll have something to eat. We'll definitely have something to drink because I think we both want a little liquid courage. And then, after we're both feeling loose and comfortable with each other, I'll seduce you."

My entire body perks up at the words seduce you. I know I was the one who just told him we needed to slow things down, but hmm...

Maybe I was wrong about that.

"You'll seduce me?" My voice is small, only because my brain has gone into immediate overload, thinking of all the things Jordan could do to seduce me.

"See?" It's his turn to sound smug. "I just scared you."

"No." I shake my head. "You really didn't."

He so didn't. I want it.

I want him.

"You up for it then?" He sends me a look, his gaze scorching me where I sit.

"You're talking to me like we're discussing a pickup game of basketball or whatever." I roll my eyes, barely able to contain my smile. "You up for another round, bro? Want to meet later? Hash this thing out? Play a little one-on-one?"

He laughs, and the sound is joyous. Amazing. I love it when he laughs. He doesn't do it often enough. "Well, Mandy? You up for another round? Wanna play a little one-on-one?"

Our gazes meet, hold. My entire body feels like it just caught fire.

"Yes," I whisper.

He takes me to dinner first, most likely to torture me. Draw this thing out. He's good at that. The torturing part.

He's good at everything he does.

We go to a small Mexican restaurant in a quiet part of town, not too far from where he lives, but not in the swank area he took me to for our last date. This place is small and old, and almost every single booth and table is occupied. The lighting is dim, the atmosphere party-like with all the loud chatter and the music playing in the background. The smells that hit me the moment we walk inside make my stomach growl.

"Tuttle!" An older woman with ruby red lips and substantial curves approaches us, wrapping Jordan up in a big hug. He lets her hug him. In fact, he wraps his arms around her ample frame and squeezes tight. "It's so good to see you," she says. "We've missed you around here."

"I've missed you too." He disentangles himself from her arms and angles her so that she's facing me. "Veronica, this is...Amanda."

"Hi." I smile at her, but she's too busy turning to gape at Jordan, her mouth hanging open.

"This is Amanda?" Her voice lowers, her gaze cutting to mine. "Your *Mandy?*"

Oh my God. For whatever reason, he's talked about me to this Veronica before? I can't even begin to wrap my head around this. I brace myself, waiting for her animosity. If he's talking about me, he can't be telling her anything good.

Right?

"This is her." Jordan nods, his expression solemn.

"Mandy." She steps forward and pulls me into her arms, her embrace so tight I struggle to breathe. "It is so, *so* good to finally meet you. And please, call me Ronnie."

"Um, nice to meet you too," I say, confused by her reaction.

She pulls away from me, clutching my shoulders and giving me a little shake. "You're beautiful! Oh, I knew you would be. Tuttle's told me plenty."

Jordan groans.

"Don't you act like that." She lets go of my shoulders to turn on him, wagging a finger at his chest. "You're the one who spilled your guts to me."

"You spilled your guts?" I ask him. It's shocking to think of Jordan telling someone else, a complete stranger, all about our failed relationship.

"He told me plenty." She tilts her head, contemplating me. "Enough to know that I should tell you that you have another opportunity right now. Don't blow it."

I'm taken aback by the urgency in her voice. I definitely know I have another opportunity right now. I've just never had anyone say it out loud to me before.

"Ronnie." Jordan's voice is firm. "Leave her alone."

"She needs to hear the truth." She turns and taps him lightly on the chest with her index finger. "Follow me. I've got a special table for you two."

Her quick change of subject leaves me reeling. Well, that and the fact that Jordan told her about our relationship.

Talk about weird.

The moment Ronnie hands us our menus and walks away, I'm leaning across the table, my gaze locked on Jordan's. "What was that all about?"

"I used to come here a lot, especially during my first season." He opens up the menu, then immediately shuts it and sets it on the table, as if he's already made up his mind. "I had a thing for their burritos. Still do."

"Great. Ronnie gave you a burrito and you told her all about your love life?" I arch a brow, surprised.

Jordan is not one to open up. To anyone.

"Yeah. So?" He shrugs, oh so nonchalant, and not saying much else, which is so typical. I used to hate how mysterious he would act back in the day. Even now, I sort of want to punch him.

And I also sort of want to hug him.

Okay, fine. I really want to hug him. That he felt the need to pour his heart out to a woman at a restaurant is sweet yet sad. Knowing that I'm the one who drove him to confess makes my heart ache for him.

I made so many mistakes in the past. That he still wants to spend time with me is like some sort of miracle.

"I'm surprise," I say.

Now it's his turn to lift his brows. "Really? Why?"

"You don't even know her," I point out.

"I do too. She's nice. Nicer than my mother's ever been." His tone is bitter, and my heart now feels like it cracked wide open.

I never liked his mother. Or his father. They always treated Jordan like a commodity, and never a person. Their own child who never felt loved by his parents. Thinking about them makes me feel fiercely protective of him.

"Is Ronnie like a mother figure then?" I ask gently, not wanting to pry but still curious.

I'm curious about everything that's happened to Jordan during the time we weren't together.

"During my first season, I came in here at least once a week. She'd always tell me I was so handsome and ask me why I didn't have a woman in my life. I guess that led me to confess about our relationship and what happened," he admits, his cheeks turning ruddy, which is totally adorable but still...

I feel like absolute shit.

Sighing, I drop my head, studying the menu, though I'm barely focused enough to read my dinner options. "Great. She probably hates me."

"She doesn't hate you," he assures me.

"I'm surprised you told her everything. That's not like you." I decide on street tacos with carnitas and shut my menu.

"I was hurt." He shrugs.

In my head, I calculate how many years are between our break up and his first season. "But that was what? Three years after we split? Four? And you were *still* hurt?"

He rests his hand over his heart, his expression sincere. "You've always had a major effect on me."

"Are you trying to make me feel terrible? Or is it just happening by accident?" Because it's totally working.

Jordan drops his hand over mine, completely engulfing it. "No, I'm just being honest. You had your issues, and I had mine."

I blink at him, hating the sting of tears that appear out of nowhere. I don't want to cry. Not here, in the middle of his favorite Mexican restaurant with Ronnie the mother figure watching over us. My timing is all wrong. "I never meant to hurt you," I admit, the words thick in my throat.

He squeezes my hand but doesn't say anything.

"I figured you were so busy, that you'd get over me quick. Forget all about me," I continue.

His eyes dim and he slowly shakes his head. "I don't know how you ever believed that was possible."

Ronnie suddenly appears, a tiny notepad and pen in hand. "Are you two done living in the past and ready for me to take your drink order?"

Her words make me sit up straight, and Jordan removes his hand from mine. I order a glass of water, the words coming out of my mouth automatically, though I'm thinking of something else. What she said. How she said it, the tone of her voice no-nonsense.

Are you two done living in the past?

The past is there. Undeniable. But Ronnie's right. I'm too hung up on it. Too worried about what I did to him versus thinking of what we could possibly do together. Here.

Right now.

Ronnie asks what Jordan wants to drink. He orders a Modelo and looks at me, silently asking if I want one too. I nod my answer, and he tells Ronnie, "Make that two," before she bustles away, headed for the tiny bar in the far corner of the room.

"You okay?" he asks, his voice low and his gaze only for me.

Taking a deep breath, I nod, smiling faintly at him. "Have you forgiven me for what I did to you?"

"It took me a long time. I was mad at you for years, Mandy. Though you breaking up with me also pushed me to work harder at football." His smile is rueful. "I wanted to show you how great my life could be without you."

"Do you still feel that way?" I steel myself, waiting for bad news. A cruel word. A tiny insult.

I don't know why though. That's never been Jordan's style.

Slowly he shakes his head. "No. Not anymore." He leans back, his brows drawn together. "I've forgiven you. I had to. I couldn't hang on to what happened between us forever. I'd be a fucked up mess."

The very last thing I wanted to do was leave him a fucked up mess. "You know there's no way we can move forward unless you can truly say you've forgiven me for breaking your heart."

He touches the back of my hand again, just his fingertips skimming my skin, making me tingle. "Trust me, Mandy. I've let it go," he says, his deep voice extra low.

Intimate.

Despite the loud conversations surrounding us, the music, the not-so-distant sound of Ronnie yelling at someone back in the kitchen, it feels like we're the only two people in this room. "Okay. Good." I feel lighter, as if a weight has been lifted from my shoulders. That tried-and-true cliché is most fitting for this moment.

"Have you forgiven me for what I did to you?" he asks.

I frown. "What did you do to me?" He's still stroking the top of my hand, and his touch feels so good.

I never want him to stop.

"I ignored you. Made you feel neglected. I never meant to hurt you either. I was just so...overwhelmed with everything. That first year in college, it was rough. I didn't handle it right." His exhale is ragged, his expression full of regret.

Oh. My heart races at the look on his face, the sincerity in his voice.

"I forgive you. Of course, I forgive you," I whisper and he shoots me a small smile just before he ducks his head. I decide to change the subject. "Ronnie's right, you know."

"Right about what?" His head is still bent, and he's drawing circles on the back of my hand, making it hard to focus.

"We can't live in the past."

He lifts his head, our gazes locking. His vivid blue eyes gaze into mine, nearly undoing me. All by a simple look. "I don't want to live in the past. As much as I loved teenaged Amanda, I want to get to know adult Amanda better."

My lips curve. I like how he just said that. I like even more that he actually used the word *love*. "I haven't changed that much."

"Yeah, you actually have." He picks up my hand, sliding our fingers together so their interlaced. Palm to palm. His thumb caresses that patch of skin between my thumb and index finger, and it's like his touch makes every nerve ending come alive. "You're much more confident."

"I don't feel it," I immediately say, and he sends me a look that shushes me.

"Trust me, you are." His fingers tighten on mine. "You're even more beautiful."

"Flatterer," I tease, but his compliment turns my cheeks pink.

"Still modest." His smile is faint. Sexy. "I always liked that about you. There were a lot of things I liked about you."

"Like what?" I can't help but ask the question, though I guess I shouldn't. It's like I'm fishing for compliments.

"Your innate kindness. You're not mean to anyone."

"Except Lauren Mancini." His ex from high school. One of the most popular girls in our class, she was the bane of my existence back then.

"You were allowed to be mean to her. She was mean to you."

"True." Okay, I may sound like an egomaniac, but I want to hear more. "What else did you like about me?"

"Your big, beautiful, sexy brain." He brings our linked hands to his mouth and brushes a kiss against my knuckles. "You were always so fuckin' smart, Mandy."

Guys don't tell you that sort of stuff. At least not most of the guys I've dated. Except for Jordan. He was always been impressed with my brainiac ways. "You were a closet nerd too, you know. You were in all of my honors classes."

"It's true." He taps our still linked hands against his chin, and I feel the faint scratch of stubble there. Makes my fingers itch to touch his face even more. "Did you ever want to shake me?"

"Never." I liked having him in class. There were other jocks in my classes, and that's what Jordan was. A jock. The others, they were loud. Brash. Complete show offs, always performing. Some of them said dumb stuff when the teachers called on them, and all of their friends would laugh, which only egged them on.

Not Tuttle. He was quiet. So incredibly intense. When any teacher called on him to answer a question, he *always* got it right.

Always.

When he raised his hand to offer his opinion on something, his answer was thoughtful. Intelligent.

"I never wanted to shake you either. Sometimes we even sat by each other." He pauses before he further explains, "T and W aren't too far away from each other in the alphabet, you know."

Right. The first time he sat by me in science class in the seventh grade, I braced myself for an onslaught of insults. He'd been known as a bit of a bully then—smack talking everyone. Short and surly and a little chubby, with braces and pimples and just...all those horrible things that affect us when we're going through adolescence.

I thought for sure he'd take one look at me, tall and skinny and awkward and painfully shy, also dealing with pimples and braces, and think I was an easy target.

He never targeted me, though. Instead, he was...nice. He'd make occasional conversation, and I was always so nervous,

I'd end up saying something stupid. His kindness threw me off guard. More than once, I caught him smelling my hair, which at the time I thought was just plain weird.

Now I know he liked the smell of my hair. He freaking liked *me,* even back then.

"We've known each other a long time, gone to school together since kindergarten," I point out. "But that's our past. And like Ronnie said, we shouldn't linger there."

"She's right, you know. I give solid advice." Ronnie magically appears by our table, depositing our Modelos in front of us. Jordan releases my hand, leaning back in his chair. "Enjoy your drinks on the house," she says. "My treat."

"Thank you," I tell her, lifting my beer to her like a toast. Jordan does the same, murmuring his thanks.

"And let my words soak in like this beer which will eventually soak into your brain. Dwelling on the past gets you nowhere. Focus on what's happening between you two at this very moment." With those wise words, she leaves.

"Want me to tell you what I like about you now?" Jordan asks after he takes a sip of his beer.

I nod, bracing myself. Do I really want to hear this?

Um...yes.

"I like that deep down, you're still the same Amanda that I've known since I was five." He takes another drink, and I can tell that's all he's going to say.

"What do you mean?" I ask after too many beats of silence. I take a drink of my beer, hoping the alcohol will eventually calm my sudden frazzled nerves. "You said just a few minutes ago that I've changed."

"You have." He points the top of his beer bottle at me. "But you're also the same."

"So are you," I tell him. "Different, yet the same."

A single brow shoots up. That same sexy move he's done since he was my teenage dream. "Is that a good thing or a bad thing?"

"A good thing," I say without hesitation.

"I think it's a good thing too."

"We agree, then, that we've changed yet stayed the same?" Not sure how that's possible, but I get what he's saying.

"I totally agree." He smiles. Drains half his beer in one pull, then sets the bottle on the table between us. "Want a burrito?"

"I'm ordering street tacos."

"You can't go wrong with their tacos." His gaze never leaves mine. "I can't believe you're here. With me."

My heart trips over itself at his raw admission. "I still can't believe it either."

"We leave for England in a few days. Are you excited?"

"Yes." Excited. Nervous. "It probably won't be a long enough trip to explore London, but I hope we see as much as we can."

"We will," he says with all that Tuttle confidence. God, his arrogance is a complete turn on. "We'll have a few days to check everything out. I've arranged a tour guide."

"Really?" I pause in my questions when a server appears, ready to take our order. I order tacos and Jordan orders a burrito, and then the waiter's gone, leaving us alone once again.

"It's a company that will take us on a private tour to all of the best landmarks in the city," Jordan explains, knowing that I was waiting for more information.

"A private tour? We won't take a hop on/hop off bus?" I wrinkle my nose, fighting the disappointment that wants to take over me. I've done some research the last couple of nights, reading articles about the best sights to see in London and how exactly a person can see them all in a short amount of time, and I figured our best option was one of those hop on/hop off buses.

I should've known Jordan had a plan already in place.

He shakes his head. "The private tour will be better."

"But the bus looks like so much fun." I mock pout.

"I can't ride one of those buses with a bunch of tourists, Mandy," he says, tilting his head toward me. "People might recognize me."

"Oh." I didn't even think of that. How much his life has changed, and how so many people want a piece of him. We haven't dealt with that sort of thing since he's come back into my life, and I wonder why. I tend to forget he's supposed to be some big-time celebrity. To me he's still just...Jordan Tuttle.

Though there's no "just" when it comes to Jordan. He's so much more than anyone I've ever met before.

"Don't you ever get recognized around here?" I ask him.

"No one cares who I am here." He waves a hand around, indicating the restaurant. "A lot of the players hang out at Santana Row, so no one bothers us there either. But when I'm anywhere else, or when any NFL team goes to another country for an exhibition game, like what we're doing next week, they'll be looking for us. Especially in London—the British tabloids are rampant. Or at least I've heard."

Mind blowing. Seriously. "Wow, I guess you're right. I didn't even consider that could be a problem."

"It's something I've had to learn to deal with," he says just before he finishes his beer. "I think I want another one."

"Do you need to get drunk because we're on a date?"

"You still make me nervous," he admits, like I should expect that.

But I don't. Big, strong football player nervous because of me? I didn't know I wielded that much power.

I ignore the nervous remark. That could open up another discussion entirely.

"So tell me." I lean across the table, my voice lowering so no one else can hear me. Not that anyone in this busy restaurant is paying us any attention. "Did you really go out with Gigi Hadid?"

TWENTY-FIVE

JORDAN

I CAN'T HELP IT. Amanda's question makes me laugh.

Loudly.

A few heads turn our way as I continue laughing, and Amanda's looking at me like I might've lost my mind. Her question is ridiculous. Of course I haven't dated Gigi Hadid. I met her once at a party about a year ago. She was perfectly sweet. Perfectly beautiful in that odd model like way. Better in photographs than in person, if I'm being truthful.

We chatted a few minutes and that was it. Next few days, all the gossip sites and mags were saying we were together.

Fucking wild, the lies they tell about people.

"Jordan," Amanda finally says when my laughter finally starts to die. "That was a serious question."

"I know, and I'll give you a serious answer." I try my best to remain solemn as I say, "No. I never dated Gigi Hadid."

"Her sister Bella then."

"No."

"Kendall Jenner."

"No."

"Kylie Jenner."

I scoff. "Come on. She's a baby."

"Not really," Amanda points out. "She's only a few years younger than us, and she's a mother now, so..."

I wave my hand, dismissing the Jenner crew. Kendall is the one I find the most attractive from that clan. Tall and thin with a beautiful face and long, dark hair.

Like Amanda.

"Miley Cyrus."

"Not my type." At all.

"Selena Gomez."

Well, shit. I did go on a couple of dates with her quite a while ago. Set up by her publicist. It was nothing serious.

I must remain too quiet for too long because Amanda starts bouncing in her seat, pointing her finger at me. "You did. Oh my God, you went out with Selena freaking Gomez? You've got to be kidding me!"

"It was nothing," I protest, but she's shaking her head, making me go quiet.

"You went out with *Selena Gomez*, Jordan. She dated the Biebs."

I remember her bringing up Justin Bieber when we were in high school too. The guy has been around for a long time. "So?"

"So the Biebs is still a big deal. Selena is too. She's gone out with a few famous guys." Amanda snaps her fingers. "She dated The Weeknd for a while."

No way do I want to go over Selena's dating history. "Who the hell calls himself The Weeknd anyway?" I make a face. "Freaking ridiculous."

"You're trying to change the subject," she accuses me with a big grin. I think she's enjoying herself. "I want details."

"Details on what?" I know exactly what she wants.

"Your relationship with Selena! Is she nice? Is she as cute in person as she is in photos? Did you have fun with her? Did you have *sex* with her? Wait a minute, scratch that last question. I don't want to know." She's shaking her head, reminding me of a little kid.

Reaching across the table, I settle my hand over hers once again, trying to calm her down with just my touch. I can still feel how jittery she is, though. "Our relationship was all of three very public dates and nothing else. She's very nice, and she's beautiful, but I didn't have any chemistry with her. Pretty sure she felt the same way. Meaning, I didn't have sex with her."

"Oh thank God." Amanda practically slumps in her chair. "I was afraid I'd end up worrying you're always thinking of Selena when you're with me."

"Not a chance." More like I always thought of Amanda, no matter what woman I was with.

Even Selena Gomez.

The server appears with our dinner plates and I can tell Amanda's surprised. My favorite thing about this place—beyond Ronnie and her sage advice—is the service is incredibly fast. Which my never-ending appetite totally approves of.

She slips her hand from mine and smiles down at her plate before she checks out mine. Her eyes go wide. "You're going to eat that entire burrito?"

The burrito is massive. Fills up practically my whole plate. "That's my plan."

"Where do you put it all?" she asks in wonder.

"When you exercise as much as I do, you can eat pretty much whatever you want." Well, almost.

We eat and talk, and she tells me about going to school. What made her want to work in sports physical therapy. I'm fascinated that she chose a career that's semi related to football. Would we have possibly crossed paths in another way? Maybe, though the last thing I want to do is get injured and end up at a place like where she works.

At least we're not talking about me dating Selena Gomez any longer. I don't want to talk about any of the guys she's dated after we broke up either.

And they exist. I know they do. She's too pretty, too smart, too goddamned nice to not attract more than a few guys in the last six years. In high school, most guys passed her over for the flashy girls. The brave, popular ones who weren't afraid to talk to boys, who enjoyed any type of attention, whether it was good or bad. Amanda always lurked in the background, doing her thing, no guy really paying her any mind.

Except for me.

Well, and that one asshole who broke her heart and had her running into my arms by pure chance. What was that guy's name again? Thad?

The fucker.

His mistake that night, the summer before our senior year, turned into my opportunity. One I almost trashed more than a few times.

Christ, I was an idiot back then. Young and dumb and, deep down inside, totally insecure. I pushed Amanda away so many times, yet we couldn't help but gravitate toward each other.

As if we were meant to be.

How'd I get so lucky that she wasn't snapped up by another guy and engaged to him by now? Or worse, married? I thought about it over the years. What if she met the man of her dreams? What if she married that guy and had his children?

Those thoughts were like a punch to the gut.

I'd look her up on occasion, though I didn't find out much about her. Social media-wise, she's pretty private. I'd ask Cannon if he knew anything, but he was clueless in regards to Amanda's whereabouts. I just hoped and actually prayed that if I ever ran into her again, she'd be single.

I'm taking it as a sign that she is. That we're here together on our, what? Second date? Talking about how we're going to give this—*us*—another shot.

It's downright unbelievable.

As we eat and she talks, I can't stop staring at her. She's beautiful, even in her work clothes. I prefer it when she wears her hair down, but I do like the braid. With her hair pulled back, I can fully see her face, and she's gorgeous. Smooth skin, high cheekbones, full, sexy as fuck lips. Those big brown eyes are sparkling as she tells me about Livvy and how she lives in Texas with Dustin, and how much she misses her old best friend from high school.

This woman is nothing like the other women I've dated recently. Hardly any makeup on her face, her hair isn't perfect, and she's not wearing a ton of jewelry. She has tiny silver hoops in her ears and that's it.

If she hadn't ended it between us, I would've bought her giant diamonds to wear in her ears. And a big fat diamond for her finger so I could claim her.

The familiar feeling rises up within me. The need to make her mine. To know that she's not interested in anyone else but me. I try to tamp it down, tell myself to fucking relax, but the more I stare at her, the worse it gets.

What is it about this girl that makes me feel so damned primal?

And why am I wasting my time sitting around eating dinner and drinking another beer while we chat when we could be back at my place? Alone?

I finish my burrito in record time, and Amanda finishes pretty quickly too since she only ordered two tacos. The moment she wipes her mouth with her napkin and drops it on top of her plate, I'm asking, "You ready to get out of here?"

Impatience laces my voice and her startled gaze meets mine. She must hear it.

Sense it.

My need to get out of here.

"You haven't finished your second beer—" She quits talking when I grab my beer and drain it in one swallow. "Okay. Guess you're done then."

"Yeah, I'm done." I rise to my feet, reaching for my wallet in the back pocket of my jeans. I toss three twenties on the table, shove the wallet back in my pocket and grab Amanda's hand when she stands. "Let's go."

We wave at Ronnie as we exit the restaurant, and I catch the knowing smile on her face just before I push open the door. Not that her reaction fazes me. Ronnie has me all figured out. She knows how much Amanda means to me. Now that she's back in my life, I'm not about to let her get away from me again.

Yeah. No chance in hell of that happening if I can help it.

"In a hurry?" Amanda asks as I practically drag her through the parking lot toward my SUV.

"Yeah." I gently push her against the side of the Range Rover, my arms going around her to keep her body from actually hitting the car too hard. "I am."

Before she can say anything, I press my mouth to hers, stealing her words, catching her breath. I turn the kiss deep in an instant, my tongue sweeping the inside of her mouth, my hands exploring, landing on her ass, squeezing her. I pull her in closer, letting her know exactly how much I want her, and when she breaks the kiss first, she's staring up at me, her eyes wide. Unblinking.

"You're taking me back to your place, right?" she whispers.

I nod. Kiss her again. Catch her plump bottom lip with my teeth, giving it a nibbling bite. "Yeah."

"You capable of driving?" When I frown, she continues, "You had two beers."

The only thing I'm drunk on is her. "I'm fine."

Now she's frowning. "Are you sure? I don't want you to put yourself at risk."

"At risk of what?"

"Of a scandal." She tilts her head back when I press my lips along the underside of her jaw. "A DUI would ruin you, Jordan."

That she's thinking of me, my career, my future, makes my heart want to crack wide open for her. She's always known how to get past my defenses.

Always.

"You want to drive my fancy car?" I murmur against her skin.

She giggles, the sound sweet. "You'll let me drive your fancy car?"

"You've got your driver's license, right?" When she nods, I lift away from her neck, my gaze meeting hers. "You're the only one I trust enough to drive it."

The giggles vanish, and Amanda visibly swallows. "I'll drive then."

"Good." I drop a kiss on her lips.

"Let's go." She pushes me off of her and I go willingly, hitting the keyless remote as I guide her to the driver's side of the car and deposit her into the seat. I give her another kiss before I slam the door and jog around the front of the car, sliding into the passenger's seat with ease. I instruct her on how to adjust the seat and mirrors and watch with amusement as she sets about her task so seriously. Her forehead is wrinkled in concentration as she moves the seat forward, her teeth sinking into her lush lower lip as she adjusts and readjusts the rearview mirror.

We're out of the parking lot in seconds. Pulling into my garage within minutes—twenty too-long minutes, to be exact. The entire drive we remained quiet beyond me giving her driving instructions to my house. The need for each other simmers between us the entire time, growing bigger and bigger until I feel like I might fucking burst with wanting her.

But I don't touch her yet. Touching her would lead to kissing her and other things, and I don't want to distract her while she's driving my car and looking vaguely uncomfortable while doing so.

Once we're in the garage, I hurl myself out of the Range Rover, slamming the door with extra force. She follows after me, both of us practically running into my house. We enter the kitchen first, the lighting dim, the room almost eerily quiet, and I catch her around the waist, bringing her in close, my mouth landing on hers.

I'm hard for her. Hell, I've been sporting semi-wood for hours. It's been too long—years since I've been inside her.

That's all going to change tonight.

Keeping my mouth on hers, I lift her up, plop her ass on the edge of the kitchen counter. She wraps those long legs of hers around my waist, anchoring herself to me, her arms curling around my neck, her fingers sliding into my hair, clutching the short strands. The kiss goes on and on, the only sound the connection of our lips, her sighs and my moans, the rustle of fabric as our hands wander.

Forget finessing her into my bed. Taking it slow. Seducing her. I want her right here, right now. I'll tug her pants down, shove the Atlas Wellness Center polo off, and fuck her in the kitchen. The mental image is so powerful, my cock jerks beneath the fly of my jeans, desperate to gain freedom.

"I want you," I whisper in her ear after I break the kiss, making her shiver. "I want you so fucking bad."

"Please tell me you have condoms," she says, her tone urgent, her hand moving down my chest, fluttering around the front of my jeans.

"I have condoms," I confirm, my mouth exploring the soft, soft skin of her neck. I bought a giant box off Amazon a few days ago. Thank Christ for Prime shipping. "Lots of them."

"Thank God." She sounds agonized yet relieved. "Maybe we should take this somewhere else?"

"Not yet." I reach for her polo, untucking it from her black pants, catching a glimpse of bare skin. I pull the shirt up and she shifts away from me, raising her arms obediently so I can completely remove the shirt, leaving her sitting on my counter in her bra.

I take a step back so I can drink her in, and she squares her shoulders, thrusting her chest out, the black lacy bra nearly doing me in. Teen Amanda would've curled her shoulders, trying to hide her breasts. Her bra size was one of her biggest insecurities. As I've said before, though, I'm not a boob man.

I'm a leg man. And her sexy legs are currently loosely wrapped around me, the heels of her feet digging into my backside.

She heaves an exaggerated sigh, breaking the spell I was falling under. "Um, Jordan? Stop looking and get to doing, please."

Like she has to ask twice.

TWENTY-SIX

AMANDA

I AM SORT OF SHOCKED by the words that leave my mouth, but I have no shame. It's Jordan, after all. He's seen me at my worst and my best.

Besides, I want him too damn much to worry about anything else. The frantic need that's building inside of me is threatening to take completely over. I haven't experienced this feeling in so long—six years, to be exact—and it's making me edgy. Shaky.

"Fuck, I like it when you're bossy," he confesses just before he takes my mouth in a commanding kiss.

Now, let's be real here. I may have bossed him around just now, but it was minor. And I don't want to be the boss. I want him in charge.

God, I *love* it when he's in charge.

His agile fingers are at the back of my bra while he kisses me, undoing the hooks. The lace-trimmed cups fall from my chest, the thin straps slithering down my arms until they land at the crook of my elbows, and I shake my bra off completely, a disappointed moan leaving me when he steps away once more, contemplating me yet again.

"They've grown," he murmurs, because of course he'd notice that. He was always extremely observant.

"I'm a B cup now," I tell him proudly.

Chuckling, he reaches for my breasts, cradling them in his hands, his thumbs brushing across my nipples, making them harden. Making me tremble. "Still sensitive?"

I bite my lip, nodding.

"Still pretty too," he says just before he dips his head and takes a lick. I tilt my head back, my hands sinking into his soft hair when he sucks my nipple into his mouth. My eyes fall closed and a whimper escapes me when he nibbles first on one nipple, then the other, alternating back and forth. Licking. Sucking. Biting. Making me want him even more.

Making me wet.

Truthfully? I don't want to have sex on the kitchen counter. Not really. The marble is cold on my butt and I still have my pants on. The angle between us seems off, so I'm not quite sure how we'd fit.

But then he grips the back of my thighs and tilts my body back, pulling me into him so his erection is directly between my legs. Showing me exactly how we fit, exactly how we'd do this.

I brace my hands on the counter behind me, lifting my hips so I brush against the front of him nice and slow. He removes his mouth from my chest and shifts away from me, his blue eyes dark, his cheeks ruddy, his hair a mess.

"Teasing me?" he asks in a rumbly growl, his intense gaze never leaving mine.

Nodding, I rub against him again, pressing my lips together when I hit a particular spot that feels extra good, so I do it again. And from the way his brows lower, I know he realizes I'm hitting that spot too.

"No way are you going to come on my jeans again," he says, reaching for the waistband of my pants. They have a drawstring, and he slowly undoes it, the black string winding around his long fingers. I watch in breathless anticipation, craving those fingers on me.

In me.

I toe my shoes off, then lift my butt so he can pull my pants down my legs, leaving me in my plain black panties and white socks. Definitely not sexy. I wind my legs around his waist again, working my socks off with my big toe, and heave a sigh of relief when I'm successful. He's staring at me again, his gaze devouring me, and he takes a step away from me so that I have no choice but to drop my legs.

"You have a condom somewhere close, right?" I ask, pressing my thighs together when he keeps watching me with that intense gaze of his.

Nodding, he reaches for me, his fingers sliding between my thighs and pushing them apart.

"You keep condoms in the kitchen?" I'm joking, but what if he says *yes, as a matter of fact, I do*? What if he keeps condoms in every corner of his townhouse? That would mean he's always prepared, and I appreciate a man who's prepared, but not if that means he's having sex all over his house with various women.

I don't like thinking of Jordan with various women. It's bad enough I know for a fact he went on actual dates with Selena Gomez.

"No, I don't keep condoms in my kitchen, Mandy. I have a condom in my wallet." His fingers tickle the inside of my thighs, making me squirm. "Not sure if I want to fuck you here, though."

I try to pull my thighs together, but he's too strong. "What are you saying? Please don't tell me you think this shouldn't happen."

Ha, and I was the one who said I wanted to take it slow.

"Oh, it's definitely going to happen. Tonight." The promise in his voice rings true, sending a delicious shiver down my spine. "I just don't know what exactly I want to do to you first."

A shiver moves down my spine and I sit up a little straighter.

There are *so* many things I want to do to him.

"I could touch you." His fingers lightly brush the center of my panties, making me throb. "Go down on you." Oh Lord, I love his tongue so, *so* much. "Or forget the foreplay and just...go for it."

I want all of it. He could touch me, go down on me, and then go for it. In whatever order he wants, I'm down. "It's unfair, you know."

"What's unfair?" He's still stroking me between my thighs, his fingers barely touching the thin fabric of my panties. But he's touching me perfectly, his fingers drifting over my clit, trying to drive me wild.

It's working.

"That you're completely overdressed," I tell him with all the sincerity I can muster.

Without a word he remedies that, whipping off his shirt, revealing all that muscly goodness. I forget all about his magical fingers for a moment and focus on his broad shoulders. His wide chest. The dark hair curling between his pecs—is there more now? Not that he's super hairy, but he's hairier than he was at nineteen.

And his abs. Oh. My. God. His abs. He has a six-pack. No, I take that back, he has an *eight*-pack. I didn't think it was possible, but his body is even more muscular, more beautiful than it was the last time I saw him shirtless. He's firm and hard and his stomach is flat, and I fixate on that thin path of dark hair that starts just below his navel and leads into his jeans.

Yes. I want to follow that path with my tongue. I have before. I want to do it again.

Now.

"Your body is unreal," I tell him, my voice reverent. I sit up and reach for him, running my fingers along first one shoulder, then the other. "God, you're hard," I murmur almost to myself as I press my hand against his chest.

"Yeah, I am," he says, amusement in his voice. He grabs my hand and places it on his denim-covered erection. My fingers curl around him automatically. "See what you do to me?"

It's a powerful thing, knowing I make this man want me so badly.

That power goes straight to my head, making me dizzy, making me bold. I cup his erection. Run my fingers along it, up and down, my gaze never straying from his face.

He's so responsive, his lips parting. Eyelids fluttering. He likes it when I touch him.

He likes it a lot.

I reach for the fly of his jeans and undo the button, then slowly draw down the zipper, spreading the denim open. I trail my fingers across the warm gray cotton of his underwear, and I swear he twitches beneath my touch.

He bites out a curse when I slip my fingers beneath his briefs, encountering nothing but hot, hard skin. I wrap my fingers around his cock and then he's quickly shoving down his underwear, his jeans, his movements frantic. I release my hold on him and he strips in record time, my fingers seeking him again just as his hand delve between my legs, slipping beneath my panties.

His fingers sink between my folds and I hiss out a long, trembling breath. I squeeze his cock and he groans. He's so long and thick, and I familiarize myself with him, my fingers tracing the veins along his length, the velvety tip of him.

Without warning he leans in and kisses me, our eager mouths sloppy, tongues everywhere as we continue to touch each other. I'm growing wetter with his every stroke. I can actually hear his fingers as he explores my depths, and when his thumb presses against my clit, I whimper into his mouth.

I'm having a serious déjà vu moment. That familiar urgency is making me remember what it used to be like between us. What it's still like. He knew exactly how to touch me, and where. The right pressure and speed. He kisses me with perfection. No thrusting fat tongues or too much saliva. It's always just enough, though when he does get carried away —like he's doing right now—it's because he's so overcome.

He's a tightly controlled man who loses control only when he's with me.

"Fuck this," he says after he breaks the kiss, and for a moment I'm alarmed.

Is he having second thoughts? Is he realizing that this won't work between us after all? I'm this close to covering my naked bits with my hands, but then he backs away, pulling me into position so I'm poised on the very edge of the kitchen counter. He falls to his knees in front of me, his face directly in between my legs. He stares for a moment, dead silent and all I can hear is my heartbeat. My harsh breaths.

His gaze lifts, locking with mine as he roughly pulls my thighs apart, shoves my panties out of the way and places his mouth right on my very center.

My head falls back at the first swirl of his tongue on my clit. Holy hell, he knows just how to work it. He licks me up and down, his fingers spreading me wide open, his tongue playing with my clit. Circling it. Flicking it. Sucking it into his mouth, applying just enough pressure that I'm seeing stars.

Oh fuck, he is so good at this. Too good.

The orgasm is barreling down on me at an incredibly fast pace, and I squeeze my eyes shut. Wishing he would slow down.

Wishing he would hurry up.

He hums against my flesh just before he begins to tongue fuck me and I blindly grasp at his hair, pulling on it, low moans falling from my lips.

I swear to God I'm about to fall off the goddamn counter.

But he grabs hold of me, his big hands gripping my butt cheeks, his mouth still on me as he licks me straight into oblivion. Until I'm a moaning, shaking, climaxing bundle of need, falling right over that delicious edge with a hoarse cry of his name.

Once the trembling has subsided, he rises to his feet, wiping his mouth off with the back of his hand. Why I find that move so incredibly sexy, I don't know, but I do.

I reach for him, pulling him in so I can kiss his magical mouth. I taste myself on his lips, on his tongue, and it makes me want him even more so I pull him in closer, my legs winding tight around him, my arms circling his neck.

"I don't want to fuck you like this," he whispers against my cheek.

"Since when do you say fuck all the time?" I ask just before I bite his perfect jawline.

He tilts his head to the side, his gaze meeting mine. "I've always loved the word."

"You never used it to say you wanted to fuck me."

"Guess I always thought it, because that's all I could think about back then. How much I wanted to fuck you," he admits. "All the fucking time."

I rear back so our gazes meet. Hold.

"I want to fuck you now," I tell him, loving the flash of heat in his gaze when I use the word.

"I want to make you come again." He touches my hair, his fingers playing with the wayward strands that escaped my braid. "You're so damn beautiful when you come."

"You know just how to make that happen, too." I press a chaste kiss to his lips. "Your tongue is magical."

He chuckles, his hands cupping my cheeks, his mouth close to mine. "You're fucking magical. Let's go to my bedroom."

Before I can say anything, he's got me in his arms, carrying me through the kitchen and up the two flights of stairs with ease. His biceps bulge, his chest flexes, and I stare at his upper body in wonder, eager to explore and lick and touch. When we reach his bedroom, he carefully places me on the giant bed, and then he's there, hovering above me, his hands braced on either side of my head as he begins his own exploration.

Butterfly kisses to my forehead, cheeks and nose. Licks down the length of my neck, gentle bites along my collarbone. He touches my breasts, flicks my nipples with his tongue, kisses a lazy path across my stomach, dips his tongue inside my belly button. I'm giggling and breathless, his mouth and hands tickling me, driving me out of my mind with want. He shifts downward, raining kisses along my inner thighs, the back of my knees, my calves, the tops of my feet.

"You have a foot fetish?" I ask when I realize he's carefully studying my pink painted toes.

"More like an Amanda fetish," he confesses, dropping a kiss on the tip of my big toe before he moves up, up, until his face is in mine. His entire body covers me, his warm, heavy weight making me sigh with pleasure as I sink into his giant mattress. "You're just like I remembered you."

His words fill me with worry for the briefest moment. "The same ol' thing, huh?" I say like a joke, though deep down I'm terrified he's already bored with me.

Stupid right? But I can't help it.

"You are perfection," he whispers just before he kisses me. It's a slow, melting kiss. Like all of that earlier frantic passion has subsided, and he's content with taking this at a languid pace.

I should be the one who feels that way since on tonight's orgasm scoreboard we're Amanda: one, and Jordan: zero, but now I'm the one who's filled with overwhelming, frenzied need.

My hands are everywhere, sliding down his wide back, gripping his extremely hard ass. His cock probes between my legs, and I spread them, wishing he was inside me already. Wishing we were connected once again. It's as if I need that connection like I need air, because I'm gasping for it, my chest shuddering, my fingers clawing at him.

"Sshhh," he murmurs against my lips. "Calm down, babe."

Oh God, he called me babe. I love it when he does that. Yes, he also told me to calm down, which coming from any other man, might've pissed me off, but not Jordan. He knows I need to calm myself. That I'm a bundle of crazed nerves.

He rises to his knees, studying me while his hands wander across my chest, his touch fleeting. "Take a deep breath," he instructs, and I do as he says, releasing it slowly. Steadily. Trying my best to calm my racing heart.

"I want you," he tells me, his gaze on mine. "So fucking bad."

"I want you too," I admit softly.

Jordan reaches over me, pulling open the drawer on his nightstand, rustling around inside of it before he pulls out a single wrapped condom. He undoes the wrapper and slips the condom onto his thick cock. I watch in rapt fasciation, my stomach twisting in anticipation of him finally being inside of me.

I close my eyes when he positions himself, his cock probing at my entry, his hands once again braced on either side of my head. I tilt my head back, my legs spread, waiting for him to push inside me, but nothing happens.

"Look at me," he commands, and my eyes automatically pop open to find him staring at me.

Slowly, surely, he enters my body, one delicious inch at a time. My eyelids waver, a whimper falling from my lips, and when he's fully seated inside of me, I exhale loudly, bringing my knees up so they press against his hips.

We lay like that, unmoving for God knows how long.

A few seconds?

A full minute?

Five minutes?

I don't know, but it's like we're reveling in the reconnection. He flexes his hips, sinking a little deeper, and we both moan. We're still watching each other, his lids at half mast, a thick lock of dark hair falling over his forehead, his expression lazy. Pleased. His jaw tight, revealing that he's holding himself back.

I want him to unleash on me.

I slide my hands down his back, resting them on his ass, pulling him closer. His gaze flickers and I whisper his name.

That's all it takes to spur him into action. He starts moving, sliding almost all the way out of my body before he pushes back in. It's excruciating, that long drag, that deep plunge. Again and again he does it, slowly at first, picking up speed after a few tries. I move with him, quickly establishing a rhythm, our bodies growing slick with sweat, my second orgasm already hovering close. I wrap my legs around his hips and he reaches between us, touching me just above where we're connected, his fingers finding my clit with ease.

"You don't play fair," I gasp, my eyesight blurring as the orgasm looms.

"You've never played fair," he reminds me, making me come with an expert thrust and a flick of his fingers.

I cry out his name, my inner walls milking him, the orgasm so powerful I swear to God I'm having some sort of out of body experience. Like I can actually hover above us, observe us in the middle of the bed, his big body nestled between my legs, his hips pumping, his skin slick with sweat.

Little shivers run through me, my nails scratching down his back, and then he's coming too, his entire body going still just before the shudders take over. He thrusts hard, again and again, his hips battering mine, and I take it.

Welcome it.

"Fuck," he mutters when he lands in a heap upon me, his head turned toward mine, his mouth at my cheek. "I came too fast." His lips tickle my skin when he speaks.

"No." I run my hands up and down his back lightly, enjoying the heavy feel of him on top of me. I didn't realize I missed this kind of connection with Jordan until I'm actually experiencing it again. "You didn't."

"Whatever you say." I can't believe he's arguing with me about this. "But trust me, I'll make it up to you."

Okay, that sounds promising. "You will? How?"

"Whatever you want, it's yours." He shifts his head closer, his nose pressing against mine. It's a sweet gesture. One that makes my heart sing in my chest, which is corny but true. That he can be both sweet yet savage is incredibly arousing.

And just like that, I'm aroused all over again.

"Whatever I want?" I repeat, just before I kiss his cheek, my lips lingering on his stubble-covered skin.

"Hell yes." The contented sigh that escapes him warms me from the inside out. "Know what you want yet?"

"Oh yeah. I do," I say with an eager nod.

He smiles again. Reaches out and grazes my cheek with his fingertips. "What is it then?"

"I want to give you a blowjob."

He blinks at me. Bet he wasn't expecting that request.

"And I want you to come in my mouth."

His smile turns hungry as his hands seek me out. "Whatever my girl wants."

TWENTY-SEVEN

JORDAN

I OFFER her whatever she wants and she chooses to give me a blowjob? Plus let me come in her mouth?

Fuck yeah, I'll give her that.

"Give me a minute," I tell her. I climb out of bed and head for the unlit bathroom, removing and depositing the used condom in the trashcan. I catch the shadow of my reflection in the mirror and blink once. Twice. Still can't really see myself.

But I know I must have a satisfied smile on my face. I can feel it there, tugging on the corners of my mouth. Yeah, I probably moved way too fast just now, but she came too. As long as my woman gets hers, that's all that matters. I'm not a selfish lover.

I've definitely never been a selfish lover with Amanda.

I slip back into the bedroom to find her on her hands and knees near the edge of the mattress. She smiles when our gazes meet. "Come here," she tells me.

I do as she says, mesmerized by the way she wags her hips, her perfect ass. Seeing her completely naked on my bed waiting for me is blowing my mind. My cock twitches, and I know I'll be hard again in a matter of minutes, though only a moment ago, I wasn't sure if I had it in me. That orgasm I just experienced fucking drained me.

Or so I thought.

The moment I'm close enough to touch her, she rises to her knees, her fingers reaching for me, curling around my dick. Her touch brings me to life, and I'm erect in seconds, a stifled groan escaping me when she strokes me up. Then down.

"You like that," she observes, her fingers tightening around the top of my dick, squeezing hard. I taught her that long ago. That she never had to be scared of hurting me. Girls were always too tentative around the dick and balls area. Always afraid they might do some damage, when really us guys want them to be a little stronger.

A little rougher.

"I like anything you do to me," I tell her, which is the absolute truth.

Her gaze flicks up to mine. "I want to try something different."

My brows shoot up, curiosity filling me. "What is it?"

She releases her hold on me and I take a step back, watching as she rearranges herself on the bed, but I can tell that's not exactly what she wants. She slides off the bed, her naked butt plopping down on the floor so she's leaning against the mattress and box spring, her nape right on the edge of the bed, legs crossed. She licks her lips and tilts her head back.

"Come closer," she urges with a sexy smile.

I move toward her and she grabs hold of me, guiding my cock toward her open mouth. The moment I make entry, I close my eyes, an agonized moan escaping as the wet warmth surrounds me.

Fuck, she feels good.

Her lips are tight as she sucks and licks, and I open my eyes. This is a must-see. Something I never thought would happen again. Amanda on the ground in front of me, my cock in her mouth. I bend my knees a little, sliding deeper, as deep as she'll let me, and then I start to fuck her mouth in earnest. I dive my fingers into her hair, messing up her braid, clutching her head, steadying myself. Her fingers curl around the base of my dick, holding me there, squeezing me, and I swear to God, this is like every fucking dream I've had over the six years since she walked out of my life.

And now it's actually happening.

I increase my pace, hips flexing, a growl leaving me. Her eyes meet mine, her gaze dark, her tongue flicking at the head of my dick again and again, and then an agonized cry leaves me. Just like that, I'm coming. Spurting on her tongue, dumping my load, all of those crude terms you can come up with for coming in a girl's mouth, it's all happening right now, and she's swallowing every last drop. I'm fucking coming until my stomach muscles heave and I've got nothing else left inside of me.

My legs weak, I pull out of her mouth and collapse on the bed, rolling onto my stomach, my arms above my head as I close my eyes. My heart is racing, my breaths shallow, and I swallow hard, trying my damnedest to calm myself down.

I hear her moving, the mattress creaking when she joins me on the bed, and then she's right there lying next to me, her hand on my shoulder, her fingers softly stroking.

"You okay?" She sounds worried.

I bury the laugh against my comforter and roll over on my side so I'm facing her. "I think you might've killed me dead."

A smile teases her lips. "You look very much alive to me."

"Just barely." I hook my arm around her waist and pull her in close. "Thank you."

I drop a kiss on her lips before she asks, "For what?"

"For that epic blowjob."

"It only lasted a few minutes." Now she sounds disappointed.

"You make me come too fast," I tell her.

"You make that sound like a bad thing."

"Is it?" I ask.

"Not to me."

"Not to me either."

"Glad we've been agreeing on everything tonight," she says with a yawn as she stretches against me, her breasts rubbing against my chest. My dick stirs, and I mentally tell it to calm the fuck down.

"You want to stay the night?" I brace myself for her rejection. She has to work tomorrow. So do I. But I'll get up early for her. Take her back to her place so she can shower and change, get ready for her day.

Having her in my bed all night is worth the lack of sleep.

Amanda blinks up at me. "You don't mind?"

I brush the hair away from her face, then reach behind her to grab the end of her mostly destroyed braid and pull the elastic off. Her hair is an absolute mess thanks to me. "Why would I mind? I asked you, didn't I?"

"But you like your privacy," she says, leaning her head to the side so I have easier access to her hair.

"You can invade my privacy anytime you want." I finish undoing the braid, then run my fingers through the silky strands, combing it until the tangles are gone.

"Really?" Her voice is soft. Her eyes are closed as I continue to play with her hair. She always did like that.

"Yeah. Give me more blowjobs like that and you're in for life," I tell her.

She laughs. So do I. She thinks I'm joking.

I'm not.

It's not just the blowjobs, though those are an absolute bonus. It's the girl she used to be.

The woman she's become.

After the incredible moment we just shared, it reconfirms my feelings. I want her back.

For good.

TWENTY-EIGHT

AMANDA

I DIDN'T FLY to London with Jordan. He went with the team the day before I was scheduled to leave. He wanted me to go with him, but I couldn't take the extra day off. I was already on the schedule at work, and they really needed me.

Work has been extra busy, and extra difficult, now that Cade is angry with me. He's very cold when we work together, speaking to me only when he absolutely has to. On the last day before I left for London, he even switched me out with Lena so he wouldn't have to deal with me.

Secretly? I was glad. When Cade likes you, he's sweet. When he's mad at you and ready to shut you out of his life?

He's awful.

But I didn't let him get me down. No way could *anything* but me in a bad mood. I was too excited about going to London, about spending time with Jordan in a foreign country. A place I'd always wanted to go, and now thanks to my

ex-current-whatever-you-want-to-call-him   boyfriend,   he's
giving me the opportunity.

I've been packing for days, constantly changing my mind,
rushing out to buy new things, including a suitcase. I rarely
use my credit card—debt terrifies me—but this trip is worth
it to rack up a few charges. Nothing too out of control,
though.

Thankfully, Jordan paid for my plane ticket, and he put me
in first class. When I boarded the British Airways plane,
took one look at the first class section with its individual
compartments that also lay out flat so I could actually sleep,
I had to contain myself from squealing with happiness.

After the long flight, I'm now in one of those iconic London
black cabs I've only ever seen on TV or in the movies,
headed for the hotel where we're staying. We're at the same
hotel with the rest of the team, and Jordan and I are sharing
a room.

Yes. Sharing a room. Another squee moment, am I right?

He asked me if I wanted my own room during our trip the
morning after we had sex, when he was driving me back to
my apartment, and I started to laugh.

Seriously? After that night we shared?

Um, no.

There's no use in pretending that we're *maybe* giving this
thing another try. It feels like we're back together. For reals.

I gaze out the window as we speed through the city. I should
be tired. I barely slept on the plane, despite how comfortable first class was. But I was too excited to see London, to

see Jordan. Too wide awake considering we left in the middle of the afternoon. The ten-plus hour trip was brutally long considering how eager I was to get there.

It's almost noon and the city is bustling with activity. Horns are honking, the double decker red buses are literally everywhere, and my head won't stop spinning.

My phone buzzes with a text notification and I smile. I know who it is.

Jordan.

Tell me you're in the taxi.

Still smiling like an idiot, I send him a reply.

Me: **I'm in the taxi. On my way to you.**

I add a heart emoji to the end of my sentence.

He quickly sends me back a smiley face emoji in response, though I see the gray bubble indicating he's typing.

Jordan: **We leave for practice at two. Let's do lunch. Unless you're too tired?**

Me: **Not tired.**

Jordan: **Good. We're in room 626. Meet me there?**

Me: **Perfect.**

He takes a minute to respond, and waiting for him makes me antsy.

Jordan: **Can't wait to see you.**

My heart swells and I'm sure I have a giant smile on my face as I stare at my phone screen.

Me: **I can't wait to see you too.**

It feels like the drive takes forever, but we finally make it to the hotel, and it's beautiful. The building appears incredibly old, and it looms above me when I get out of the taxi. A multitude of flags hang from the front of the building, snapping and waving in the wind. The air is crisp, the blue sky dotted with big, fluffy white clouds.

"Here you go, miss," the taxi driver says, setting my suitcase beside me on the sidewalk, then bows a little, like I'm royalty.

Ha.

"Thank you." I already paid him on the credit card machine in the taxi, and included a tip. I don't have any British money on me, so I'll probably need to find an ATM at some point. All the travel guides I read said I shouldn't use those currency exchange windows—the rate is too high and I'll end up getting ripped off.

Considering I need every dollar I make, I'm not a huge fan of getting ripped off.

I grab my suitcase and wheel it into the hotel lobby, smiling when the doorman nods his greeting as I walk past. I spot the bank of elevators to the right and soon I'm in one, gliding my way up to the sixth floor.

I'm tapping my foot, nerves making me jittery. Jordan and I haven't seen each other since that night we spent together. And what a night it was. I fell asleep pressed against him. Woke up to him touching me, his big warm hands everywhere at once. We had sex again, slow and half asleep, no kissing, no real foreplay involved. Just him behind me, sliding in easily since I was so wet. He filled me completely, his hand on my hip, his face pressed against my hair. His thrusts were slow. Lazy. His other hand slid up my chest, cupping my breasts, his fingers playing with my nipples, both of us eventually coming in this languid, dream-like way.

If he woke me up like that for the rest of my life, I wouldn't mind.

The elevator dings and comes to a stop, the doors sliding open. Heading left, I practically skip down the plush carpeted hall, halting when I spot room 626.

Biting my lower lip, I knock on the door, waiting for Jordan to open it.

Within moments he's there, holding the door open, his gaze hungry as he takes me in. "Finally," he says in greeting, taking my hand and practically dragging me inside the room. I clutch the handle of my suitcase in my other hand, bringing it with me.

The door slams shut behind me and he helps me with my suitcase, setting it against the wall before he turns to me. "Hi," he murmurs, his gaze lingering on my lips, making them tingle.

For whatever weird reason, I suddenly feel shy standing in front of him. All this build up over getting here, and now I'm tempted to run and hide. "Hi."

He touches my hair, tucks a few strands behind my ear. "You look pretty."

My heart flutters at his compliment, but he must be lying. My hair is a bit of a tangled mess, and I'm in yesterday's clothes. I brushed my teeth on the plane thanks to the mini sized toothbrush and toothpaste they gave me, and I splashed water on my face, so I know I'm not a complete hideous troll.

But I've definitely had better days.

"Thank you." I really take him in. He's wearing Adidas track pants, black with the signature three white stripes on the sides—surprising considering I always thought he was the Nike type. A red 49ers shirt stretches across his broad chest and he's wearing white socks. No shoes. It looks like he's recently got a haircut, though he kept it long on top, which I love.

More silky-soft hair to run my fingers through.

His face is covered in scruff, as if he hasn't shaved in a day or two and his eyes are as blue as ever. Those blue eyes are watching me watch him at this very moment, and I wonder what he's thinking.

"You look good too," I finally say when I realize both of us have been quiet.

He smiles and reaches for me, pulling me into his arms. "Are you hungry?"

I nod, though food is actually the furthest thing from my mind now that Jordan is touching me. "A little."

"We could order room service," he suggests, his arms tightening around me. "They have a pretty good menu."

"I'd like to check it out," I say just before his mouth lands on mine. The kiss is simple. Soft. Our lips part, a spark lighting between us, igniting us both. I run my hands up his chest. He runs his hands down my back until they're cupping my butt.

And then we're full on making out. Tongues and lips and sighs and moans. He walks me backward, toward the bed until the back of my legs hit the edge of the mattress. Both of us falling, falling, Jordan landing first and pulling me on top of him, breaking my fall.

We never stop kissing, and when he moves to take off my shirt, I stop him, ending the kiss, my hand covering his. "I haven't showered," I warn.

"I don't care," he says, leaning in to kiss me again, but I press my fingers to his mouth, halting him.

"I feel gross." I drop my fingers from his lips and he contemplates me, his expression serious.

"You should take a shower then," he says, rising to his feet and offering his hand to me.

I take his hand and stand, then follow him into the massive bathroom, marveling at all the gleaming white tile everywhere, the giant, sleek glass shower. He opens the door and reaches inside, turning the water on with a few quick twists of his wrist. Within seconds I can tell the water is hot, the steam already rising and starting to fill the room.

"Let's get you undressed," he says, reaching again for the hem of my shirt.

"Jordan," I warn, feeling suddenly modest, which is silly.

And he knows it too, from the incredulous look he's giving me. "I've seen you naked before, Mandy. *Plenty* of times."

"I know, but this is just like...I don't know. I've got airport funk on me and I've been in the same clothes for the last twenty-four hours or whatever." I've lost complete track of time. "I'm not sexy, like at all." I wrinkle my nose at him, but he's undeterred.

"You're always sexy to me," he says, sweeping me into his arms and kissing me senseless.

I struggle against him, batting at his chest until he finally breaks away from my lips, frowning at me like I'm irritating the hell out of him. "Please. Let me take a shower first," I tell him, resting my hands on his chest. "Then I'll be up for anything."

His brows lift. "Anything?"

I smooth my hands up and down his chest, impressed yet again with all the hard, warm muscle I feel beneath my palms. "Yes. Anything."

"Better take a quick shower then, since I have to leave soon." He drops a kiss on the tip of my nose. "How about I join you?"

I heave an exaggerated sigh, like he's really putting me out. "Fine," I say, smiling when he scowls.

"You sure you don't want me to call in an order for room service?" he offers. "So it'll be ready after the shower?"

Yeah, I'm really not that hungry. I think I've gone beyond tired and hungry, and now I'm just existing. Sparked to life by Jordan. "I'm fine. Really." I start to strip, until I'm standing in front of him in only my no-nonsense beige panties.

Definitely not sexy.

But Jordan is looking at me like he wants to eat me up, which is encouraging. His gaze never leaves me as he quickly strips too, until he's standing in front of me with absolutely nothing on. And trust me, a naked Jordan is a sight to behold. His body is absolute male perfection. He's already semi-erect, and when my gaze drops, I swear he grows even harder.

Mentally tossing my modesty out the window, I step out of my panties, kicking them away. Jordan opens the shower door and ushers me inside, slapping my ass as I enter the shower with a loud smack.

"Ow." I turn and glare at him, but he just grins and steps inside, shutting the door behind him.

He wastes no time, grabbing the tiny bottle of shampoo and opening it, pouring the golden liquid into the palm of his hand. He rubs them together, watching me as I duck under the hot spray of water. "Come closer," he says, and I step toward him. "Now turn around. I'll wash your hair for you."

Oh my God, he's going to spoil me. His fingers dig into my scalp with expert precision and I close my eyes, enjoying the head massage. He works the shampoo into my hair as he steps even closer to me, and I can feel him. He's so very warm—hotter than the shower. Skin slick with water. His erection brushes against my thigh.

"Feels so good," I say with a little moan, leaning my head back as he guides me under the spray of water.

He helps me wash the shampoo out, running his fingers through my hair again and again. His touch makes me tingle, and it's not even sexual.

Well, not *really*.

But all he has to do is look at me and I want him, so this is no surprise.

"There you go," he says, and I pop my eyes open to see him reach for the bar of soap. "Now I'll wash you."

"I need conditioner first," I tell him.

Jordan rolls his eyes and grabs the conditioner, opening the tiny bottle and squeezing a dollop of the thick white liquid into his palm. He distributes it throughout my hair, combing it in with his fingers thoroughly. When he's finished, I'm the one who picks up the soap and starts running it all over his body, exploring.

I've never had sex in the shower before, not that I'd tell him that. I'd rather keep my sexual activity of the last six years a mystery. Let him imagine all the many men I've been with since we broke up. Let him think I've been doing all kinds of interesting things.

The reality? My dating and sex life wasn't that interesting. I dated some really nice guys—and some not-so-nice ones too. But none of them held my interest like Jordan. None of them made me want to pursue something deeper, more serious.

It's like I've been waiting all along, knowing that he would eventually walk back into my life.

And look at me now.

TWENTY-NINE

JORDAN

I TOOK a shower right before Amanda arrived at the hotel, not that she needs to know this. No reason to stop her from running that bar of soap all over my body since I'm already clean, right?

Her nails graze my skin as she lathers me up, causing goose bumps to rise, and I swear to God she's going to make me combust. Though I can also tell she's tired. The long flight and major time change are finally getting to her. Her movements are slower than usual, and her eyes are droopy. I even caught her hiding a yawn only a minute ago. I feel a little guilty, bossing her around, forcing myself into her shower.

But not guilty enough to back out and let her shower on her own. The thing is, I can't resist her. The moment I opened the door and saw her standing there, a wan smile on her face, her fingers clutching the suitcase handle extra tight, like she might be nervous to see me, all I could think about was getting her naked. Getting her beneath me, on top of me, whatever. I just knew I had to have her before I went to practice.

Maybe having her with me will help me play better. Practice yesterday was a bitch—we were all sloppy, and I heard that whistle blow so many times I wanted to punch something. Everyone blamed the time change for our mistakes. I slept like a baby on the plane, so I knew that couldn't be it.

Yeah. I think I was just missing Amanda.

I needed her with me.

I push all thoughts of yesterday's practice out of my brain and focus on the here and now. Amanda standing in front of me with water streaming down her naked body, making her skin glisten. Her hands are bubbly with soap as she runs them along my stomach. Then lower. Lower still. Shifting away so she can wash along the sides of my hips.

The tease.

Finally, those soapy hands touch my cock, and I clench my teeth. She sets the bar of soap on the nearby ledge, and then her fingers grab hold, sliding up and down. Nice and slow. She glances up at me, her once-sleepy eyes now sparkling with heat, her lips quirked in a devilish smile. She knows what she's doing.

I say nothing. Neither does she. The only sound is the water hitting the tile. Keeping her grip on me, she carefully falls to her knees, her other hand curving around the back of my thigh, tugging on me.

"Get under the water, Jordan."

I do as she tells me, the soap washing off my dick the moment the water hits it. Amanda licks her lips, her gaze intent as she leans in and takes my cock between her lips.

Jesus. My knees nearly buckle and I brace my hand against the tile wall, watching my shaft slide between her lush lips. Suction tight, her mouth is hot, her tongue wet as she pulls me all the way out and licks the tip.

I could come like this. Easily.

But I don't want to.

She wraps her lips around the head of my cock and sucks extra hard, making me waver. Making me reconsider coming like this after all. She's good. Knows just what to do to send me over the edge. Back in the day, we experimented together all the time. She wasn't afraid to ask me what I liked, what felt good, what could she do to make it better. I always liked that about her—in bed and out of it. Her inquisitiveness. Her constant need to do something good, better, best.

Like giving head. She's fucking fantastic at it.

The coy look she sends my way tells me she knows she's damn good at it too, and that's the deal breaker. She's doing this on purpose. Giving me an orgasm so...what? She can fall into bed and I'll leave for practice a satisfied man?

We both can end up satisfied in this scenario if she gave me a chance.

I grab her by the shoulders and reluctantly push her away, her mouth falling off my cock. A fucking tragedy.

But I can remedy this.

She's frowning, her swollen lips forming into a pout, the water running over her, and she blinks rapidly. "Why'd you make me stop?"

"Not like this, babe," I tell her, hauling her into my arms. She weighs nothing. I turn and readjust her, pressing her back against the cool white tile. Her legs automatically go around my waist, her pussy poised just above my dick, and I slide into her with ease.

"Oh God," she whispers, the back of her head knocking against the tile. She winces. "Ow."

"Careful," I murmur, slipping my hand behind her head, rubbing it gently. Otherwise, I don't move. I'm fully embedded in her tight, hot body, my cock twitching, eager to get moving and make the magic happen.

Because that's what it is between Amanda and me. Magic. Sparks fly every time we fucking touch. Almost like we were...

Made for each other.

I pin her in place with my body and start to move. Push inside of her deep, savoring that slow drag as I pull almost all the way out. Her legs wrap tighter around me, like she might be afraid I'll disappear, but I'm not going anywhere.

I'm going to see this through.

"Jordan." My name falls from her lips, encouraging me to go faster. She sounds lost. Overcome. I watch her, unable to look away as I continue to fuck her. Her eyes are closed, a little whimper falling from her lips every time I thrust. I remove my hand from the back of her head and touch her cheek. Her mouth. Her lips part, sucking my fingers in between them, and her eyes pop open.

Emotions swamp me at the glow in her eyes, and I'm tempted to say something. Those words. Three of them. So simple, yet they would change everything.

Not too sure if I can say them yet.

I've never been one to say them. In my house, love wasn't something given easily. My dad was never around. If he wasn't working himself to death, he was out with one of his many mistresses. Mom was too worried over where her husband was, what others thought of her. Too wrapped up in her own problems, she didn't have time for me.

No one ever really did.

With Amanda, I finally understood what real love was. Until she left me too.

Her abandonment reminded me that love was a joke. Something I could never count on.

So yeah. I'm not going to tell her I love her.

I'm thinking she'll have to say those words first.

THIRTY

AMANDA

I SLEPT like the dead once Jordan left the hotel to go to practice. The plane ride, the taxi ride, the shower, the sex, the orgasm, it all had a mind-numbing effect on me, and the moment my head hit the pillow, I was out.

Not sure how long I slept, but when my eyes blink open, I can tell it was nighttime. The hotel room is dark, the curtains still parted, so I can see the lights from the city just outside the window. I sit up, pushing my wild hair away from my face. Glance down to see I'm wearing Jordan's red Niners T-shirt.

Huh. I don't remember putting that on.

My phone sits on the bedside table, plugged into its charger. Funny, I also don't remember pulling my charger out of my purse. Jordan must've done that for me.

I start to smile when I think of him. Always taking care of me.

That's just his way.

Glancing around, I look for any sign of him, but he's not in this room. I just know. His presence radiates, and I gravitate toward him like he's the sun and I'm this bumbling planet lost in space.

But where could he be?

I grab my phone and check it for notifications. I have four texts and two missed calls from Jordan, plus a voicemail notification.

You awake? Team is going to dinner, wanted you to join me.

Mandy? You must be still sleeping.

I'll bring you back something to eat. This restaurant is amazing.

Miss you.

I check my voicemail next.

You're sleeping. I know you were tired. That's why I left you alone and didn't wake you up when I came back to the room. But I wish you were here with me. Cannon wishes you were too.

In the background, I hear Cannon making fun of Jordan for telling me that. I can even hear Cannon making exaggerated kissy noises.

Anyway, I'll be back in the room soon. In about an hour or so. Hopefully you'll be awake by then.

The voicemail ends.

A sigh escapes me and I listen to the voicemail again. His voice is deep. Low. Intimate. Warmth spreads through me at hearing it, making me tremble. There's emotion there, just beneath the surface. When we had sex earlier in the shower, he'd been so tender with me. So sweet. And when he came inside me...

I drop the phone, blinking in shock. Yeah. He came inside me. I felt it. As in, he didn't wear a condom.

And I'm not on the pill.

I fall back onto the bed, my head sinking into the pillow as I stare up at the ceiling. Shit, shit, shit! I didn't even think of asking him to put on a condom. He didn't think of it either. We both messed up with this one.

I try to think of the last time I had my period. A week ago? Two weeks ago? Okay, let's be real here. I'm like clockwork. My period shows up every twenty-eight to thirty days. And it warns me too. It was two weeks ago, give or take a few days. Which means I should be ovulating.

Right.

Now.

"Oh God," I say out loud, and close my eyes. Press my hands against them, rubbing hard. Maybe it was all a dream. Maybe we really didn't have amazing shower sex. I imagined the entire thing. My hands fall away from my eyes as I continue to stare at the ceiling. Yep, that's what happened.

There's rustling at the door, a click sounds and then the door swings open, letting in a bright beam of light. I close my eyes and turn my head, thankful when the door quietly shuts.

"Amanda?"

I sit up. Offer a little wave. "Hey." My voice is weak. I sound pitiful.

Jordan sets a takeout container on the desk and approaches the bed. "Hey, sleepyhead. Did I wake you?"

"No, I woke up a few minutes ago." I run a hand over my hair, wincing. I went to bed with it wet and now it's all over the place. Great.

"You sleep good?"

"Yeah. Really good." I try to smile, but I give up quick.

I'm quietly freaking out here. How do I tell him this? I mean, it could be nothing. I have no idea how fertile I am. What if I'm not fertile at all? What if it turns out that getting pregnant won't be easy for me? What if I end up having to do in-vitro or whatever?

Oh my God, talk about putting the cart before the horse.

Hmm, I could also—do something to ensure I won't get pregnant. There are plenty of options out there.

But this is with Jordan. The boy you loved. The man you probably still love. The man you want to be with forever...

"Are you okay?" He settles his big hand on my shoulder, giving it a squeeze. My skin warms from his touch and I waver.

Should I tell him? He needs to know. My chances of getting knocked up are high.

I'm also panicking. Worrying over potentially nothing. So...yeah.

For now, I need to keep this to myself. No use in getting him worked up too.

"I'm fine. Still a little out of it," I assure him with a faint smile.

"Hungry?" he asks.

My stomach chooses that moment to growl. Loudly. My nervous laughter mixes with his deep chuckle.

"I take that as a yes." He stands and goes over to the desk, grabbing the to-go box he brought in with him. "Can I turn on a lamp?"

"Go for it," I tell him, and he does. The bright light makes me blink, holding a hand over my eyes like a vampire. "Oh God, that's awful."

"You'll get used to it. You need to wake up anyway. You need to adjust to the time change." He pops open the box and the room instantly fills with the delicious smells of the dinner he brought. "Come over here and eat."

I crawl out of bed, tugging the shirt down as I do, though I don't know why I'm worried. It's so large, the hem almost comes to my knees. I pad over to the desk and look inside the box. There's baked chicken and roasted potatoes, plus a side of green beans flecked with slivered almonds. A flaky roll sits next to the chicken and my mouth literally starts to water.

"Oh my God, I'm starving. This looks amazing."

Jordan pulls the chair away from the desk for me and I plop my butt onto the seat, realizing quick that I'm not wearing any underwear.

Well. I have a feeling I should get used to this. We're going to sightsee all over London, but I anticipate us spending a lot of time in bed together too. Using condoms every single time, I might add.

No more accidental protection-free sex for us. No way.

I just hope our one time without protection doesn't result in something too big for us to handle.

"THIS PLACE IS PACKED," I say in wonder, gazing out at the field, at the majority of the seats filled in Wembley Stadium. There are people everywhere. I knew the NFL had been hosting exhibition games in the U.K. to gain interest in the sport, but I had no idea it was becoming so successful.

"We're one of the most popular teams in the NFL right now. Of course they're going to come out in droves," says Harvey Price, lead publicist for the 49ers. He's wearing a black three-piece suit, accompanied by a bright red tie. He's a fast talker, slick looking, and I'm not sure I can trust him, considering what he said to me when Jordan introduced us earlier:

"Ah, so you're the new mystery girl in Tuttle's life."

Harvey Price's words and his skeptical tone left me unsettled. More in the way he said it, versus what he actually said.

"I just didn't realize football has taken off so well over here," I tell him. We're in a borrowed suite at Wembley, and it's filled with all sorts of people. Family members of the team. Employees. Friends. Guests. Someone whispered Prince

William and Kate—excuse me, the Duke and Duchess of Cambridge—were possibly going to show up later.

Now that I'd like to see.

"They like to watch, but I don't believe any of them want to actually play," Harvey explains. "They're fans of the super-star players, the most visible ones, including Tuttle. But I doubt the NFL will ever really take off here. They prefer their own football. Soccer. Whatever you want to call it."

I smile at him, then return my gaze to the field. The game starts at two-thirty, and it's already two-fifteen. Yesterday was my first full day in London, and I didn't get to spend as much time with Jordan as I wanted. Not only did he have practice, but the team also made a public appearance, a sort of meet-and-greet early last night that I attended, but then left after about an hour when the crush of people in the room overwhelmed me.

I was so incredibly tired. I'm still not fully adjusted to the time difference. Besides, Jordan barely knew I was there. He was talking to so many people—correction, so many people were talking to *him*. He's popular. Everyone wants a piece of him.

Including me.

Those old, lingering insecurities threatened at one point, but I pushed them away. I was going to be fine, I told myself. Jordan wants me there.

I know he does.

But Harvey Price had a special request. He asked before the event started that Jordan and I not stand together or take any photos with each other. "I don't want this exhibition game to turn into the Jordan Tuttle New Romance Show," he said matter-of-factly. "The British paparazzi love to chase anyone from the US, because they know sites like TMZ will pay big money for scandalous photos. We don't want to give them anything to talk about. This weekend should be about the team."

I didn't protest. Neither did Jordan. He did pull me aside, full of apologies, but I told him I was fine. I understood.

Doesn't mean I liked it, but I definitely understood.

I kept my distance during the time I was there, and it hurt. Every time Jordan caught my eye, he'd wink at me, or smile. I'd smile in return, but I felt lonely.

So lonely.

He made up for my loneliness by kissing me fiercely the moment he slipped into our shared bed when he finally made it back to the hotel. I could feel the urgency in his touch, his lips. By the time we came up for air, I was pretty much naked, Jordan pushing inside of me after putting the condom on, making me cry out in pleasure.

"Don't ever think I'll abandon you," he told me, his eyes bright, his tone serious. *"That was Harvey's idea. Not mine."*

"You two dated before," Harvey suddenly says, startling me.

I turn to look at him, noting the shrewd expression on his face. "Yes," I say, keeping my tone nonchalant. "We did."

"You're the girl from high school. The one who got away." When I frown, he continues, "What Tuttle said in the *Inside Football* interview."

"Oh. Right." I don't know how much Jordan has told Harvey, so I really don't want to delve too deep into this conversation.

"How'd you two reconnect?" His tone is casual, but I'm not stupid. He's digging for information.

"Social media." I don't bother telling Harvey that episode of *Inside Football* spurred me into action.

"A modern love story then," Harvey says, a slight smile curling his thin lips. "Sorry. I'm always looking for an angle."

"I'm sure," I murmur, glancing around the room. I don't really know anyone here. And I'd rather be talking to anyone else, even a complete stranger, if I'm being honest. This guy makes me uncomfortable. Like he's watching me, waiting for me to make a mistake.

He's judging me too. Seeing if I'll measure up.

"You don't like me very much, do you." It's not a question Harvey's asking. More like a statement.

I turn to face him once more, my gaze meeting his direct. "More like I don't think you like me."

"Honestly?" I never like it when people use the word *honestly*. To me, it means they lie—maybe more than they tell the truth. "I don't know how I feel about you yet." Harvey crosses his arms, contemplating me. "Lots of questions run through my mind. Are you using Tuttle? Trying to get a piece of his fame?"

My lips pop open but I can't find any words to say. His accusation takes me aback.

"Any other woman would've stomped her feet like a toddler and thrown a major hissy fit last night after I told you two that you couldn't be seen together." He tilts his head. "But you didn't."

I shrug. Why make our lives more miserable by acting like a baby?

"You earned a few points for that," Harvey continues.

"Gee, thanks," I say sarcastically.

"Listen." He takes a step closer, his voice lowering. Like he's going to tell me a big secret. "This life isn't easy. It's not for the faint of heart. Most of the women who come after these guys are in it for the money. Or the fame. That's it. They don't give a shit about the man himself. They want his money. They'll do whatever it takes, even make up lies about being pregnant with their baby. They care more about what the man can give them in their quest for celebrity."

My bravado wilts a little when he says the word *pregnant*.

"I'm not out to become a celebrity," I start to say, but he silences me with a look.

"The ones who stick with their girlfriends from high school? Those long-term relationships tend to work better than any other. These guys know that the girl who stuck by their side since he was a teenager actually fell in love with them, not the celebrity version of themselves."

Then I should be trusted, right? Isn't that what he's telling me?

"But you're an unusual case. The high school sweetheart who sweeps back into his life out of nowhere, just when his popularity and worth are about to skyrocket? Not so sure about that one." Harvey starts to walk away, patting me on the shoulder as he passes. "We'll keep in touch."

I watch his retreating back, see how he stops and talks to a woman who looks about my age, maybe a little older. She gives him a hug, and his gaze meets mine when they're mid-embrace.

Harvey mouths, *A good one*, and points at the back of her platinum blonde head.

Turning away, I face the field once more, contemplating everything Harvey just said. He doesn't trust me. He thinks my motives are possibly shady when they're anything but.

Huh. Like it matters, what that guy thinks about me. He's the team publicist. I won't let him dictate my life.

I blink my vision into focus, excitement filling me when I see the team already out on the field. Specifically Jordan. We're so high up, he's like a tiny speck of white and red, the number eight on his back telling me exactly where he's at.

Taking out my phone, I snap a pic of them down on the field, then open up Instagram, putting together a quick post.

Enjoying my favorite pastime live and in person. Back with the old crew. #eightisgreat #jordantuttle #cannonwhittaker #ninernation #london

I add my location—Wembley Stadium—and post the photo of the team on the field.

Hopefully Harvey won't care if I made that post. Not that I should let him dictate what I do. But still. Now he's got me thinking about my every move. Worrying over my behavior, how I might look. How I should act.

And that sucks.

His words linger throughout the first half. To the point I can barely concentrate on the game. Not that it's a big deal—they're winning so easily, it's almost embarrassing for the opposing team.

Yet I can't shake the fact that the team publicist doesn't trust my motives for being back in Jordan's life. Do I look that sketchy? Does he really believe I'm out to cash in on Jordan's fame? I don't want to deal with the fame thing at all. Jordan is a private person, but guess what? So am I. He signed up for this from the beginning. He knew what he was getting into.

Just because I care about the man doesn't mean I can handle the celebrity that comes with him. Maybe I can't. Maybe this will all prove to be too much.

"Hello. Please tell me you're Amanda."

Whirling around at the lilting female voice, I find a petite dark blonde standing in front of me, clad in a beautiful pale blue dress. The dress matches her eyes perfectly. They're icy blue, sparkling and friendly.

I have no clue who she is.

"Yes, I'm Amanda," I say carefully.

"Oh, thank goodness." She rests her hand against her chest, her shoulders slumping in relief. "Cannon told me to come in search of you, and I was afraid with the mad crush of people in here, I'd never find you."

She's British. Her accent is sharp, her pronunciation almost exaggerated. Her posture is perfection. She has an elegant air about her, her hair pulled back into a sleek ponytail, her lips covered in a becoming shade of pink.

Oh, and she mentioned Cannon's name. How does he know this woman?

"You're a friend of Cannon's?" I ask.

Her cheeks blaze a deep pink at the mere mention of his name. "We only just met yesterday, but...yes. I'd like to consider him a friend."

"And you are?"

"Oh, how absolutely rude of me! I haven't even introduced myself." She smiles. Does a little curtsy. "I'm Lady Susanna Sumner."

Lady Susanna? "Shouldn't I be the one who curtsies to you?" I ask as I take her offered hand and shake it.

She lets go of my hand and laughs, shaking her head. "No, never. I'm not one for all that formality. I can't help it if I was born the daughter of an earl."

An earl? That means she's royalty. From a noble family or whatever. "I don't mean to be rude, but how in the world did you meet Cannon?"

"At the event yesterday. I accompanied my parents to the meet-and-greet gathering. My father is a huge fan of American football, and he wanted to meet some of the team members. I tagged along because I didn't have anything else better to do on a Friday night." She smiles, her cheeks still pink. "My father introduced himself to Cannon, even complimenting him on his massive arms, which was so incredibly embarrassing. I chastised Father for his ridiculous statement, and Cannon took great offense. Said he couldn't believe his arms didn't impress me."

Oh Cannon. "In other words, he was flirting with you," I tease.

She rolls her eyes. "Right. I told him he was so obvious. Father drifted away after a few minutes of our silly conversation and we ended up chatting for the rest of the night. He even, um, took me to dinner."

Hmm. I wonder if *took me to dinner* is code for something else entirely.

"Anyway." She waves a dismissive hand. "Cannon invited me to the game, and told me I should find you so we could keep each other company. I almost thought I wouldn't make it, I was running so late, but now here I am."

A new friend. I already adore her. She's chatty and nervous and very unsure about this entire thing, I'm guessing. In other words, we can totally relate. "Perfect. Let's sit together during the second half of the game."

She wrinkles her nose, looking like a cute little bunny. Maybe it's the pink cheeks and the dark blonde hair. Her teeth too. The front ones protrude slightly. Kind of like a... bunny. "The second half? I'm ashamed to admit, I don't know much about American football. Or any other sport, for that matter. I just shout at the TV with the rest of my family when they're watching a game at the appropriate moments."

I smile and hook my arm through hers. "I'll give you a lesson in American football. I just have one question. Should I call you Lady Susanna?"

She appears horrified by my suggestion. "Heavens no! Please just call me Susanna."

"Perfect." I tug her closer to me, our arms still hooked. "Let's go sit down and watch the game."

We settle into our seats, Susanna chattering away, her hands fluttering. I get the sense she's kind of a Nervous Nelly. Or maybe she's just excited, I don't know, but I like her. She'll be the perfect distraction for the rest of the game. At least I won't have to worry about Harvey lurking around, watching my every move. Or worry about the fact that there's a chance I could be...

Pregnant.

Ugh. I'm worrying over nothing. I need to stop.

So instead, I focus on Susanna and start explaining the basics of American football.

My favorite subject.

THIRTY-ONE
AMANDA

AFTER THE GAME—THE Niners won—and the interviews and the photo ops, Jordan and Cannon were finally set free. Susanna and I stayed together the entire time, like sweet little groupies, eager to catch sight of their men.

Us patiently waiting around for them reminded me of high school. When Livvy and I would linger outside the locker room until her boyfriend at the time, Ryan, would finally emerge.

And I, of course, was there for Tuttle. Not that I ever wanted to admit it back then, before we were officially dating. What we had before our actual relationship was so complicated and confusing. He drove me insane. So much push and pull. All the, *I want to be with you but I don't know how to love* stuff. He made my teenage heart ache.

He still makes my heart ache, but for entirely different reasons.

Jordan and Cannon approach us, and I can sense Susanna tensing up. She presses her lips together, a vaguely desperate humming sound coming from her, and when she turns to look at me, I see the panic written all over her pretty face.

I have so been in her shoes. That unsettling feeling of "where do I belong in this equation?" I know that's what she's experiencing.

"Hey." Jordan greets me with a hug and a quick kiss on the lips. "Sorry to keep you waiting."

"You have a job to do." I smile up at him. "I get it."

That familiar nagging feeling hits me, though. One I remember from when we were younger. Will he always keep me waiting? Is that my role in this relationship? To stand on the sidelines while the bright light constantly shines on *the* Jordan Tuttle?

"What are your plans tonight?" Cannon asks us, thankfully forcing me to stop thinking about the negative parts of dating Jordan.

We both turn to face him and Susanna. They're standing next to each other, Susanna looking a little uncomfortable. A lot awkward.

"Not sure," Jordan answers, slinging his arm around my shoulders and pulling me into his side. "All I know is I'm starving."

"Same," I add.

"All four of us should go to dinner," Cannon suggests, slipping his arm around Susanna's waist. Aw. "What do you think?"

Susanna stares up at him adoringly. I think she wants him to be all lovey dovey, which isn't normally Cannon's thing. At least, it wasn't when we were in high school. "That sounds fantastic," she tells him.

Jordan is watching the two of them in confusion. I'll have to update him on what's going on later, but for now we have to just roll with it. "Yes, let's go to dinner. Have any suggestions, Susanna?" I ask.

She grins and nods. "Definitely. I can even drive us! I brought the family car."

The family car?

We walk out into the mostly empty parking lot, headed straight for an older, silver Mercedes sedan.

"It's a beastly thing. My father drove it when he was a teen, if you can even imagine," Susanna explains while we walk. "It's one of the safest cars on the road. That's why he insists I drive it."

"Protecting his baby girl?" Cannon asks, tugging on the ends of her hair.

Susanna darts away from him, her heels sounding loudly as she walks. "That and, well, I wasn't the best driver when I first started out."

Jordan grabs hold of my hand and tugs me close, whispering into my ear, "She's not going to kill us, is she?"

I shake my head, trying to contain my laughter. "I hope not."

We pile into the vehicle, Jordan and I taking the back seat while Cannon barely fits his huge frame into the passenger seat. Susanna pulls a pair of glasses out of her purse, putting them on before she starts the car.

"My driving glasses," she explains when Cannon looks at her funny. "They really do help."

"Holy shit, you're adorable," Cannon says just before he leans over and kisses her on the cheek.

They keep talking as she starts to exit the parking lot, and Jordan sends me another one of those confused looks. He ducks his head, our cheeks practically touching as he says, "You need to tell me what's going on. Unless you're just as clueless as I am."

"Lucky for you, I'm not clueless." Thankfully, Cannon turns the radio on, and Susanna starts bopping her head to the music. "They met last night."

Jordan's frowning. "Last night? I didn't know Cannon could move so fast."

"Well, he did. I guess they really hit it off. He invited her to watch the game, so here she is."

"And who, exactly, is she?"

"Lady Susanna Sumner. Youngest daughter of an earl. She's twenty-three and doesn't know a thing about American football." That's about all I know. "Oh, and I get the sense that she grew up very sheltered on her family's estate."

"Estate?"

"I did mention she's the daughter of an earl? Meaning she's nobility."

"Actually, we're distant relatives of the queen, so yes. We're technically part of the royal family." Susanna's gaze meets mine in the rearview mirror, her eyes looking huge behind her glasses. "Sorry, didn't mean to eavesdrop."

"I should apologize. We're the ones blatantly talking about you in the back of your car," I say.

"Saying only good things, I hope." Susanna appears truly worried.

"Just giving Jordan the rundown." When Susanna frowns, I continue. "He didn't know who you were, so I was letting him know."

"She's my future girlfriend," Cannon says proudly.

Susanna pushes his shoulder, not that he's going anywhere. He's such a giant hulk of a man. "Please. You're leaving in a few days."

"I'll miss you." He sounds sincere. "You'll spend the next few days with me, right?"

"Um..." A horn honks and Susanna jerks the steering wheel, causing the car to veer sharply. Another horn honks and she hits the brakes, glaring at Cannon once she has the situation under control. "You're distracting me."

"Stop distracting her," Jordan tells Cannon, his voice firm. "I want to make it to the restaurant in one piece."

Jordan's scowling so hard, I almost start laughing, but don't.

This is going to be an interesting night.

WE END up at an Italian restaurant not too far from our hotel, and the food is amazing. The place is packed when we arrived, but the maître d' is an old family friend of Susanna's—and the son of the owners of the restaurant. We're whisked to a table almost immediately, and given extra appetizers and wine.

"I'm so full," I say, pushing my plate away from me. I ate almost every bit of my carbonara, especially the bacon. I love bacon.

"Aw, you can't be full." Susanna mock pouts. She's sitting directly across from me, her half-eaten plate already pushed aside. "You must save room for dessert. Their cannoli are to die for. Or the tiramisu."

"You should've warned me. I wouldn't have eaten all this." I wave my hand at my plate. "Tiramisu is my favorite."

"We'll share a dessert," Jordan suggests, resting his hand over mine and giving it a squeeze.

I smile at him, enjoying how relaxed, how happy he looks tonight. The game is over and they won. Now we're just two people with friends, on vacation in one of the most exciting cities in the world.

"Let's order the entire dessert menu," Cannon says as he looks it over. "They all sound amazing."

"That's because they *are* amazing," Susanna says, plucking the menu from Cannon's fingers. Her eyes bug out when she takes in the entire list. "But we can't eat them all, Cannon. There's so many!"

"We can try," Cannon says with a shrug, taking back the menu. Our server happens to choose this moment to stop by

YOU PROMISED ME FOREVER 267

our table and check on us. "We want every dessert on the menu."

The server frowns. "Excuse me?"

"The dessert menu? We want all of them. One of each," Cannon explains.

Susanna starts giggling, then takes a sip from her wine. I think she's drunk. I barely touched my glass, not that anyone noticed.

Thank goodness.

"Are you serious?" the server asks incredulously.

"He's serious," Jordan says, his voice firm. He's scowling at the server, and I almost feel sorry for the guy. "One of each, like he said."

"Right away, sir." The server nods once before he buzzes away.

A shiver moves down my spine as I gawk at Jordan. I love it when he takes command of a situation, which is often. He's a natural born leader, and it's so damn sexy I sort of want to throw myself at him.

Fine, I *totally* want to throw myself at him.

"You are so demanding," I tell him, resting my hand on his rock-hard thigh.

Jordan turns to look at me, his scowl immediately softening. "I got tired of hearing him argue with Cannon."

"He wasn't arguing. I think he was in shock by the order."

"Whatever. They were annoying me." Jordan shrugged.

I squeeze his thigh, my fingers trailing up. "You are so sexy when you act like that."

His brows lift and he leans in closer. "When I act like that?"

"Like you own the world." My fingers brush the front of his jeans.

He grabs hold of my wrist, stopping me. "Wine making you daring tonight?"

Nope. I barely drank a drop. I'm a little too freaked out by our having sex with no condom to want to drink. "*You* make me daring," I tell him, trying to work my wrist out of his grasp so I can touch him again. He's smirking, looking far too cocky for his own good. Susanna and Cannon aren't even paying attention to us. They're too engrossed in their own intimate conversation. "Stop being so sexy all the time and maybe I won't try and grab you."

"Is that what you're doing? Trying to make a dick grab?" He's smiling as he lets go of my wrist.

I smack his shoulder lightly. "So crude."

"You're the one trying to maul me at the table in a public restaurant." His smile is wicked. "Not that I mind."

His words, the look on his face, leave me breathless. "We should go," I whisper. "Don't you think?"

"We still have approximately ten desserts coming to our table," Jordan reminds me, just before he leans in and kisses me. His lips are soft and warm, and taste vaguely of wine. "Then we can leave."

Those four words are so full of promise, I have to press my thighs against each other to stave off the sudden want.

"Do you two want to go out with us after we finish dessert?" Cannon asks, interrupting our moment.

We both turn to look at him, then at each other. "Sure," I say as Jordan says, "No," at the same time.

"What are your plans?" I ask, my cheeks hot. I'm sure they could guess what our plans are.

"Not sure." Cannon turns to look at Susanna. "What were you thinking?"

"I don't know. Go to a pub?" The color in her cheeks is high, and I'm wondering if she's thinking of doing something else.

Like some alone time with Cannon.

Jordan yawns, his movements exaggerated, and he covers his mouth. "I think we're going to have to pass. I'm exhausted."

"No problem," Susanna chirps, her gaze meeting Cannon's. "I'll take you to my favorite pub."

"Sounds fun." Cannon smiles down at her. I can't help but think these two are making a possible love connection.

"You okay with going back to the hotel?" Jordan asks me.

"Yes, sure. Of course. I totally understand if you're tired," I say sympathetically. "Do you want to leave now?"

"And miss dessert? No way." Jordan leans in, whispering in my ear, "Though you're the dessert I want to taste later."

My cheeks go hot at his words.

I can't freaking wait.

THIRTY-TWO
JORDAN

I COULDN'T HUSTLE Amanda out of that restaurant fast enough. Susanna wasn't lying—the desserts were delicious. And after the game I played, I allowed myself to totally indulge. In the food. The wine. The cannoli.

And as soon as we get back to the hotel, I plan on indulging in the woman beside me.

The moment we exit the restaurant, we're immediately bombarded by flashing lights. Cameras. Shouting, insistent voices.

Paparazzi.

I throw up a hand at the line of people with cameras, slipping my other arm around Amanda's shoulders and pulling her into me. She presses her face against my chest, trying to shield herself, and I glare at the small group of three men and two women who continually snap photos of us.

"Tuttle! Tuttle! Tell us who's your new lady love!" one of them yells, his voice seemingly in time with the flash of the cameras.

"None of your damn business," I tell them, guiding Amanda beside me, headed toward the black Mercedes SUV I requested via Uber a few minutes ago. The driver must've seen what was going on, because he hops out of the car and rounds the front of it, opening the passenger door for us.

"Get in," I tell Amanda and she does as I say, sliding inside quickly, averting her face, her hair falling against her cheek.

The cameras are still flashing as Cannon and Susanna approach me, concern written across both of their faces. "What the hell is going on?" Cannon asks, wincing from the cameras' flashes.

The photographers start yelling his name—and Susanna's.

It appears they're even more interested in them.

"Better go find her father's car and get her out of here," I tell Cannon grimly. "Looks like the paparazzi found us."

"We're out," Cannon says, grabbing hold of Susanna's hand and pulling her toward him. "Text me later. Let me know you two made it back to the hotel."

"You do the same," I tell him before I get into the car and slam the door, watching through the window as Cannon and Susanna hurry away, hand in hand.

The flirtation was strong between those two tonight. I can tell Cannon's totally into her—something I'm not used to seeing. He's a pretty quiet, keep-to-himself guy. But I have a strong feeling they aren't going to end up at her favorite pub.

More like they're going to end up in Cannon's hotel room bed. That's my plan for ending our night too.

"Hey, you all right?" I ask, turning to face Amanda.

She nods, her eyes wide when they meet mine. "That was…intense."

"Yeah, I didn't expect them to find us." Or to care. I rub my jaw, trying to ease the tightness there. "Don't know how they did."

"They must've followed us," she says, her voice soft.

"They must've." I glance at the driver, our gazes meeting in the rearview mirror. "Hey, thanks for helping us get away from the photographers."

"No problem, mate," the driver tells me, his eyes even wider than Amanda's. "Aren't you one of those American footballers?"

"No comment," I tell the driver grimly, refocusing my attention on Amanda. I pull her close, so she's pressed snug against me, and she rests her head on my shoulder. I place my hand on her knee, giving it a reassuring squeeze.

The driver remains silent, zipping through the still busy streets like a mad man, and I'm grateful for his speed. I'm anxious to get back to the hotel and away from the chaos.

"You're awfully quiet," I tell Amanda after a few silent minutes, hoping she's not too shaken up over our earlier encounter the media. "Don't let what happened with those photographers bother you."

"Okay." She says the word slowly. It's clear she's doubting my reassurance. "Can I ask you a question?"

"Go for it."

She glances up so our gazes meet. "Does that happen often?"

"Sometimes." With Selena Gomez it did. Hell, I'd meet a beautiful, famous woman anywhere and the photogs went nuts. The media would label us as a couple when all we did was chat for two seconds at an event.

It's frustrating as shit, how they constantly leap to conclusions. My fictional sex life is way more exciting than my real one.

"Only with other celebrities?" Amanda asks.

I think of Mia. "Pretty much with anyone I'm seeing."

"Oh." Her voice is hollow. She's quiet for a moment before she says, "Harvey told me he didn't want us seen together while we're in London."

I'm immediately irritated. "Who cares what he wants?"

"Um, I do. He questioned me today."

Sitting up straighter, I remove my arm from her shoulders, trying to fight the irritation rising within me. That guy needs to keep his nose out of my private life. "Questioned you about what?"

"My intentions." She pauses when I frown. "Toward you."

I gaze off into the distance. "That's none of his damn business."

"He seems to think it's his business."

"What exactly did he say?" I ask, turning my attention toward her once more.

"He thinks I might be using you. He finds it suspicious, how I all of a sudden came back into your life. He believes I want something from you," Amanda explains, looking uncomfortable.

"Yeah, you want something from me all right." She blinks, clearly shocked. "My body." I smile, trying to lighten the moment, but she's not having it.

Amanda scowls at me, shaking her head. "Seriously, Jordan. He doesn't trust me. At all."

"So?"

"So, if he sees photos of us together coming out of a restaurant splashed all over the internet, he's going to flip."

"I don't care if he flips. He can talk to me if he has a problem." She starts to protest again, but I touch her lips, silencing her. "Don't worry about Harvey, Mandy. I mean it. I'll take care of him."

She blinks up at me, worry filling her dark eyes. "But I don't want to make things hard on you."

"I can handle anything Harvey throws at me," I say with confidence. And I mean it. I'm not scared of Harvey Price.

I don't want Amanda scared of him either.

"Forget Harvey. Forget the photographers. Forget everyone." Reaching out, I brush a few wayward strands of hair away from her cheek, lightly caressing her skin. I need to distract her. "We good?"

"Of course, we're good." She smiles faintly and I tug her close to me once again, wrapping my arm around her shoulders. Having her so close, it feels natural. Right. "I'm also kind of sleepy," she murmurs, nestling her cheek against my shoulder. "I think it was all the food."

"I'm not that tired."

She lifts her head, her gaze meeting mine in the dim light. "Wait a minute. You said you were exhausted earlier. In the restaurant. That's why we left."

I shrug. "I lied."

Her lips curve. "You were just trying to get me alone."

"Well, yeah. I thought you knew that after what I said to you earlier." I touch her cheek. Her skin is so soft. Everywhere.

"Well, I thought that's what you meant, but you confused me. One minute calling me dessert, the next minute saying you were exhausted."

"I'm never too tired for you." I touch her lips, her chin. Back to the corner of her mouth. I love this mouth. I've kissed it so many times, I've lost count. When I was a kid, I would fantasize about kissing that mouth. What she might taste like. I'd also fantasize about those lips on other parts of my body.

Turns out the reality is way better than the fantasy.

"So it's true? You're going to feast on me when we get back to the hotel?" She's talking in hushed tones, like she doesn't want the driver to hear what she's saying.

I'm sure he can understand every word, not that I'm going to point that out to her.

My voice drops an octave, my dick twitching at the glow in Amanda's eyes. She's aroused, I can tell. "Is that what you want?"

She nods. "Yes," she breathes.

"Then that's what you'll get." I tilt my head, my lips hovering above hers. "Whatever you want, I'll give you."

She angles her head and lifts her chin, trying to connect her lips to mine, but I shift away, not kissing her yet.

I want to draw this out. Torture us. I'm a glutton for punishment.

"You're mean." She pouts.

"You won't be saying that when I've got my face between your legs," I point out, feeling evil.

"Jordan." Her tone is faintly accusatory, though her eyes flash with heat.

"You know you want it," I tease.

"I always want it," she admits, her fingers landing on my jaw, caressing me there. "I always want you."

I grab hold of her wrist and bring her hand to my mouth, kissing her knuckles. She spreads her fingers wide and I turn her hand over, my mouth on her palm, her fingertips on my cheek. I let go of her hand, but she doesn't stop touching me. Her fingers are still on my cheek, dropping to my mouth. I gently kiss them and she smiles just before her hand returns to her lap.

We remain quiet, never looking away from each other, and I'm tempted. So tempted to tell her how I really feel. Right now, in the back of an Uber. That I'm in love with her, that I've never really stopped loving her. Does she feel the same?

How would she react if I actually said those words out loud?

I'm not sure if I'm ready to find out.

THIRTY-THREE
AMANDA

I WAKE up the next morning completely naked and sore in the best possible way. Jordan kept me up most of the night. He was insatiable.

He was amazing.

Keeping my eyes closed, I stretch my legs out, surprised my toes don't bump into Jordan's muscular, hairy legs. I raise my arms above my head, the bones in my neck cracking with satisfaction, then roll over, reaching across the mattress to find it...

Empty.

As in I'm the only one in the bed.

Huh.

I sit up, pushing my tangled hair out of my face, yanking the sheet up with me to keep my upper body mostly covered. The room is quiet and dark, and I know I'm alone. Jordan isn't here. He's not even in the bathroom.

Where did he go?

Reaching for my phone on the nightstand, I check my notifications to see I have a text from Jordan.

Meeting with Harvey. Be back soon. xo

He sent me the text almost an hour ago.

I chew on my lower lip as I contemplate answering him, my sudden nerves making me anxious. He's having a meeting with Harvey? God, this has to be about me.

Us.

The restaurant.

The photos.

Immediately I bring up a new browser, Google Jordan's name and then click images. The photos from last night pop up, one after the other, and while yes, there are quite a few of me and Jordan—though you can barely see my face thank goodness—there are even more of Cannon and Susanna.

The headlines are all about *Lady Susanna* this and *Lady Susanna* that. One of the tabloids calls her *Lady Suz*, and for some weird reason, it sounds kind of lewd. As I read one of the articles, I realize she's a bit of a minor noble celebrity here in Great Britain. And to think she played it off yesterday like she was no one important.

Clearly, she was being modest.

It's almost like everyone in London—everyone in the United Kingdom—knows exactly who Lady Susanna Sumner is.

But I can't be distracted by the Lady Susanna and American Footballer scandal for too long. My paranoia kicking in big time, I finally give in and send Jordan a text.

Me: **Are you almost done? Is everything okay?**

He takes a few minutes before he finally responds and I work on destroying my thumbnail with my teeth while I wait.

Jordan: **Everything's fine. See you in a few.**

I set my phone on the bedside table with a sigh and glance around the empty room. Well. I can't sit around and let the morning slip by. I'll make myself crazy. So I climb out of bed and take a long, hot shower. Ponder my outfit choices before I finally get dressed. Blow dry my hair till it's nice and smooth. Curl the ends. Carefully apply my makeup—because hello, now every day in London is going to possibly turn into a photo op.

After all that, Jordan still isn't back yet.

In fact, it takes *another* thirty minutes for him to finally return. I'm seated on the edge of the bed, eating the breakfast I ordered from room service because I was starving, when he opens the door and strides inside our room, his steps hurried, his expression...grim.

"Hey. Sorry to keep you waiting," he says, his gaze flicking to mine for the briefest second before he heads straight into the bathroom and closes the door.

He could barely look at me.

What gives?

I shove my worry aside and continue eating, though it feels like I'm chewing cardboard. My stomach is twisted in knots, my hunger evaporating with every bite and I feel like crap for not finishing such an expensive yet basic meal, but I can't do it.

I just...I can't.

Is he mad at me? Did Harvey fill his head with lies? I'd hope to God he'd believe me before he ever believed Harvey, but who knows? Jordan's image is very important. He doesn't just make his money playing football. He also has extremely lucrative endorsement deals. One wrong step and he could lose out on millions.

But what's wrong with having a steady girlfriend? Especially if the steady girlfriend is someone from his past who's loved him for years? Seriously, what's wrong with that? What's wrong with me?

Jordan's in the bathroom only a few minutes, and when he finally emerges, I'm already on my feet, pacing back and forth in front of the window that overlooks the city. I come to a stop when he blocks my way, a solid wall of sexy muscle that doesn't so much as budge.

"Hey." He grabs hold of my shoulders and gives me a little shake, but I keep my head bent. I know I'm being ridiculous, but it's like I'm almost too scared to face him. "Mandy. Look at me."

I lift my head, my gaze meeting his, and I see nothing but kindness there. He's so completely open with me—he has been since the moment we reentered each other's lives. And that's such a difference from our previous time together. Young Jordan was full of mystery. Turbulent. Brooding.

Sometimes even...heartless. He drove me crazy, especially in the beginning of our relationship. He ran so hot and cold. When I was with him, I never knew what I was going to get, or who I was dealing with.

"I talked with Harvey," he says firmly. "I set him straight."

"Set him straight how?" My voice is weak. A little shaky. I know I'm overreacting when I shouldn't.

"I asked him about the conversation yesterday between you two and he said he was just looking out for me. That he was protecting my best interests," Jordan explains.

I'm sure Harvey believed that. I'd go as far to say that I believe it too. Jordan Tuttle's image is very important to the franchise.

"But I told him it was more like he was protecting the *team's* best interests, and what you and I are doing, doesn't affect the team whatsoever." His expression turns thunderous. "And I also warned him that he couldn't bully or insult you. That if he has a problem with anything, he should take it up with me, since we're together." When I remain quiet for a beat too long, his eyes narrow. "Amanda. We *are* together, aren't we?"

"Is that what you want?" My voice is weak.

His hands fall away from my shoulders and he takes a step backwards, as if he needs the distance. "Isn't that what *you* want?"

"I—but we promised to take this slow." God, why did I just say that? I sound like I'm backtracking, when I'm so not, but it's just...

It's so scary, realizing Jordan wants to be with me. I want to be with him, but so much comes with being in a relationship with Jordan Tuttle. Am I capable of handling it?

He laughs, but the sound lacks humor. "You're with me in London. We've been together as much as possible since you reached out to me on Instagram. You know I don't make time for just anyone. So yeah. I'd call what we're doing pretty fucking serious."

He sounds angry, and I have to confess—a pissed off Jordan Tuttle is hot. This is exactly what my teenage self would've thought. I remember having these exact same thoughts when we were together in high school. All that pent up anger and frustration spilling out of him is downright sexy.

My lust-driven thoughts probably mean I have a mental problem.

I also realize he's waiting for me to respond.

"It's just that everything is happening so incredibly fast. Only a few weeks have gone by since we first saw each other again," I explain, throwing my hands up in the air. I'm frustrated, but not with him. More like I'm frustrated with myself. "I mean really, are we sure this is going to work between us the second time around? There are no guarantees in life, Jordan."

"It's been a few weeks and the six years before that," he reminds me, completely ignoring my last question. "You want me to be honest with you right now?"

"Of course I do," I say.

"I never stopped thinking about you. Ever. I always wondered where you were, what you were doing. Even after we split and I was so damn mad at you and fucking miserable, I knew if I saw you again, I'd want you back," he admits.

I blink at him, shocked by his words, the passion behind them, the intense gleam in his eyes. He means every word he says. He still cares. Dare I think...he still loves me.

I still love him.

But is it too soon to admit our feelings to each other, when things are so unsure between us?

"Did I just freak you out?" he asks, tilting his head to the side as he contemplates me.

"You didn't freak me out." I'm a total liar. He freaked me out a little. "I'm more worried about Harvey. He said some pretty awful things to me. What if he's saying those same awful things to other people?"

"Fuck that guy. Who cares what he thinks?" Jordan's mouth goes thin. "Swear to God Mandy, if he's bad mouthing you to other people, I'll kick his ass."

"That is the absolute last thing I want you to do." I go to him, resting my hands on his chest, desperate for him to listen to me. "But I care about what Harvey thinks. I can't help but care about what *everyone* thinks. I don't want people to see me as some gold digger or famewhore out to get whatever I can from you. I'm just—an average girl, okay? An average *woman*." I put emphasis on the last word. "It's kind of scary to be thrust into this world where the spotlight is always on us. On me. I'm not used to it."

"This is exactly what drove you away last time," Jordan says grimly.

I curl my fingers into his shirt, feeling the warm, hard skin beneath. My knees go a little weak but I need to stay focused and get my point across. "Image is *everything,* Jordan. Maybe Harvey's right. Maybe we should keep a low profile until we know for sure that we're—serious about each other."

Oh God, what am I saying? Of course, I'm serious about him. I'm fairly certain he's serious about me.

But there's always that niggling doubt in the back of my mind, lingering there. Reminding me that maybe, just maybe I'm not the woman for him.

"You want to keep a low profile? Because we're not *serious* about each other?" he asks incredulously.

"Maybe?" I release my hold on his shirt and take a step back, feeling helpless.

He rubs his hand along his tight jaw, glowering at me, just before he starts heading for the door. "I'll be right back," he calls over his shoulder.

"Wait, where are you going?" I ask but the door slams shut before I can even get the last word out.

He's already gone.

———

"I BLEW IT," I tell Livvy, who's yawning in my ear. I called her within minutes after Jordan stormed out of our hotel room, not even feeling bad for waking her up at the crack of dawn. She's woken me up countless times since she moved to Texas, so this is total payback. "I don't think he's coming back."

He's been gone for almost two hours. He hasn't texted, he hasn't called me, nothing. I'm lying on the bed, wishing I could go after him, but considering I have no idea where he went, I wouldn't know where to start.

Instead, I wait in the hotel room, hoping he'll show up.

"You keep repeating yourself," Livvy says, yawning yet again. "And he's definitely coming back. His suitcase is there. He needs his stuff."

"Right, but maybe he doesn't need *me*." Tears spring to my eyes, and I blink them away. I haven't cried over this yet, and I don't want to start now. But as more time passes, the more worried I become. "I should've just told him I loved him."

"Do you love him?" Livvy asks, sounding genuinely curious.

"I've always been in love with him," I admit. "It's like my feelings for him were lying dormant in my mind and the minute I heard from him, talked to him, saw him, all those old emotions came flooding back. They never really went away."

"You should tell him that, every single thing you just said to me," Livvy says. "The minute he returns to your hotel room, you need to spill your guts."

"What if he comes back mad?" I practically wail, flopping backwards on the bed. I stare up at the ceiling, my mind racing. I wish he would walk through that door right now. I want him in this room, standing in front of me so I can tell him how sorry I am for saying all those stupid things. And then I can kiss him and touch him and admit my true feelings for him.

"You're being ridiculous," Livvy says, being the blunt, tell-it-like-it-is friend I need in situations like this. "Maybe you should top wallowing in self-pity and go find him."

"How can I find him? I'm in a foreign city, and it's huge, Livvy. I have no idea where he is, or where to start looking for him," I say, feeling helpless.

"Text him. Call him and profess your love. And if he doesn't answer, leave him a voicemail and tell him how you feel. He won't be able to resist you if you cut your chest wide open and bleed out your love for him," Livvy says.

What an image. "That's somehow grotesque and beautiful, all at once," I tell her.

"That's what love is. It's messy and beautiful and awful and exhilarating." Livvy's voice goes soft. "It's really scary. But wouldn't you rather take the risk and tell him how you really feel versus possibly losing him forever?"

Her words make my heart hurt. "What if I've already lost him forever?" I whisper, my stomach twisting at the mere thought.

I can't lose Jordan.

Not again.

"You haven't lost him," Livvy says without hesitation. "He hasn't given up on you that quick. Trust me."

Her words linger in my head long after we end our call. She's right. I need to tell him how I feel. I need to pour my heart out to him and reassure him I'm really not scared. I just...he was right. I freaked out a little and said dumb stuff that I wish I could take back.

Grabbing my phone, I call him, waiting anxiously for him to answer.

But it goes straight to voicemail. I clutch the phone tightly as I listen to his deep voice say, *Sorry I can't take your call right now. Leave me a message and I'll get back to you as soon as I can.*

The tone sounds, and I start talking.

"Hey. I don't know where you are, but I hope you're not mad at me. I just—panicked. And I said stupid things. All those old insecurities resurfaced, when I should've never doubted what you said. I don't really believe we're moving too fast." I hesitate for only a moment before continuing. "I've always had feelings for you, Jordan. I missed you so much these past six years, and having you back in my life feels so...right. So *perfect*. I don't want to lose that. I don't want to lose you. I—"

Another tone sounds, the phone clicks, and the call is over.

"Shit!" I toss my phone onto the bed in frustration and close my eyes, fighting my tears yet again. I don't want to cry. I refuse to cry. He'll show up. I know he will. I know he...

A horn sounds once. Twice. Over and over again, insistent. Urgent.

I hear a voice.

"Amanda!"

Jordan's? Over a *loudspeaker?*

I climb out of bed and go to the window, shoving the curtains back. There's a double decker red tour bus idling by the curb. The second level is uncovered, the seats filled with people, and Jordan is standing in the middle of the aisle clutching a microphone, his focus zeroed in on our hotel window.

His gaze immediately finds me and he speaks into the microphone.

"Open the window, babe."

Reaching for the lock, I undo it with shaky fingers and the window swings open, a gasp leaving me when the cold air hits my face. I can smell the exhaust from the idling bus, hear the traffic in the near distance, even the low murmur of the tourists on the upper level of the bus talking to each other with their heads bent close.

"She opened the window," Jordan tells them and they all lift their heads, their gazes on me as they start cheering.

My cheeks go hot and I slap my hands against them, not sure what to do or say. My heart is thumping wildly and Jordan's gaze never leaves mine as he starts to talk.

"Yo, Mandy," he calls out to me with a giant smile.

"Yo, Tuttle," I call back, grinning stupidly as I rest my hands on the edge of the window and lean my head out.

"Remember how I told you I didn't want to ride one of these buses because I didn't want anyone to recognize me?" he asks.

I nod. "Yeah." I'm shouting, but how else can he hear me?

"Well, I don't care if they recognize me. Some of them know who I am, but most of them don't, because they're from another country. None of that matters, though. You want to know why?" he asks.

People are stopping on the sidewalk to watch him, since it's not every day this kind of thing happens, you know? The side street our hotel is on isn't very busy, but there's a car waiting behind the bus. And then another.

"Why?" I ask when I realize he's waiting for me.

"Because you're not with me. Nothing really matters if you're not by my side. I didn't realize that until you came back into my life. Before, I was just living. Doing my thing. And it wasn't bad, you know?" He chuckles into the microphone and I can't help but laugh too.

I can't believe he's doing this.

I never want him to stop talking.

"But then you slid into my DMs and the message you sent me was just so...you. It made my heart ache in the best way." His voices goes a little deeper, and he rubs at the center of his chest, as if it's hurting right now.

My own heart wants to melt at his words.

"*You* make my heart ache in the best way," he continues. "You said earlier maybe we're moving too fast, but if I'm being real with you right now, I don't think we're moving fast enough."

I wait for him to continue, but he remains quiet.

As in, he's killing me.

"What do you mean?" I finally ask.

He moves the mic away from his face and clears his throat before he resumes talking.

"I love you, Mandy. I will always love you. Till the end of fucking time." He glances at his captive audience on the bus, his expression sheepish. "Sorry." Then he looks up at the window. Looks up at me. His eyes, his entire face is shining with emotion. All of it aimed right at me. "But it's true. I know it's only been a few weeks, but when you're ready to spend the rest of your life with someone, why not start right now?"

The tears finally flow down my cheeks and I rest my hand over my mouth, trying to contain the sob. "Oh Jordan," I practically wail.

His brows furrow and he brings the microphone so close to his mouth I can hear him breathing. "Get your pretty ass down here right now, Amanda," he practically growls.

I leave the window. Dart out of the room and run down the hall, frantically hit the down button for the elevator. It feels like it takes hours, but I'm finally outside in front of the hotel, and Jordan is standing there waiting for me, the bus directly behind him, a line of traffic filling both sides of the street, a few cars honking, the drivers impatient. The sidewalk is crowded with onlookers too and yep, there's even two photographers taking photos and calling out Jordan's name.

He ignores them all. He doesn't look at anyone else.

Just me.

"I love you," he whispers as he steps toward me, taking my hands in his and interlacing our fingers together. "If this isn't proof enough, I don't know what is. I hijacked a tour bus and made an ass of myself in front of everyone on this street. All for you, Mandy."

I sniff, ready to say I love him too but then he pulls me into his arms and holds me tight, my face pressed against his chest, my tears soaking his shirt. He tangles his fingers in my hair, his mouth at my temple. I'm so overwhelmed, so freaking relieved, all I can do is stand on this sidewalk and cry in Jordan's arms.

THIRTY-FOUR
JORDAN

I WAIT for Amanda to say something. *Anything.* My entire body is tense, nerves buzzing inside of me, making me feel antsy. I grab hold of her slender shoulders and take a step backward, causing her to tilt her head so her gaze meets mine.

Her dark eyes shine with tears and her cheeks are flushed—and damp. She smiles at me and shakes her head, a little laugh escaping her. "You hijacked a tour bus, Jordan. For me?"

"For you." I gave the driver a huge tip and when I spoke to his manager on the phone, I promised I'd film a commercial for the tour company. I was that desperate to prove my point to Amanda.

I'd do anything for her.

Anything.

The laughter dies, and she smiles, her eyes glowing. "I love you too," she whispers. "I've loved you for what feels like forever."

Before she can say something else she's back in my arms, my mouth fused with hers. The crowd on the sidewalk, on the bus, even the people waiting in their cars start cheering and I can hear the click of the cameras taking our photo.

This is the biggest declaration I can make. She can never doubt me again. I am completely and totally in love with Amanda Winters.

And she's in love with me.

"Come on," I whisper against her lips when I break the kiss seconds later. "Let's go inside."

We rush into the hotel lobby, her hand still clasped in mine as I lead her over to the elevator, thankful when the doors slide open immediately. We slip inside and I press the number six button, Amanda wrapping her arms around my neck just as the doors slide closed, her mouth on mine before the car even begins its ascent.

Her kiss is hungry, her tongue seeking mine, her fingers playing with the ends of my hair. I return the kiss with matching hunger, guiding her out of the elevator when we reach the sixth floor. I tear my lips from hers and practically drag her to our room, my shaky fingers having a hell of a time pulling the card key out of my wallet.

She laughs and takes the key from me, as if she knows I'm having difficulty, and she unlocks the door with ease. We enter the room in a rush, me pressing her against the door as soon as it shuts, my mouth back on hers, my hands sliding beneath her shirt, encountering warm, bare skin.

I tug the shirt up, and she helps me shed it, tossing it onto the floor. Her bra is white. Trimmed in satin and lace. Virginal when she's anything but. I shove the cups up, exposing her breasts, her rosy pink nipples hard and begging for my mouth. I draw one in, sucking and biting, licking away the sting when I hear her harsh intake of breath. I do the same to the other nipple, my hand dropping in between her legs, rubbing her there, pressing the seam of her jeans against her pussy.

She writhes against me, her legs squeezing around my hand, like she never wants me to escape. With my other hand I undo the button, pull down the zipper, and then I'm delving my hand inside, brushing my fingers against her panties.

They're damp. She's so fucking wet right now.

All for me.

Our overeager hands start pulling at each other's clothes, and within seconds we're naked. I pick her up, carry her to the bed and deposit her there, following after her. Our kiss is long, full of circling tongues and heat, my cock ready to plunge inside her wet depths and just fuck her already, but I hold myself back.

I want to savor her.

Without warning I roll us over, so I'm lying on my back and she's on top of me, her legs splayed across my hips, my cock nudging against her. My hands find her ass and I grip her firmly, trying to get her to move.

She rests her hands on my shoulders and lifts up, staring down at me, her brow wrinkled. "What do you want me to do?"

"Sit on my face." I smile.

Her mouth drops open in shock, but come the fuck on. She's got to be pretending. "Jordan."

I mimic her. "Amanda."

Her cheeks turn pink. I guess she is actually a little...what? Embarrassed? "Are you serious?"

"Serious as fuck," I tell her in my most solemn tone. I tug on her ass again. "Come on."

"Oh God." She releases a shuddery breath and closes her eyes, her entire body trembling. Pressing her lips together, she moves away from me, and my hands fall away from her ass. Now it's my turn to frown at her in confusion. But the confusion evaporates quickly, because she crawls closer, so she's right next to me, my mouth mere inches from her thigh. She rises up on her knees, grabs hold of the head-board, swings her leg over my head and straddles me so that we're face to pussy.

I place my hands on her lower back, lift my head, and make first contact.

THIRTY-FIVE

AMANDA

THE MOMENT his tongue touches my clit, I'm gasping. His hold on me is firm, and I can't make my escape even if I wanted to.

Not that I want to.

His tongue takes deep, dragging licks across my skin. Back and forth. Up and down. No part of me is untouched, and I grip the headboard tightly, my knuckles white, my thighs trembling.

God, his tongue feels so...incredibly...*good*. I can hardly stand it.

We used to do this all the time. Back when we were younger and couldn't seem to get enough of each other. Every chance he got, he'd go down on me. I think he enjoyed turning me into a screaming, gasping mess. It wouldn't take much—he'd slip his fingers deep inside me, suck my clit, and bam. I'd go off like a rocket. Again, and again, and...

Again.

It feels the same way at this very moment. This entire trip, it's like we're young and insatiable. Like we can't get enough of each other. I thought that would calm down with time and age, but I guess I was wrong.

I'm just as frantic, just as needy as I was when we were eighteen and dying for it—for each other.

His tongue flicks against my clit, ratcheting the tingly sensation that's a warning my orgasm is coming soon. I lift up a little and start to move my hips, tilting my head down so I can watch him.

And what a sight it is, having Jordan Tuttle lying between my thighs. His big hands squeeze my butt, his fingers perilously close to my crack, his lips sucking my clit. Throwing my head back, I close my eyes and rub against him unashamedly, desperate for release, knowing it's close. Right there, on the horizon. I'm reaching for it.

Reaching...

His hand is suddenly there, his fingers toying with my clit, searching my folds, slipping inside of me. He curves them, hitting that mysterious spot deep within, and that's it. I'm coming all over his face, sobbing his name as the tremors rack my body. He keeps going, though, never stopping, and oh my *God,* another orgasm is there, just behind the first one.

Meaning I'm coming again. I swear tears form in my eyes and I can barely breathe as I beg him to stop.

"Do you really want me to stop?" he asks once I've calmed down some. I can't even look at him right now. It's like I don't want to face the one who tortures me the most. "I can make another one happen." His voice is brimming with arrogance as he pinches my clit between his fingers. Like he's trying to prove a point, making me shudder.

"I don't know if I can take it." I'm breathless. I can barely talk. Glancing down, I watch as he gently circles my clit with his tongue, his touch light, his fingers sliding in and out of me slowly.

"You can take it," he says in that confident way of his before he lays his tongue flat against my clit and drags it up and down.

"Yes," I whisper, knowing he's one hundred percent right. I can totally take it.

"Hmm, fuck you taste so good."

His words make me shiver. The sounds he makes as he basically devours me make my entire body tighten. And then I'm coming for the third time, this one somehow the most powerful orgasm of them all. It's like a slow wave taking me over, taking me down. My entire body is completely focused on the point where his tongue makes contact with my flesh, and I'm shaking. Shivering.

It's like I have no control over my body anymore.

He grabs hold of my waist and flips me over with ease, not that it was a difficult thing to do, considering I'm a boneless mass of quivering flesh. I lay there, trying to catch my breath, and he's already inside me, filling me to the hilt. Fucking me hard. He grabs hold of my hands, interlaces our fingers, and lifts our arms above my head. Keeping me pinned as he rams inside of me. Again. Again. And again.

Fast. Faster. Until I'm lost to the rhythm and he's shouting my name, just before he goes completely still, spilling inside of me. I can feel it. Feel his come and—

Wait a minute.

Oh.

My.

God.

We forgot to use a condom.

Again.

"Jordan." I'm shoving at his shoulders, trying to push him off of me, but that's impossible. He's huge. Like a massive wall of solid muscle, and he's still lost in his own orgasm, his chest covered in sweat, his muscles gleaming in the dim light, making him look like some sort of sex god. I'm not lost to the moment anymore. No, I'm totally awake, no residual effects from the drugging orgasms I had only a few minutes ago affecting me.

Nope, I'm totally, one hundred percent aware we forgot to put the condom on again, and now we just *doubled* our chances in getting me pregnant.

"What's wrong?" He's staring down at me, his brows lowered, his breaths labored. I'm still shoving at his shoulders and he rolls over, slipping out of me, and when we both flip to our sides to face each other, I can feel the semen spill from my body, leaving the inevitable wet spot on the mattress.

"You uh...didn't wear a condom." I send him an imploring look.

What the hell is wrong with us? We're acting foolish.

Irresponsible.

"Wait, what? We forgot the condom?" When I grab his hand and bring it to the wet spot between us, he shakes his head and mutters, "Fuck."

I crawl out of bed and go use the bathroom, remembering advice I read on a Reddit forum once.

If you pee, more semen might come out and there's less chance of you getting pregnant!

Yeah. That sounds like some piss poor advice if you ask me —excuse the pun.

But I'm desperate, so I'll try anything.

Once I'm finished, I exit the bathroom to find Jordan sitting up in bed, the lamp on the bedside table on, casting the room in harsh light. I blink him into focus, freaking over-whelmed by the fact that he looks so goddamn beautiful just sitting there with the white sheet covering him from the waist down. The sweaty sheen on his chest and arms enhances his muscular build and I can't help it.

I yearning sigh leaves me.

He's got his head bent and hands in his hair, and when he drops them to look at me, I notice his lips are swollen, his eyes full of unrecognizable emotion. He looks so despon-dent I can't help the sudden alarm racing through me.

"I'm sorry," he says when he spots me standing there in the bathroom doorway. "I'm an asshole."

Sighing, I walk over to him and climb into bed. "You're not an asshole," I tell him as I slip between the sheets.

"It was totally careless of me, not to use a condom." He slips his arm around my shoulders and hauls me in close, so I'm plastered to his side.

"We didn't use one in the shower either," I tell him quietly, resting my hand on the center of his chest. His heart is beating so fast. I smooth my fingers back and forth, wishing I could calm him down.

"Shit," he mumbles, turning his head so our gazes meet. "I'm sorry."

I lift up to kiss him. "Don't apologize. It's both our faults."

We're quiet for a while, the both of us overthinking everything, I'm sure. I know I am. The curtains are still open, letting in light from outside, and my eyes start to get heavy. Maybe we could take a nap. This day has been so totally overwhelming, in both the best and scariest possible way...

"Would it be such a bad thing, though?"

Jordan's deep, rumbly voice wakes me up, and I blink up at the ceiling, confused. "Would what be a bad thing?"

"You getting..." His voice drifts and he hesitates for a moment before he spits out the word. "Pregnant."

I pull away from him and sit up, shocked awake by what he's saying. "Are you serious right now?"

He sits up too, leaning against the headboard. "I don't know. You're acting like what I'm suggesting could be the end of the world."

"It wouldn't be the end of the world, but it would be...a lot. You know? We've only just walked back into each other's lives."

"And we love each other," he adds, his voice low, sending a shiver down my spine. "I'm in love you. And you're in love with me."

Okay, I dreamed of having babies with him when we were younger. Because I was a romantic teen who wanted to give Jordan Tuttle my whole entire world.

"What about Harvey?" I ask.

He snorts. "What about Harvey? Who cares what that pompous ass thinks? Besides, we don't even know if you're pregnant."

"Harvey might think I'm just an opportunistic female looking to earn a payout upon having a famous football player's baby," I remind him.

"If he so much as alluded that to me about you? I'd tell him to go fuck himself," Jordan says fiercely.

His protectiveness melts me.

"After everything we've been through, we can survive it, Mandy. We can survive anything," he continues.

"We're not perfect," I point out.

"We're pretty goddamn perfect together." He rests his fingers against my lips before I can protest. Drops them when he realizes I'm going to be quiet. "Hear me out. I couldn't tell you this when we were out on the street with everyone watching us, but when you sent me that DM on Instagram, I couldn't believe it was you. At first, all I wanted to do was show off how great my life was and rub it in your face that you could've had your chance. If you hadn't broken it off, your life would be pretty fucking great too."

Wow. I always assumed that, but to hear him say it...I believe that's the most brutally honest Jordan has ever been with me.

Not gonna lie, it hurts.

"I invited you to my game, fully prepared to diss you afterward. I figured you'd bring a friend with you when I offered up two tickets, but no. You actually brought that guy. *Cade.*" He spits his name out, like it's a dirty word.

"Jordan. You *told* me to bring Cade," I remind him, and he waves a hand, dismissing my words.

"I know. Like a fucking idiot. Seeing you with him, I was consumed with jealousy. I wanted to kill him. I didn't like how he stood next to you. Or when he touched you. It pissed me off. *He* pissed me off," Jordan explains.

"Did I piss you off?" I ask quietly, surprised by the anger in his voice.

"No. Never. I took one look at you and realized you were even more beautiful than the last time I saw you. I just wanted to steal you away from him. That's the moment when I realized." He hesitates, his gaze lifting to mine. "I wasn't over you, not even close. I've *never* been over you. Spending these last few weeks together has been so incredibly *easy*, Mandy. It proved to me that we belong together."

His new, more heartfelt admission makes my head spin. And my heart hurt. But in a good way. "I-I don't know what to say."

We watch each other for a moment before he murmurs, "You know exactly what to say."

Emotion threatens to choke me and I shake my head, feeling helpless. "I already told you that I'm not over you. Is that what you want to hear?"

I feel like I'm about to fall apart, yet he's sitting there *grinning* at me. And Jordan Tuttle rarely grins, trust me on this one. "That works, yeah."

"What else do you want me to say?" I ask, feeling a little feisty. "Do you want me to admit that I'd love to have a baby with you, but the thought of actually having a baby scares the shit out of me?"

His eyes grow darker, reminding me of that look he gets when he wants me.

Uh oh.

"A baby scares the shit out of me too," he says, scooting closer. "But if it happens, we can figure it out. Together."

"What if it doesn't happen?" I ask warily, watching as he shifts even closer. He's within touching distance. Neither of us reach for each other yet.

"Then we'll still be together and have kids later. When the timing's right."

When the timing's right. Oh. That sounds...

Perfect.

But he's right. Even if the timing is wrong, it would still be perfect.

As long as I was with Jordan.

"Preferably after we get married, I guess," he continues, dropping the words *get married* like the most casual of bombs.

My jaw falls open and I tug the sheet up when I realize I'm sitting here with my breasts on full display and he's talking about actually marrying me. If he's for real, I don't want to remember how I was *naked* when he proposed to me.

What is this life anyway?

"After we get *married?*" My voice squeaks.

He nods. "Married."

"You want to marry me?"

His gaze locks with mine. "Pretty sure I've wanted to marry you since I was thirteen."

I scoff. "Impossible."

He grabs hold of me out of nowhere, showing off those quick reflexes he usually saves for the football field. I'm pinned beneath him, my head on the pillow, his hands around my wrists, holding them against the mattress, his legs straddling my hips. I can feel his erection pressed against me and I silently marvel at his stamina.

Luckily enough, the man never, ever seems to stop wanting me.

"Why are you being so difficult?" he asks just before he dips his head and delivers a too-quick kiss to my lips.

"I'm trying to tell you how I feel," I say, squirming beneath him. He's heavy, but I love feeling him on top of me. I actually *crave* the weight of him pressing me into the mattress.

Always.

"I'm trying to do the same thing. But then you start snorting at me or whatever and saying my feelings are impossible." He thrusts against me, nice and slow. A total tease. "You're kind of rude."

"You're rude for making me lay in the wet spot," I say with a sniff.

His eyes grow dim. "I *am* rude for forgetting the condom."

"Stop worrying about the condom." I blink up at him, my mood turning serious. "You're clean right?"

"Yeah." He nods, his gaze dropping to my lips, lingering there. "Totally clean. I get tested regularly."

He dips his head, kissing me before I answer him, "I'm clean too."

"Good." He kisses me again. "Now that we got that out of the way, I need to ask you a question."

"What?"

"Amanda." He clears his throat. "Will you marry me?"

I touch his face, my fingers sliding down his cheek. My chest is tight. I'm afraid I might burst into tears at any moment. "Yes," I whisper. I'll marry you."

Jordan grins. "I knew you'd say yes."

"So arrogant." He tries to kiss me yet again but I turn my head, his lips landing on my cheek. "You just asked me to marry you. Now we have things to do."

"Like what?" He dips his head, his mouth resting at the spot where my shoulder meets my neck.

Ugh. I can't think when he kisses me like that. "We'll need to find somewhere to have the ceremony. And all the other things that come with it, like a reception. Weddings don't plan themselves."

"Can't we just run away somewhere and get hitched? I vote for a tropical location." He's running his mouth up and down my throat. Hot, damp kisses that are making me melt.

"Won't your parents be angry?"

"Fuck 'em." His voice is muffled against my neck. "I don't care what they think."

"My mom wants me to have a big wedding," I confess. "I'm her only daughter. She's always wanted to see me walk down the aisle in a white wedding gown."

Jordan lifts away from my neck, his tender gaze meeting mine. "What do you want? Elope, or a big ceremony? Whatever you want, we'll do." He smiles. "I'd like to see you walk down the aisle in a wedding gown too. Beautiful and knowing you're all mine."

I blink up at him, fighting the tears that threaten to spill. "Are you being serious right now? Are we really talking about wedding plans?"

He doesn't say anything. Just nods his answer.

"But we've only been back together for a couple of weeks. Maybe a month? That's not long enough—"

He presses his index finger against my lips, silencing me. He's always pulling this trick. But I guess I'm always trying to talk over him too, so I guess I deserve it.

"I already said this, but I'll say it again." Jordan removes his finger from my mouth. "We've been apart for the last six years, Mandy, yet I knew the moment I laid eyes on you again after my shitty game that I was still in love with you. Isn't that long enough? Why waste any more time?"

Oh God, he busted out the word *love* again. It's kind of unbelievable that he's still in *love* with me.

And I'm still in love with him.

"Jordan." My chest hurts. I'm so going to cry.

"I love you. I've never stopped loving you. So yes. I want to marry you. And if by some miracle you're pregnant, then fucking fantastic. I think we'll make great parents. We might not be ready, but we'll have each other, so we'll be fine. We'll be better than fine. And if you're not pregnant, that's okay too. We'll have lots of fun practicing with all the amazing sex we'll have until you actually are pregnant," he continues, his voice fierce, his eyes blazing with determination. And love.

So much love.

Yep, here come the tears.

"I want at least four kids, okay? Two boys and two girls. Matching sets," he says as he releases one of my hands and cups my cheek, his fingers extra gentle, like he's afraid I might break apart.

Funny, since I feel like I am breaking apart, but in the best possible way. All because of his sweet declarations.

"Four?" I gasp, the tears now coming in full force. "That's *so* many."

"Yeah, well, I love you so goddamned much, I want everyone to know it. And if we can show our love for each other by having a bunch of kids, then that's awesome." He leans in, so close our noses touch. "You do love me, right, Mandy?"

This time it's my turn to nod as my answer. I'm too busy trying to control my sobs to actually say anything.

God, this man.

How did I get so lucky to have him come back into my life?

"I need to hear you say the words," he whispers, and I close my eyes when he slips inside of me, connecting us. Forging us together as one.

I sniff, blinking my tears away when I open my eyes to find him watching me, his face in mine. "I love you," I whisper. "I love you so much, Jordan Tuttle."

My earlier fears about possibly having a baby with him evaporate. Why would I be scared when I'm with the man I love? The man I'm supposed to be with? Nothing's scary with Jordan by my side.

"I love you too. You're my everything." He starts to move, a little smile curling his perfect lips. "You okay with this?"

"Okay with what?" I frown, a whimper escaping me when he slides deeper. He knows just how to do this.

"I forgot to put on the condom."

My eyes fly open and I mock glare at him. How can I be upset after what we discussed? We love each other.

He wants to marry me.

No matter what happens, we're in this together.

Forever.

"You did that on purpose." I lightly sock his shoulder with my fist, then close my eyes when he hits a particular spot deep within me, making me whimper.

"Mmm, yeah. I did. It feels good, being inside you with no condom on." He's still moving at a languid pace. Trying to drive me out of my mind, I'm sure. "I like the idea of having a baby with you right now, Mandy."

"I'll get fat," I warn him.

"Not fat. Full of my baby."

My belly flutters at his possessive tone. "Don't go caveman on me, Tuttle."

He laughs. "Busting out the last name, huh? Figures."

I grab hold of his shoulders, making him pause. I stare into his eyes and ask, "Are we really doing this? Declaring our love for each other? Planning on getting married and having children?"

He doesn't even hesitate. "Yeah. We are. It's what I want more than anything in this world."

"It's what I want too," I whisper.

"Then let's do it." He's grinning again. He looks so happy. So gorgeous. And he's all mine. "You in?"

"I am so in," I whisper just before he kisses me.

EPILOGUE

JORDAN

"I HAVE one last gift for you," I tell Amanda as I reach behind the massive Christmas tree and pull the tiny box from its hiding place.

Her mouth drops open, her eyes sparkling with excitement. She's bouncing around like a little kid. "What is it?"

"You'll have to open it and find out." I settle in next to her where she sits on the floor. It's Christmas morning, and we're at my house in Sonoma. We just opened our gifts to each other, save for this one last present.

"You spoil me." She nudges my side, then holds out her left hand to study the giant diamond on her ring finger. "I still can't get over this ring. It's so beautiful."

I steal a kiss from her. "You're beautiful." I gave it to her two months ago and I still catch her staring at it like she is right now. "You're worth twenty of them."

"Oh, stop." She shakes her head.

"It's true."

"I didn't expect another present." She smiles. She doesn't have a lick of makeup on, her hair is piled on top of her head in a sloppy bun and she's wearing holiday-themed pajamas. They're green and red and it says *Oh Deer* on the front of the long-sleeved shirt. She wanted me to get a matching set, but I refused.

A man can only deal with so much.

I relented and wore red and green plaid pajama pants for this special occasion—pajama pants she bought for me. That's about as much Christmas spirit as I can get, which made her incredibly happy.

That's all I want in life.

To make Amanda happy.

I fucking love her so much. She is my entire world.

"This gift you'll love." I flick my head at her, encouraging her. "Open it."

She pops off the red bow and then tears away the gold wrapping paper, revealing the small black velvet box. Her gaze lifts to mine briefly before she pops the box open.

A gasp escapes her when she spots what's inside, and she presses trembling fingers against her mouth, her gaze lifting to mine. "Where did you find this?"

It's the very same promise ring I gave her at Christmas during our senior year in high school. It's small and delicate, and there's the teeniest, tiniest diamond set in the center. I didn't want to scare the crap out of her or her parents by giving her a ring with a large stone in it, so I went for discreet. And it worked.

She loved it. Her parents didn't freak out.

Everyone was happy.

"I called your mom and asked her if she knew where it was. And she did," I explain. "She gave it to me when we were there for Thanksgiving."

"Oh my God, you two are so sneaky!" She's staring at the ring, smiling down at it. "I wonder if it still fits."

"Of course it will." It belongs on her finger.

Just like we belong to each other.

"I left it in my old jewelry box when I moved out to live on my own. Mom said she'd keep it in the closet." She's blinking back tears, I can tell. "At first, I wanted to take the ring with me, but it felt like such a sad reminder of what I lost, I left it behind. It was...easier that way."

"You didn't lose me. You never really did." I reach over and pull the ring out of its velvet setting and hold it out to her. "Can I put it on your finger?"

She holds her right hand out to me. "Please."

I slip the ring on her shaking finger, rubbing my thumb across the tiny stone. "We promised each other forever that night."

"Then I broke up with you less than a year later." Her voice is tinged with sadness.

"Yet here we are now. Together." I lean in and kiss her briefly, my lips lingering on hers. "I guess we kept our promise to each other after all."

Amanda's staring at me, her eyes shining with tears. And love. So much love. "I have one more gift for you too," she whispers.

Excitement fills me. "Yeah? What is it?"

Leaning in, she kisses me, then leaps to her feet. "I'll be right back."

She's gone for a minute—I have no idea where she went. And then she's back, clutching something behind her, stopping to stand directly in front of me. "Guess which hand I'm holding it in."

I point at her. "Your right."

Rolling her eyes, she reveals her right hand has nothing in it. "Guess again."

"Your left?" I ask with a chuckle.

"Ta da!" A small, flat present is clutched in her fingers. It's wrapped in simple white paper, with a shiny silver ribbon tied around it. "I was going to give this to you as a New Year's present, but I couldn't wait any longer."

"A New Year's present? Who does that?" I tease as I take the present from her. It's flimsy. Almost feels like a piece of paper wrapped up in...paper. I open it carefully, worried I might tear something.

It's a slick piece of paper, just like I thought. Black and white, with tiny writing in the top right corner. I can make out Amanda's name. The date. It's a photo of some sort.

Oh.

Shit.

It's a photo of...

"That's our baby," she whispers.

My head jerks up, my eyes going wide when they meet hers. "We're having a baby?"

"I had an ultrasound a few days ago." Amanda nods, smiling tremulously. "It happened when we were in London. The baby's due on the Fourth of July."

"Serious?"

She rolls her eyes and snatches the ultrasound photo from my fingers. "Serious, Jordan. There's our baby's head. Right there." She points.

I stare at the blob in the photo, squinting. It sort of looks like a head. Maybe. My heart swells despite my confusion. That little blob is mine and Amanda's baby.

Our first child.

This moment, my life right now, is mind blowing.

"Is it a boy or girl?" I ask.

"We don't know yet."

"I want a girl. So she's smart and pretty like her mama." I reach for her, take the photo of our baby from her fingers and place it on the coffee table before I pull her into my lap and hold her close.

"I want a boy so he's strong and handsome like his father," Amanda says, her head nestling into the crook of my shoulder.

"Don't forget smart," I remind her.

"And smart." She holds her hand out, fingers splayed, staring at the tiny ring on her finger as she sighs. "I love this ring even more than my engagement ring."

I squeeze her close, resting my chin on top of her head. "Why?"

"There's so much more meaning behind this ring. The promise we made to each other. Turns out it all came true."

"Yeah, it did. I'm a lucky son of a bitch, knowing you're mine forever," I tell her, making her laugh.

And I mean it. She *is* mine.

Forever.

ACKNOWLEDGMENTS

This one, as always, is for the readers. The Tuttle lovers who want to #cuddlewithTuttle and think #eightisgreat – especially to Nina, who is the ultimate Tuttle lover. Just when I thought I was finished with Amanda and Jordan's story, Nina convinced me I should write a book for them as adults. So here you go. Hope you all enjoy!

ALSO BY MONICA MURPHY

The Callahans

Close to Me
Falling For Her
Addicted To Him
Meant To Be
Making Her Mine

Forever Yours Series

You Promised Me Forever
Thinking About You
Nothing Without You

Damaged Hearts Series

Her Defiant Heart
His Wasted Heart
Damaged Hearts

Friends Series

Just Friends
More Than Friends
Forever

The Never Duet

Never Tear Us Apart

Never Let You Go

The Rules Series

Fair Game

In The Dark

Slow Play

Safe Bet

The Fowler Sisters Series

Owning Violet

Stealing Rose

Taming Lily

Reverie Series

His Reverie

Her Destiny

Billionaire Bachelors Club Series

Crave

Torn

Savor

Intoxicated

One Week Girlfriend Series

One Week Girlfriend

Second Chance Boyfriend

Three Broken Promises

Drew + Fable Forever

Four Years Later

Five Days Until You

A Drew + Fable Christmas

Standalone YA Titles

Daring The Bad Boy

Saving It

Pretty Dead Girls

ABOUT THE AUTHOR

Monica Murphy is a New York Times, USA Today and international bestselling author. Her books have been translated in almost a dozen languages and has sold over two million copies worldwide. Both a traditionally published and independently published author, she writes young adult and new adult romance, as well as contemporary romance and women's fiction. She's also known as USA Today bestselling author Karen Erickson.

f facebook.com/MonicaMurphyAuthor

○ instagram.com/monicamurphyauthor

BB bookbub.com/profile/monica-murphy

g goodreads.com/monicamurphyauthor

a amazon.com/Monica-Murphy/e/B00AVPYIGG

p pinterest.com/msmonicamurphy

Made in the USA
Las Vegas, NV
27 July 2023

75312824R00194